I wandered back to my dorm, trying to figure out how I felt. What happened yesterday could easily have killed me, but Ms. Graz was acting like I was throwing a hissy fit over a prank. A lot of things had happened since I started school and for the most part the staff hadn't been particularly helpful. In fact, some seemed to think I was the problem. Not a fun situation to be in. But I had to stay. Hyde needed at least one human to stay open.

The room was quiet when I got back. Ilse was still asleep, of course, and I was still more sensitive to cold because of yesterday's events. After cocooning myself in blankets, I wrote a quick email to my family. I mentioned having a quick brush with hypothermia, but not how it happened or how bad it got. Just as I finished sending my email, another one popped up. From Jesse.

Hey, Vi,

Just wanted to let you know I got accepted to Hyde. So plan on my joining you after Christmas. You'll introduce me to your roommate, right?

Jesse

I buried my head in my hands and tried to ignore the feeling that things were about to get worse.

KNIGHTFALL

The Hyde Chronicles: Book Two

By H. J. Harding

Acknowledgements

Every book that exists has multiple parents. Thank you to Katie who wanted me to write this in the first place, and will someday read one of my books. Thank you to Wallace who fell in love with the universe and believes me one of the best writers in the world. Sometimes, anyway.

Thank you to everyone who read this book in its' early stages, particularly my editor, Petticoat Betty.

Thank you to everyone who reads this book, buys this book, or tells someone else to buy this book. If you've done all three, thank you thrice.

Last but certainly not least, thank you to my Lord and Savior. Nothing can be accomplished without you and if it could, it would be meaningless. May this book honor You.

Chapter One
A Typical Day

"Attention all students! The blood-seeking creeper vines are loose. All students are to head to the nearest shelter with all due speed. Students inside shelter are not to leave until the all clear has been announced. Trained faculty, please meet at the arranged points to corral the plants. Thank you."

When the announcement started, I looked around trying to figure out where it was coming from. Once again, I failed to notice any sign of visible speakers. Maybe it was magic; wouldn't be a surprise in this school. No one else in the crowded cafeteria was looking for speakers, so I stopped before I looked any dumber.

Swallowing the soup I had in my mouth, I looked at my friends. None of them seemed overly concerned about the announcement, so it probably wasn't a major deal. "Okay, stupid question time. What exactly are 'blood-seeking creeper vines' and how does a plant escape?" Being the only human in the group, actually in the entire university, meant I was often forced to play catch up. Of course, since the population of the school came from all different dimensions, everyone had a turn at being ignorant sometimes.

I was a little surprised that Adrian was the one to answer. While he was the only non-freshman at the table, the panther shifter also came from my dimension so he shouldn't have had that much of an advantage over me. Of course, he grew up knowing more about the dimensions than I did.

For example, it wasn't until I came to Hyde University that I learned there were twenty major dimensions, each of which had diverged into little related clusters, and there were nexus points where dimensions shared space. Our dimension was 13A. Adrian knew that before attending.

"Blood-seeking creeper vines are mobile, intelligent plants. I think they come from one of the 2s or 3s. Plants are smarter in those dimensions. Anyway, like the name suggests, they're vamparic, like your roommate. Unlike your roommate, they rarely hesitate to attack anyone they come across. They have a very shallow root system that lets them uproot themselves and move to a new location. May not have much in the way of speed, but they can cover nearly three meters at a time, and the creepers can extend up to five meters from the plant. Don't ask me how, but somehow they can sense when someone nearby is bleeding. And if someone nearby isn't bleeding, well, the thorns can take care of that. A single plant can't kill you, but they travel in packs and somehow communicate with each other. No one knows how they do it. That's one of the reasons they escape so often. That and they learn. Every time someone uses a certain technique to prevent them from escaping, once the plant learns to get past it, they all know it in hours."

I shivered. "Why keep them around then?"

Adrian took a sip of his soda. "Lots of reasons. The different parts are useful. The leaves and sap in the vines have medicinal uses. The flowers are used in certain magic ceremonies, and perfumes, I think. The roots are made into tea for medicine, magic, or luck. Besides, Dr. Ash is the head of the botany department, and he likes them for some reason. He's a dryad, so they can't hurt him." He took a bite of his burger, swallowed and continued. "You're a bio major, right? Then you'll study them in Advanced Botany. Allison did a major report on them in her senior year, and drove me nuts telling me all about them."

I smiled. "Your sister was a bio major?"

"Nah, psychology. Her paper was on learning behaviors."

"So how are they going to stop the plants?" Kara asked. The werewolf had finished her lunch and been about to leave when the announcement was made. If her massive grin was any indication she was not at all unhappy that she had to stay and socialize with her friends instead of going to class.

"Magic, plant elementals. Stuff like that." Adrian shrugged. "They're afraid of fire. Again, like your roommate."

I shook my head but didn't say anything. After more than a month of distrust, Adrian and Ilse had finally come to some kind of truce, wispy as it was.

"Speaking ill of a lady when she is not present to defend herself is the actions of a–"

"He wasn't insulting her. It's a known fact that vampires are cautious of fire. Like most intelligent people." Interrupting Tim may have been mildly rude, but I was sure that letting him and Adrian get into *another* fight would be worse.

Tim had unfortunately been… out of it, during most of the time the rest of us made friends with Adrian, and the yeti still had to warm up to the shifter he had believed a threat for so long. I couldn't exactly blame him, and Adrian did seem to take a little too much enjoyment in tweaking people's noses, but this wasn't the place for a fight. Though perhaps that wasn't the reason for this particular fight. Last Friday, the 21st of October, had been the school Halloween dance. Tim and Ilse had spent most of that dance together, but neither had said anything about being more than friends before or since.

I decided to change the subject quickly. "So, these plants. Are they cold resistant? It's almost November." Hyde University was on an island in Wollaston Lake, Saskatchewan, far closer to the North Pole than I really wanted to be. I think it might have been a whole thirty-five degrees Fahrenheit today.

"Some. Soon it will be too cold for them, but they can manage now." Adrian leaned back as Kara's roommate, Denise, stole his empty plate. The dragonfly shifter made what she called 'table sculptures' at most meals. This one was particularly impressive, standing almost four feet off the table in places.

"How long does this normally take? Any chance they'll cancel my Foundations of Literature class?" I was more hopeful than expectant.

"Doubtful," Denise said, trying to balance a cup on a fork stretched between two plates. "Your class isn't for an hour, and I doubt Professor Argus would cancel class unless it was more than half over by the time they caught the creepy vines."

"Shouldn't take that long. Not unless it really gets away from them." Adrian said, keeping a tight hold of his cup lest it join the rest of ours in the table sculpture.

I sighed, causing Kara to give me a sympathetic smile. "Not looking forward to your test?" She asked, looking up from the napkin flag she was making for Denise.

"I've been studying and studying. The past three days I've been cramming like crazy. But I still can't understand half of it." Studying literature from multiple dimensions is tough. Especially when some of the concepts and authors aren't even pronounceable in

English. Kara commiserated and Tim assured me that I'd do better than I thought.

Adrian just shrugged. "Could be worse."

I winced at the reminder. Yes, even failing a massive test was better than what was going on last week, or most of the month. No one was hurt, everyone was mostly getting along, and as far as I could tell, no one was trying to kill me or get me expelled. It had been a rough month. I was still having nightmares. "Yeah, I know."

He looked a little sheepish at my reaction. "You'll do fine."

Before I could answer him, the announcement came that we could leave our shelters. They had corralled the 'creepy vines' as Denise put it. Considering the circumstances, I wasn't sure she was wrong. There was plenty of time for me to get to class.

I pushed all those thoughts away as I got to class. Foundations of Literature was hard enough when I wasn't distracted. I was early, but not the first one there. Stifling a groan, I slid in my seat, next to Arie, the harpy that lived a couple doors down from me.

She was stretching her blue eagle wings, looking rather pleased with herself. I half expected her to start preening feathers with her beak. Evidently she wasn't nervous about the test. Then again, why should she be? As far as I could tell, she was one of the best in the class.

"Professor Argus? Will there be extra credit on the test? *Some people* might need it." She gave me a syrupy smile that was belied by the contempt in her eyes.

I tried to ignore her, making sure I had two working pens. Professor Argus's extra credit questions were notoriously difficult so I wasn't relieved when he said there was.

"Class, pull out your weapons of orthographic destruction and commence." The teacher's grin was demonic. Rattled, I flipped over my test and had to resist the urge to scream.

***

Adrian was waiting outside when I got out of class, like usual. "How'd it go?" He smirked.

I shook my head. "Considering it's nothing compared to *some things* this month… it was evil."

Arie was leaving then, and must have heard me. She tossed her blue hair and walked away with smirk making sure to tell her friend that she was certain she aced it, at a volume that seemed unnecessary unless her friend was profoundly deaf. While I didn't know Tatiana well, I knew the pixie had hearing that was at least as good as mine, probably better.

Adrian ignored them. "Really?"

"Worst thing this week so far. Hopefully it will stay that way."

"It's Tuesday," Adrian pointed out, holding the door for me.

I thanked him. "Yeah, I know." I sighed. "I know, I know. I shouldn't complain. It's a perfectly normal part of school. No one got hurt, and I might even have gotten one of the extra credit questions right." A pause. "I still hate that class."

Adrian was trying not to laugh at me, I could tell. "Five Hydeonians says you got a B+ or better."

"No bet." That came out to around twenty-five U.S. Dollars. I didn't want to risk that, even if I didn't think I had done quite that well. A few times I ended up doing better in that class than I expected. Hyde arranged for the grades to be counted the same way another college in one's home dimension would, hence why my grades were the letter grades I was used to. Almost. Canada had slightly different grading than American schools, having A+ be a normal grade, leaving a B to be the equivalent of a C by my usual standards. We got to my math class. "Gotta go. See you later?"

"Probably," Adrian said, leaving.

I got to my seat just before Professor Pod, the seven and a half foot centipede, started taking role. There was just enough time to nod to Krystal, the ice elemental whose room was right next to mine. She smiled back.

Math was easier than Lit, at least for me. For one thing, it hadn't changed with new dimensions. Math was math no matter where you were. Well, mostly. Besides, I didn't have to figure out deep themes and symbolism. Krystal didn't seem to agree with me, but we studied together sometimes, like last night. Good thing, because Professor Pod decided today was a good day for a pop quiz. Sneaky teachers.

This quiz I was less worried about. For one thing, it didn't count for a quarter of my grade like the one in F of L. Two, it was much easier. Krystal seemed to agree, if the smile on her face was any indication. Of course for all I know, she finds Lit easier.

All in all, except for the vines getting out, it was a pretty typical day at a normal college. If you ignored the fact that everyone else wasn't human, I could actually tell my family about most of the day. My dimension was called a 'shade' dimension, meaning the majority didn't know about the multiple dimensions and all the other types of beings out there, and it was against the rules to tell people about it. Probably Inter-dimensional law too, because the school made/tricked all the students into signing a magically binding contract swearing they wouldn't reveal the secrets of the school. Though my family would think I was nuts if I did try to tell them anyway.

I got back to my room and was surprised to see that Ilse was awake. Being a vampire, she was almost entirely nocturnal and normally wouldn't be up for several more hours. She didn't seem particularly happy to be awake now, either. The phone in her hand suggested the explanation. "Here she is. She just walked in."

I took the phone in surprise. I hadn't expected a call. Mouthing an apology to Ilse, I turned my attention to the phone. "Hello?"

"Hey, Vi."

"Jesse?" That was a surprise. My oldest cousin on Dad's side, Jesse and I lived in the same neighborhood until he went to college, but we were never that close. He was two years older than I, but our interests were usually very different. It wasn't that we didn't get along, but I wouldn't have expected him to put much effort into trying to talk to me. "Is everything alright?"

He laughed, relieving me a little. "You don't want to talk to me? I'm hurt."

I smiled. "Of course I want to talk to you, you goof. I'm just surprised. Besides, I think you woke up my roommate."

"It's five in the evening."

"Three over here. We're two time zones over. Besides, she takes night classes."

"Fine, fine. I apologize to your roommate. Is she cute? She sounds cute."

"Jesse!" I fought back laughter. Ilse had gone back to her room, so I went to mine, both for privacy and to cut down on noise. "She could be a model," I said honestly.

"Realllly?" He managed to draw the word out for almost a minute.

"Oh, why do you care? It's not like you're coming here."

"Well, that's the thing." I froze. "I'm thinking about transferring. Hyde's been brought up a few times, and I wanted your opinion. Violet? Are you still there?"

Chapter Two
Family and Friends

I swallowed twice. "Yes, I'm here. Hyde? You want to come here? Are you sure?"

"Well, I'm not positive. That's why I'm asking you. You seem to be enjoying it."

Jessie at Hyde. Oh my. Could he adjust to everything? "You're pre-law, right? The pre-law program isn't what you'd need, being a different country and all." Not to mention the dimensions. "Besides, I doubt you'd get a baseball scholarship. I don't think they play that here."

"It was in their brochure."

"Oh, then I guess they do." I thought some more. "I'll be honest; Hyde required a lot of adjusting. More than I expected. Yeah, I do love it, but it's so very different. Is your mind mostly made up, or are you considering other options? Why are you transferring anyway?"

"Oh, different reasons. My favorite professor retired, and I don't like some of the ones who stayed. The baseball team is pathetic. Tuition is on the rise. I feel like a change. Do you know that I've never left the state of Virginia? Ever?"

"Neither had I before I came here."

"Anyway, I have a few options. Hyde is on the list, but not the only one. Uncle Kevin seems to think it's a good idea."

I closed my eyes, having a pretty good idea why my dad would want Jesse at Hyde. "If the only reason you're considering Hyde is to play nursemaid to me, then no, you shouldn't come here. It wouldn't be best for any of us."

"Whoa, retract the claws." His joke calmed me a little. I suppose it had come out testier than I meant to. "It's not the only reason and I'm not going to play nursemaid. So, what do you like best and least about Hyde?"

I had to think about it for a few minutes. Especially how to word things so that I could say what I needed to. "The best would probably be how very much there is to learn. Plus I've made some great friends. Least would be the snobs. There are a few who don't like me, just for being different." That was an understatement, but I could hardly tell him that someone was trying to drive me away from the school, or even kill me.

"Huh. Wouldn't have thought there'd be many Americaphobes in Canada."

"It's not always because I'm American. There's other reasons." Like being human.

"I guess that happens everywhere."

"I suppose." Not to this extent.

"I better go. This call is going to cost a fortune."

"Well, let me know what you decide," I said. Jesse at Hyde. Oh my.

***

"Would that be beneficial or detrimental?" Ilse asked, taking a sip of her drink, food, red substance I tried not to think too much about. Dinner, unlike lunch, was often just the two of us. Probably because I had to wait until nine or ten for her to be up and ready.

I had to think about it. We had recently found out that Hyde University required there to be at least one human at the school to stay open, and some people seemed determined to make sure it didn't. Two had recently been caught, but my friends and I knew there were at least two more people involved. We had to keep quiet about it, but Taria, my student advisor claimed the faculty had everything under control. I wasn't sure I believed it.

"Jesse coming? I'm not sure. Both I guess. I like him okay, though he is a bit of a tease. Having another human, or more than one, would be great. I think. But I honestly don't know how well he'd adjust. Plus there's the prejudice. It's not fair to ask him to put up with that." I rearranged my pasta some more; probably hadn't had more than three bites all night. Judging from Ilse's reproachful look, she had noticed. "Though it might get my parents off my back. They aren't happy with how little I tell them about school. Maybe having him here will reassure them. Or he'll get as close-mouthed as I am, they'll decide the school is brainwashing us and force us to come home." I shrugged and forced myself to have another forkful of noodles.

Ilse shook her head at me. "If he would be completely unable to adjust, Taria will know and refuse his application. It might be wise to speak to her in any event."

I brightened at that. "You're right. Good idea. I'll have to talk to her after class tomorrow." Hopefully she would be in a better mood. She still seemed to have some lingering suspicions about me. After being able to prove that I wasn't responsible for the… disaster earlier this month, things had gotten even more awkward. Still, she was my advisor, and since she had been the advisor for every human student in the past hundred years, if Jesse did come, she would be his as well.

"How was your literature test?" Ilse asked, deciding the topic was done.

I pushed my plate forward, set my arms on the table, and buried my head in my arms, groaning. It did nothing to drown out her laughing.

***

The next day I had Interdimensional History with Taria. It was my most crowded class, with nearly three hundred students. But the purple telepath shapeshifter managed to keep order nicely. After class, I waited until the rest of the students had left to talk to her. Maybe it was my imagination, but she had seemed to be watching me during class. I don't know if that was lingering suspicions or her way of saying she wanted to talk to me. After all, her telepathy didn't work on me anymore.

Not the most socially adept at the best of times, nerves left me utterly 'graceless' as Arie put it once. "My cousin is thinking of transferring to Hyde," I blurted out as soon as I got to her desk.

Her wings switched from looking like sheets to becoming ribbons intertwined above her head. "Yes, I've received his application."

No one spoke for a minute. I couldn't think of anything to say. Fortunately, Taria continued before I could lose my nerve entirely. "Do you believe your cousin would be unsuited to Hyde?"

I opened my mouth, closed it, and after a pause, opened it again. "I'm not sure. It would definitely be a challenge. Jesse doesn't even read fiction for fun. I think finding out he was wrong about, well, the nature of reality would be hard for him. If he did manage, I think he'd be fine. He's always been pretty culturally sensitive to others. He usually manages to pull off being understanding without being condescending."

Taria nodded. The wings separated, morphing into large bells. "That coincides with our findings."

"How can you tell who can adjust? I mean, the application was weird, but I still…"

"Several ways. The paper itself is magical, allowing us to know if someone lies or hedges the truth. In addition, the applicant leaves a bit of their aura on it which is then read by an aura reader." I suspected there was more to it than that, but didn't ask.

Much as I wanted to ask if Jesse would be accepted, I didn't think she'd tell me. It wasn't really my business. So I was surprised when Taria brought it up. "Do you believe we should accept your cousin?"

Closing my eyes, I tried to think objectively. "It's not my place to say. I don't know all the circumstances. I can say this, Jesse is not the type to be a loose cannon. If he can't take it, he'll go back home. But he won't try to cause problems. That's just not who he is."

Taria nodded. Her wings formed an extra set of arms that started picking up papers on her desk. "If your cousin was completely unacceptable we would not be having this conversation. Nor would we be discussing this if he was unquestionably acceptable." Her eyes pierced me. "There is no reason to mention that to anyone else."

I nodded.

"Good. You should get to your next class."

I didn't have another class for several hours, but I didn't argue. Tim would be meeting me for lunch soon; maybe I'd feel better after eating. After thinking about it, I decided not to mention the possibility of Jesse coming to anyone else yet. Nothing was set in stone, it could wait until more was decided.

***

The cafeteria was crowded, and I took long enough getting my food that Tim had gotten a table first. "Sorry I'm…" I cut off when I noticed who else was sitting at the table.

"Oh, Violet. I'm glad you're here. Have you met Arie? She's in my literature club. Arie, this is Violet, a friend of mine," Tim introduced us.

"Um, yes, we've met," I said carefully, trying to ignore Arie's poisonous glare. "In fact, we're only a few doors down from each other." Price Hall was the freshman girls' dorm.

"You are already friends? How fortuitous." Tim smiled.

I had never mentioned Arie to Tim, had I? "Well, maybe that's a slight exaggeration. Did you two want some privacy? I can…" Denise and Kara had a lab today. Adrian got roped into doing something either with or for his sister. I had no idea about Krystal or her twin, Bria, but I never saw them in the cafeteria. It was here or likely alone.

"Of course not." Tim seemed surprised I even asked. "We would love for you to join us. Wouldn't we?" He turned to Arie, who pulled her beak into something that was probably supposed to approximate a smile.

"If you don't have other plans," Arie said, looking like she hoped I did.

"I am rather certain you don't." Tim was up and pulling out a seat for me. There was no way out without it being extremely awkward.

"Thank you." I sat down and tried to think of something, anything, to say. I had never had trouble talking to Tim before. But I had never tried talking to him in front of the harpy before either. "I didn't know the school had a literature club."

"Oh yes, it's *very* exclusive," Arie said. "You have to be invited in by a professor. Didn't you get an invite?" Her smile showed no doubt as to the answer.

I swallowed my first three responses. "No, I have to admit that Literature is not one of my better classes."

"Oh? You're better at some of the other ones?" Arie asked.

"Fortunately, yes," I said dryly.

"Say, are you two in the same Literature class?" Tim asked. "You both mentioned recent tests."

"Yes, we sit near each other." Arie said. "How did you do, Violet?"

"I won't know for sure until I get it back, but I think I got one of the extra credit questions."

"Yes, they were *so* easy, weren't they?"

I think Tim was finally getting the hint that maybe things weren't exactly amicable between us, because he hurried to change the subject. He asked Arie about someone, presumably some author, who I had never heard of. It was something being discussed in their club, evidently.

For the next hour, I said nothing as the two of them discussed authors, books, symbolism, themes, and other concepts that went over my head. I didn't understand a quarter of it, and there was no way to break into the conversation if I had. I felt more alone than if I had sat by myself.

While I was trying not to slip into a sulk, I watched them. I might not understand what they were saying, but I could see that Tim was really excited talking about it. It was his passion and he loved having someone who shared it. Arie had lost almost all of her venom and seemed to be having a grand time.

They liked each other. The idea slapped me in the face like a cold fish, but it was obvious after just ten minutes. I gripped my spoon so hard it hurt, swearing that I wouldn't ruin this for them. Arie would get one chance without my interfering. If she hurt him, though, all bets were off.

So when they left together, barely remembering I was there, I said nothing. When Tim came back for the notebook he had forgotten and asked me what I thought of Arie, I told him the only thing I could. "I hope you will be very happy."

Chapter Three
Questions and More Questions

Once I got out of lunch, I had about an hour to kill before Biology at three and Fitness for Life directly after that. Not having any better ideas, I decided to spend some time looking at registration for next semester. While I couldn't sign up for classes until next week it wouldn't hurt to make a plan. I had been lucky this semester. Most of my classes were in the afternoon, and I only had one eight o'clock; Music of the Dimensions on Tuesdays and Thursdays.

I would need another math class, Biology II, Magic for Non-Magic Users, and Prominent Forms of Government. Sooner or later I would need another arts class, but that could be music, visual arts, or theater. I had enjoyed music with Professor Shale, and she was a really cool teacher, but she didn't seem to know what to do with me anymore. She was obviously uncomfortable with me, but I didn't know if that was because she still thought I was guilty or because she now knew I wasn't. Maybe it would be best to leave it for now.

Looking at the classes offered, I made a note to ask Doctor Gronk if freshmen could take Basics of Genetics. I would see him in Bio. I would also have to pick a minor at some point. Shaking my head, I started to shut down the computer before suddenly freezing. Terror swept through me in waves, cold sweat prickled at my neck and back, and my breath caught in my throat. The room spun as I tried to stand, causing me to nearly fall on the floor. Then it was over.

What was *that*? Huddled over the chair, I tried to remember how to breathe normally, waiting for my pulse to get back to human range instead of say, small mammal frightened by a cat range. Was that a panic attack? I had never had anything like that happen before. I would be perfectly happy if it never happened again.

The computer was still asking me if I was sure I wanted to shut down. Apprehensively, I clicked 'yes' but it didn't cause another attack. I had to get to Bio or I'd be late. Maybe I should ask Dr. Gronk about it. My last thought was to be grateful I had gone back to my dorm instead of the school computer lab like I had considered. That could have been embarrassing.

***

There was only ten minutes between Biology and Fitness. Long enough to ask Dr. Gronk if I could join his genetics class, but not long enough to ask him about panic attacks. By the time class got out, it didn't seem as big a deal.

The bright orange troll stroked a craggy chin. "Basics of Genetics is usually an upper level class. However your grades are good and I think you can handle it. If you get at least an A in this class I'll admit you." I barely had time to thank him before dashing off to the gym.

Dr. Gronk was great. A brilliant mind, a wonderful sense of humor, and he had never blamed me for the disturbances earlier this month. No wonder he was my favorite teacher. I could do without the giant prank war in the science department, but even that wasn't too bad since the teachers were careful not to let any of the students get hurt in the middle of their pranks.

Fitness for Life had spent the whole semester so far in learning how to river dance and Coach O'Rater showed no signs of having us do anything else. The leprechaun was also coach of the football team, but I had a feeling we wouldn't be playing football this semester. I was enjoying river dancing, but it was exhausting, and probably the reason I had lost ten pounds since starting school.

I stumbled out of the gym an hour later. An hour of dancing will do that to most people. To my surprise, Adrian was waiting for me. While he was often waiting for me after several of my classes, Fitness wasn't one of them.

"Hi." I gave him a closer look. "You okay? You look tired." 'Tired' was a bit of a compliment. He looked ragged.

"I'm fine. Look, we need to talk." He glanced around. "All of us."

The ones who swore the oath. It was the only thing he could mean. "Same place as before?"

"Probably best. Allison knows, she suggested it. Says the sooner the better."

"Okay, I can get the other girls." After all, they all lived on my floor. "But Ilse won't be up for a few hours. I can wake her if it's an emergency…"

"Think you'd better. What about the yeti?"

Did Adrian have something against calling people by name? "I don't have his number. Kara might."

He looked surprised. "You don't?"

"No, I only have Kara's. Come to think of it, Ilse might know his number. She contacted him once." I tried not to think about the night.

"Worse comes to worse, I'm sure Allison can figure out a way to look up his number." Adrian shrugged. "One hour."

"Okay." Once again I was involved in cloak and dagger stuff without knowing why or what I was doing. Joy.

***

Gathering everyone was harder than I anticipated. Bria was in class, so Krystal wrote a note for her to meet us. Kara was in one of her clubs so I had to ask her roommate where she was. Fortunately Denise knew. Though how Kara could participate in a club called Ultimate Frisbee Deathmatch was a mystery to me. The name was only slightly an exaggeration. When I got there, almost half the team was on the injured list, either temporarily or for the rest of the game. Kara had just been tackled and told she out for the rest of the game. I think she was pretty disappointed about being side-listed until she saw me.

"Violet can take me to the infirmary. I'll see you guys tomorrow, good luck!" She called before limping hurriedly to me.

"Do you need the infirmary?" I asked as soon as I thought we were out of earshot. She was holding her arm protectively, so I took her bag.

"Nah, I'll be fine by tomorrow. Just need to bandage up a bit." Her limp did decrease as we got out of sight. "So, what's up?"

"I can get my first aid kit when I wake Ilse." I explained quickly.

"Okay, I'll meet you down there. You better go ahead of me." She had a point. Our meeting place was in the basement of our dorm, and I had to go to the top floor to get Ilse and the kit. In addition to being inefficient for us to go together, it was also a little suspicious. Since I had further to go and we were running out of time, it only made sense to hurry.

"Fine, see you in a bit. Oh, do you have Tim's number?"

"No, I don't." Kara winced. "We better exchange numbers at the meeting."

"Definitely." I sped up.

My first aid kit was under my bed, so I could get that easily. Waking Ilse was not difficult, but it was a little riskier than I liked.

"What is it?" An irritated voice demanded, cutting off my knocking on her door.

"We're having a meeting."

"Who's 'we'?"

"The ones who swore the oath. Allison called it. We're supposed to be meeting in less than ten minutes."

There was a loud groan. "I'll be out in five. Make sure the blinds are closed."

"They are." They usually were, in the common room anyway. Besides, it was already dark. Dark came early in winter when you were close to the Arctic Circle.

Ilse stepped out a few minutes later, looking like she stepped off a magazine cover despite it being her equivalent to having to get up at three in the morning. She stopped rubbing her eyes when she saw the box in my hands. "You are injured? I smell no blood."

"I'm fine. This is for Kara. She got a little beat up in her Frisbee game." I explained, trying not to look at my watch.

"Ah. Let's meet with the others then."

"Right. By the way, do you know Tim's number."

Ilse didn't, so it was a good thing Allison was able to look it up. Yet another reason why we needed to exchange numbers.

I don't have a lot of medical training, but I have some. Mom had me take some first aid classes in hopes that I would think about being a doctor instead of a geneticist. It succeeded. Succeeded in convincing me I didn't want that kind of pressure. Or exposure to injured people, blood, etc. on a regular basis. However, my meager training was more than anyone else had, so it wasn't a surprise that it was up to me to help Kara 'bandage up'.

Bria was running a little late, but she slipped into the room sitting next to her twin not long after Ilse and I arrived. "So, what's so important?"

That was indeed the question of the day. Everyone looked to Allison for the answer. Well, I was still trying to apply hydrogen peroxide to Kara's skinned elbow, but I did glance up briefly.

Allison sighed. "We may have a major problem."

"Such as?" Tim asked.

"We all took a magical oath, remember?" That wasn't the sort of thing one forgot easily. "What did we agree to?"

"To not betray each other or the school." Tim answered. He had been the one to suggest the wording.

"Exact words," Allison prompted. Out of peripheral vision I saw her running her fingers through her hair, sending brown ribbons flying through the air.

Bria pulled out a scrap of paper and read aloud. "*I solemnly swear to uphold the standards of justice, friendship, and tolerance. I will not betray the principles this school was founded on, or my fellow oath-takers.*" She shrugged. "So?"

I gasped. "We are so stupid!" Everyone stared at me. "What principles was the school founded on? It was, what, a thousand years ago? How have they changed from today? Was there an original code of conduct? What does it say? I don't know. Does anyone else?" Judging from the looks I was getting, everyone else was starting to realize the same thing. We could be found in violation of the oath for breaking a rule we didn't know existed. I didn't know what happened if you broke an oath like that, but I had learned enough to know it was serious.

Ilse took a deep, unnecessary breath. "Very well. We made a magical oath. As that is not something we can go back on, the first order of business is to discover exactly what we agreed to. Allison, you said yourself that this oath was a good thing, therefore it's doubtful that we agreed to anything too horrible or contradictory."

"The library is sure to have some information on the founding of the school. That's bound to tell what the founding principles were. It might also give some hints on why someone wants the school to close," I suggested.

"Good idea," Kara said. "We also need to figure out who 'Morgana', like you nicknamed her is. All we know is a female magicus, sophomore or up, who's conspiring against the school."

"You know, thinking about it a little more," Which I hated to do, "no one ever said she was one of the people involved last year. I assumed, but that might be wrong," I admitted. "Meaning we can't eliminate the freshmen."

"Perhaps we can," Ilse said. "When the first spell was cast on our door, the school compared the magical signature to that of every magic user in our dorm. That would eliminate every freshman girl, ten magici."

Leave it to Ilse to know that. "So how many are left?"

"Probably around forty female magici," Allison said. "Possibly up to fifty if you count faculty, staff, and live-in alumni."

"If only we had more information about what happened last year," Kara sighed, examining the bandage on her arm. "A witness or something."

My head snapped up from the tape I was applying. "We do."

In seconds everyone was looking at Adrian. He leaned away from the weight of our attention. "I don't remember any of it. You know that."

"Nothing? At all?" I asked.

"A couple of scraps. Nothing that makes sense."

"Someone did that deliberately, to lock up your memories, right?" I barely looked in his direction, mind whirling. "Then there must be a way to undo it. Or at least help you remember more."

"Maybe not 'must', but it is a possibility. Though if there was a way, one would think the faculty would have found it," Tim pointed out.

Adrian shrugged. "They gave up when I became an almost closed mind. Besides, the faculty didn't figure out about Morris or…" he stopped as he saw me try and fail to repress a shiver, "or everything else that's been happening this semester."

"Are you willing to try?" Allison asked. "If we found something that we thought might work, safely?"

"I've been trying. Nothing is working," Adrian admitted. "I've even tried going back there. But…" He cut off and eyed his shoes. "Sure, whatever."

"We'll see what we can do," I said softly. "There are nine of us. What if we split into groups of three? Three to look up the school's history, particularly the founding. Three to research the magici, how many there are and how to eliminate possibilities and three to look up ways to block or restore memories."

After a few minutes, we had it divided up. Denise and the Ice Twins would look up the school's past, and Ilse, Kara, and Allison would focus on the magici. Which left Tim, Adrian, and I working on Adrian's memories. Oh, lovely. The meeting ended with us exchanging contact information.

Chapter Four
Uneasy Suspicion

The next night was a full moon. That wasn't something I paid much attention to before Hyde. Outside of Hyde it was mostly a case of looking up and thinking, 'Oh, it's full moon. Huh. Pretty.' Here, there were three major campus clocks that kept track of lunar phases, and major campus events were planned around full moons and day after. Actually, considering Weres of any kind averaged only about ten percent of the school population, at best, it was a little surprising how much effort went into considering full moon.

The majority of the students and faculty had scarcely more reason to care about the average lunar phase than I did at home. Most of the Weres were jittery the day of, went to bed early, and were tired and hungry the next day. They used a drug called zealopor to sleep through the night, but that didn't cancel out everything.

There were only two Weres on our floor, Kara and Felicity, a werecat who lived on the other side of the hall. So, the other nineteen girls should have been mostly unaffected by the whole thing. Yeah, right! Maybe in a few months, but the entire floor remembered far too well what happened *last* full moon. There was a tension in the air like electricity. No one wanted to talk about it, but from the darting eyes, heightened reflexes, and sentences that would be cut off without warning, everyone was thinking about it.

Kara was a nervous wreck, and insisted Denise stay somewhere else until the zealopor kicked in and Kara fell asleep. Denise agreed, but that seemed to be more for Kara's sake than anything else. Ironically, Denise seemed to be the calmest person on the floor.

Then again, I couldn't remember ever seeing Denise really upset.

Because of last month, Thylica, the RA, had to supervise the transformation. The wood elf arrived about twenty minutes before Kara had to transform and promised to tell Denise when Kara was asleep and she could come back in.

That was why Denise was currently in our sitting room, as the three of us pretended we weren't trying to see through the walls to know what was happening in Kara's room. Or maybe it was just me.

"She'll be fine," I said, wishing I knew what was going on. "Kara inspected her zealopor earlier, right?"

"Just before I left," Denise confirmed. "I don't think it was the first time either."

"Have you begun your research yet?" Ilse asked, probably so we'd stop glaring at the wall.

"I'm meeting with Tim and Adrian to work on it tomorrow," I said, before looking to Denise.

"We've started, but we keep hitting dead ends," Denise said. "For some reason the library doesn't like it when you accidentally freeze the table."

I bit a lip while trying to nod wisely. "I can't imagine why."

"Anyway, we'll be allowed back in the library Saturday and can get back to it then. I keep looking for videos of the founding, but the librarian says there weren't any time travelers with cameras."

I was pretty sure she was joking, but decided not to say anything. Ilse didn't seem to know how to respond either. "Well, I wish you luck. We have begun investigating magici. Allison is investigating any alumni who have been on campus this semester. I am looking into the faculty, and Kara is doing her best to befriend every female magicus student in the school, in hopes of getting a lead."

There was a knock on the door then. Being the closest, I opened it to find Thylica. "It's done. She'll sleep until morning."

"Right, thank you," Denise said. She stood up even as Ilse and I invited her to stay a little longer. "I have to be up early tomorrow. Besides, don't you have the class of no sleep?"

"I do have music at eight," I admitted. Professor Shale had some original methods of making sure students didn't fall asleep in class. I had lucked out so far, so I hadn't had snakes licking my ear, but Denise did have a good point.

When Denise left, I turned to Ilse. "We have to figure this out. Quickly."

"We will."

***

"Well, this was… less than helpful," I said, after about two hours of looking through every single book we could find on memories or mind magic.

Adrian looked even more frustrated than I did. Not surprising, considering it was his mind we were trying to 'crack', as it were. Tim didn't seem as frustrated, but he also hadn't said a word in the past half hour. That one might have been my fault, though. I had threatened to leave if they didn't stop sniping at each other.

"The library does seem ill-equipped for our particular pursuit." Tim sighed.

"It doesn't make sense." I buried my head in my hands, tugging at my hair. "Every time we come to the library to look up something important, we can't find what we're looking for. Does someone come ahead of us and check out everything useful?"

I heard, more than saw, Adrian sit up sharply. "Catalogue. English, please."

Head still resting in my hands, I turned to face him before sitting up when a light film suddenly filled the space in front of him. "I didn't know there was a catalogue." I had spent the first two months here painstakingly learning my way around the library. Emphasis on the 'pain' part.

"Yeah, but you have to know how to ask. Ms. Graz should have told you on your first visit," The panther shifter answered absently while trying to find what he was looking for. It was probably magic, but the catalogue functioned like a touch screen.

"She informed me," Tim said. "Were you not told?"

"No, she never mentioned it at all. Odd, she had to know I was a freshman. I was asking for basic information about the school and dimensions." I thought back to my first visit to the library and meeting the thirty-foot long chartreuse dragon. "Maybe she forgot." Her achievement plaque said she had been librarian for over four hundred years. I didn't know much about dragon aging, but it stood to reason that they'd forget things sometimes after several hundred years. Besides she had to be an incredibly busy woman, er, dragon. "So, how do I ask for the catalogue?"

"Say 'catalogue' your language, and 'please'. The magic of the catalogue doesn't always work well with the translation spell, so you name your language. Besides, it makes it less likely you'll call for it accidentally." Adrian was frowning at the catalogue. "We're missing some things. There are books in this list that we should have found but haven't. Maybe they've been misplaced."

I called for a catalogue, absurdly pleased that it worked. Now I just had to figure out the classification system. "Maybe we should write down the titles we need, and split up to look for them."

We considered splitting up the list, but decided against it since there was no way of knowing who would find what. Conveniently, the catalogue let you make a list of books. It also highlighted where they were *supposed* to be, but that wasn't a lot of help when they were mis-shelved. I got first floor, Adrian took second and offered to do the third, but Tim said he'd take third and fourth because the fourth had less books than the others.

I hated the steps in the library. Hated them with a passion. They gave me a horrible sense of vertigo and I had nearly had a bad fall on them before. Of course, I'm pretty sure I had *help* with that fall. Yet another reason to be nervous on the stairs.

Last week I found out there was an elevator, but I still couldn't find it on my own. Maybe it moves. I know the shelves move, I've seen them do it. After a few minutes of looking for the elevator, I gave up and took The Evil Stairs of Doom. Hate the stairs.

The first floor is darker than the others, using candles instead of light bulbs. It seemed like a fire hazard to me, but apparently they had ways of protecting the books. No idea why they used different lighting here, but I'm sure there was a reason.

It was also the most likely place to find Ms. Grazletz. It wasn't that I disliked the dragon librarian. I had no problem with her. But she didn't seem to like me much and still acted like I was a troublemaker. I couldn't walk into the library without her breathing down my neck. She wasn't at her desk, maybe she was helping a student somewhere. On a different floor. Or maybe she was getting some sleep. Just because the library was always open didn't mean she was always there.

I started with the section closest to the desk, in hopes that I'd be finished by the time she came back. This appeared to be a section on music. Or rabbits. I really couldn't tell. Either way, it wasn't particularly helpful.

As I moved to other sections, the library got darker and more shadowy. I could hear the bookshelves moving. Sometimes I thought I could hear the books muttering, but that was just me spooking myself. Probably.

Then I spotted it. *The Art of Mind Magics* was on a bookshelf between *Death: The Unexplored Doorway* and *Ritual Safety and Sacrifices*. I snagged the mind book, then, on further consideration, reached for the ritual book. Maybe if we could figure out what they had been trying to accomplish, it would tell us what they wanted.

My fingers brushed the spine when a voice behind me made me jump. "My, my. Such... *interesting* reading choices."

I spun around quickly and tried not to shriek in surprise at the glowering dragon head inches from mine. "You startled me." Now why did I say that? It was clearly obvious, from the jump to the blush, to the quick breathing.

"Perhaps because you knew you shouldn't be here?" Ms. Graz. peered through her pink glasses at me. "This is advanced reading for strong magic users. Why are *you* here?"

"I was doing some research. For a friend." Words stumbled over themselves in haste.

Long claws plucked the book from my hands. "I would recommend against it. Some could get the wrong idea." She gave a puff of frigid air that made me shiver before she leaned in closer. "I'm still watching you. Now go, and don't let me catch you in such dangerous sections again."

"I didn't realize it was forbidden." I tried to worm away. "There was no warning, they aren't kept secret." Her glare intensified and I shut up.

Ms. Graz didn't say anything, but after freezing me with her eyes, she backed off enough to let me scurry upstairs. It wasn't until I was back at the study room that I wondered what I was running for. I hadn't done anything wrong. Then I thought about the last month and realized that it might not matter.

***

"What do you mean, she took the books away?" Adrian asked, as if the four previous times I told him were some joke or misunderstanding, and if he kept asking the books would appear, possibly in a flash of sparkles and a trumpet flourish.

"For the *last* time, she said I wasn't allowed in that section. No, actually, she said some could get the wrong impression, and I shouldn't let her catch me there."

"How very extraordinary," Tim mused. "I have heard there are certain reserved works, but they are not kept in the library at large. There was no reason for her to deny you access to this section."

"Maybe, maybe not." I eyed the ceiling. "I was nearly framed for performing a very illegal ritual. She, and maybe others in the faculty, may think it's better if

I'm not researching rituals at all. But I thought only magic users could work rituals. So, it really shouldn't matter."

"Unless you were working with someone," Adrian agreed.

"There is no way to become a magicus, right? You're born one, or you aren't?" I looked at my study partners, seeking clarification.

Tim frowned, furry brow wrinkling. "There are legends, unconfirmed ones, of ways to steal another's magic. They contradict and likely have little basis in fact. Such a process, if it even existed, would undoubtedly be a capital crime in all dimensions."

"That's.... strict. Do they hurt the magic user?" I asked.

"The legends I am familiar with are more or less unanimous in stating that the one losing magic doesn't survive the process."

"That would do it," I agreed.

"They're stories. Lore and fables for children." Adrian barely looked up from his list of the titles we had found. "I wouldn't put much faith in it."

"Do you know how much of Hyde I would have dismissed as fairytales back in July?" I asked. "Still I'm certainly not planning to kill anyone and steal their magic, and neither are either of you, so it doesn't matter. Back to the major issue; how do we get Adrian to remember?"

I left the library an hour later, wondering if we had accomplished anything other than a deep, throbbing headache.

***

November 1st was Founding Day at Hyde, one of the few holidays the school actually celebrated. Considering the number of dimensions, never mind the number of countries the Hyde body came from, that made sense. Though there was a winter break that covered Christmas and New Years. Apparently that was a common holiday period for numerous dimensions for various reasons. I suspected it had to do with Winter Solstice, but I hadn't done enough research yet to confirm or deny it.

The celebration committee is the group that plans events. Allison was on the celebration committee, and despite coming late in the year, seemed to be the driving force. Not surprising, considering her personality. Personally, I thought she was a little overly optimistic about the Founding Day plans. Allison wanted an outdoor concert from the school orchestra, various outdoor sports competitions, and a picnic for dinner. In Wollaston Lake, in November. The week before had averaged about twenty degrees Fahrenheit. Needless to say, it snowed all day. Heavy, can't see three feet in front of you, blizzard, snow.

According to Adrian, after Allison threatened the weather with various dire threats (and it snowed even *harder)*, she unleashed her back-up plan. The no-holds-barred, free-for-all snowball fight. Students and faculty participated, though some managed the safety zones where one could warm up with various hot beverages, and sometimes, a bonfire.

I preferred the safe zones; drinking hot chocolate, and trying to warm up from having had a snowball dropped down my back. Krystal was really getting into this. Normally she was shy.

Having lived in Virginia my whole life, I hadn't had many opportunities for snowball fights. Oh, it wasn't like I had never seen snow, but we didn't usually get deep snow or snow that lasted a long time. More likely, we'd get a few inches that would stay for a day, maybe two. Needless to say, I was pretty lousy at this snowball fight thing, even if I was quite proud of myself for nailing Professor Argus. I think it was him, anyway.

Still, the hot chocolate was good, and from the screams and shouts all around, I'd guess a lot of people were having fun. Allison had picked a good backup option. If I actually saw her in any of this blizzard, I'd tell her so.

"You appear to be amused," A voice nearby said.

I managed not to jump but it was a close thing. "Tim! I didn't see you there." His white fur blended too well into the snow. Probably it was a survival trait for yetis.

"My apologies. Startling you was not my intent." He took a coffee. "I was wondering if perchance you had seen Arie today?"

I felt a stab of something then. It wasn't quite hurt and wasn't quite jealousy. All I knew for sure was that I wasn't happy he was looking for her. But, I had promised I'd stay out of it, and had talked to the other girls about doing the same. "No, I don't recall seeing her. Sorry."

"Ah." He smiled, probably to try and hide his disappointment. It didn't work. "Thank you."

"Was there a specific reason you were looking for her?" I asked him, as he seemed to be trying to see through the sheets of snow. Our area was protected, but surrounding it was practically a white-out.

"Oh, nothing specific." He trailed off.

Somehow that made it worse. Though not quite as bad as when Arie did shuffle in. She was still wearing an outfit that belonged on a beach, one with lax dress codes, and her wings were clogged with snow. She must have been freezing. Tim visibly brightened when he saw her, before becoming very concerned that she might be chilled. I was quite proud of myself for not saying a word about how she probably would have been warmer if she had actually tried wearing a coat.

I don't know how susceptible harpies are to cold or what the symptoms are, but I suspected the shivering and the fact that she was bluer than normal weren't good signs. Tim was trying to help her brush snow off, but it wasn't enough. "What's your hot beverage of choice?" I asked.

Arie's eyes focused on me, slower than I liked, and narrowed. "What?"

"Hot drink. You're cold. Coffee, tea, chocolate? Something else? I don't know what you want."

"Why?"

"Because you're cold. Are you hypothermic?" I tried cataloging the symptoms of hypothermia. Signs of mild hypothermia included shivering and mild confusion. Moderate hypothermia was evident by more violent shivering, confusion, slow movements, and victim becoming pale, with extremities turning blue. Severe hypothermia affects breathing rate, pulse, inability to think clearly, skin turns blue, and the body starts to shut down. In some cases the victim starts to take off clothes in the last stage. Could that be what happened to her coat?

No, I was exaggerating. There was no reason to assume that harpies reacted the same way to cold as humans do, and she didn't seem that bad off.

"Coffee. I believe Arie would like some coffee." Tim cut in, giving me a grateful look.

Assuming that he would know what she drank, I hurried over to the booth. The frost sprite managing it looked in their direction worriedly. "Is she going to be alright?"

"I certainly hope so. One coffee, please. That is safe for harpies, right?"

"Ours is." The coffee was practically thrust into my mitten-ed hands. "We have some blankets too, if needed."

"Thanks, I'll keep that in mind." I scurried back to Arie and Tim as quickly as I dared without splashing the coffee. "Here."

Arie looked suspiciously at the cup I placed in her hands. "What is this?"

"Coffee. Remember? Do you need blankets? Or the infirmary?" Maybe confusion was a symptom for harpies too. I was starting to get really concerned.

"I remember. Why did you get it?"

"Because you're freezing." I almost threw my hands up in exasperation but restrained myself at the last moment.

"Just drink it, please," Tim said. He was wrapped around her, trying to warm her with his body heat. He'd done that for me once, under less serious circumstances, so I could attest that he was a lot warmer than a coat.

With a suspicious look, Arie drank the coffee. Slowly the blue was receding to her normal coloring.

"Need another?" I asked.

After a moment of hesitation, she nodded. I could feel her watching me the whole time until I got back and handed her the drink.

Three coffees later, Arie had definitely thawed out and was proving that her tolerance for caffeine wasn't any better than her resistance to cold. "Thank you for your help, I'm not sure I could have made it back to the dorm on my own, you are so brave and selfless, and I am really impressed, and would you walk me back to my dorm please?" I'm not sure she breathed at all during that. I'm not even sure she put spaces between the words. She was clearly talking to Tim, as my role as 'Coffee Girl' wasn't worth mentioning. Admittedly, Tim's role was harder, but still.

Tim offered to escort us both back to the dorm, but I turned him down. The last thing I wanted was to get between Tim and Arie like this so I was trying to come up with an excuse when I saw it. Kara appeared out of the snow and beckoned me to follow.

Odd. I shot a quick look at Tim, but he wasn't looking in the right direction. I looked back at Kara who gestured more frantically. What was going on? I opened my mouth to say something to Tim, but closed it again. If Kara wanted Tim involved, she would have come here. Either that or she was avoiding Arie. If something was going on, I didn't want Arie involved either. Besides, she would be more susceptible to hypothermia after her recent brush with it. "I've got to go." I said a quick goodbye to them, and headed into the blizzard after Kara.

She didn't even wait for me to get to her but immediately started leading me somewhere. On one hand, it would be difficult to talk in the middle of a blizzard. On the other, Kara wasn't the quiet type. I would have expected an explanation.

It wasn't until I got to the creek that I got suspicious. The creek had frozen over, but my weight was enough to break the ice. The creek was shallow, but this must have been one of the deeper spots, meaning I was up to my shins in frozen water. I shrieked in shock, but managed to stumble my way out.

There was no sign of Kara. No way. There was no way that was Kara. Blizzard or not, Kara was a werewolf. She would have heard me cry out, and would make sure I was alright. She wouldn't ignore that. Unless something happened to her.

I wasn't sure if the chill that went through me was fear, wind, snow, or water. Probably all of the above. My feet were becoming blocks of ice as I stumbled up a slight incline. Normally I wouldn't notice it. Today it might as well have been Mount Everest. Never mind that I couldn't handle Everest on a good day.

I managed about three feet with no signs of Kara or anyone else. Even the footprints were being covered by snow. Guess that's what happens when you try to track someone in a blizzard. There wasn't any sign of a struggle that I could see, but that didn't mean much.

Suddenly I wondered why I had stopped. Shouldn't I be trying to follow the footprints as long as they were at all visible? That made the most sense. I took a few more steps. Had I stopped again? No, I was moving. Wasn't I?

Confusion. A major symptom of hypothermia. My coat wasn't warm enough when it wasn't a blizzard and my feet were soaked. Besides, I had been outside for over an hour. I had to get inside.

But what about Kara? If that really was her, she was probably in danger. If it wasn't her, then she might still be, depending on how the imposter made sure she wouldn't show up at the wrong time. Or not.

My head was too fuzzy to think. Get inside. Then I could figure out what to do. A few more steps. I wasn't shivering anymore. I wasn't even as cold. A few more steps. Maybe I should take off the coat. I started to unzip it, but my fingers wouldn't work. I blinked at my hand. Green. Was it supposed to be green?

I didn't have time to puzzle over that, as gray and white swept over my vision and the snow rose up to meet me.

Chapter Five
Cold Comfort

I woke up with something large and hot on top of me. Large, hot and black. Large, hot, black, and looking at me with green eyes. "Adrian?" I managed to croak out.

The black panther nodded at me. My brain started to analyze. I was still outside, and it was still snowing. The snow on the ground was curved around me, probably done by Adrian to protect me from the wind. Add the large cat on top of me acting as a living blanket, and voila, one unfrozen Violet. I must have been close to freezing to death if my memories were accurate. Paradoxical undressing, scary. Good thing I was too confused to take off my mittens.

Why hadn't he gotten me inside? Maybe he couldn't carry me. Or maybe by the time he found me, he had to warm me up in a hurry. Cellphones don't work on the island, something about being the nexus point of multiple dimensions wreaks havoc on cellphone signals; so he would have had to leave me to call for help. Yeah, I could see why that wasn't a preferred option. I didn't bother asking how he knew to look for me. That's what defender psychics do.

Besides, he couldn't talk in this form, so no point asking questions. He'd have to change back to answer me, and then we would both be at the mercy of the cold. Of course, Adrian was a black panther at the moment. A black phase of a jaguar. A tropical cat. He might have a nice thick fur coat, but I wasn't sure how long that would help him. Plus I wasn't going to truly warm up while lying in the snow.

"I think I can walk. We need to get inside," I said, teeth chattering like a mariachi band.

The cat looked at me and nodded. Carefully he pushed himself up, trying not to put too much weight on me. I hadn't even realized he had spread out to avoid that before. Considering his panther form weighed about four hundred pounds, by his own admission, I was grateful for his care.

I managed to stand up, with great difficulty, and almost fell again because I was shaking so hard. Adrian changed back to human and immediately started taking off his duster. "Here, put this on. It's got some cold protection woven in."

Huh, magic coat. Cool. No pun intended. Wait, I knew his coat was magic. He had mentioned fire protection. Still confused. I needed to get inside. "You'll need it," I stammered out.

"I'm shifting back as soon as you have it on. Keep a hand on me and I'll lead you to Stevenson History building. It's closest. We can take the tunnels, get you back to your dorm."

It was too cold to argue with him, and I could feel myself getting more confused, so I just put on the coat. Since I was already wearing a coat, I didn't think the duster would fit, but it went over my coat fine. Maybe it's bigger than it looks. Or, if it's enchanted to resist cold and protect from fire, it could be enchanted to fit, no matter what. Maybe I'd ask later. Or maybe we should get inside before we froze to death despite his coat.

White streaks prevented visibility more than three feet in any direction, so I desperately hoped Adrian knew where he was going. Though I wasn't sure how. I doubted he could see any better than I could, and he shouldn't be able to smell anything in this storm.

I was disoriented enough to go around in circles without knowing it, but my guide cat didn't seem confused. Just as I was starting to get to the point where I wasn't shivering again, we got to the building. Well, I actually walked into one of the columns in front of the building. Which is how I learned cats can snicker. Well, jaguars can. Or at least they can if they are actually shifters.

We got inside without further mishap, where it was much warmer. I could tell because I was suddenly in intense pain from my limbs trying to melt. Frostnip, the early stage of frostbite, is very painful and dangerous. I don't recommend it. To anyone. I think I tried to tell Adrian that. I don't think he understood, considering the sharp cries I was making.

Adrian dragged me over to a chair and had me sit down. I saw him go to a phone, but black started creeping into my vision.

***

I remember snatches of voices, bits of white and black, and a few other colors. I remember it was warm, and someone moving my clothes. I think I tried to fight that, but I'm not sure.

When my mind finally restored itself, I felt horrible. And cold, even though I was surrounded by warm water. A bathtub. Judging from the familiar toiletries, it was the bathroom in my dorm. I had been wrapped in a towel to preserve some modesty, but it was only semi-successful at relieving my embarrassment. Especially since Kara and Ilse were also crammed into the small room, presumably to make sure I didn't drown or slip into a coma or something.

"You're awake!" Kara clapped her hands. I winced. She continued in a quieter voice, "Sorry. How are you feeling?"

"Ugh." That said it all.

Ilse handed me a cup of hot chocolate. "Drink this, it shouldn't be too hot."

It was tepid, but as cold as I was, it might have been molten steel. Still, it revived me enough to ask what happened.

"Adrian found you," Kara started. I nodded, remembering that part. "He managed to get you to Stevenson, but you couldn't walk. So he called Tim and me. Tim helped him get you here, Ilse called the infirmary to find out what to do, and we brought you here. You need to stay in the water," She added when I tried to stand.

I subsided, realizing I really wasn't ready to get up yet. Kara and Ilse were both stronger than the average human of their size, so they could easily carry me. Unless I needed extreme measures, water was probably the fastest, safest way to warm me up, but Ilse had issues with water. I still didn't know the details, but at very least, it was uncomfortable for vampires. So having Kara for help made sense. If I was making the judgment call, I would have said to take the victim to the infirmary, but they did call, and by now it probably wasn't a big deal.

Adrian had actually called Tim for help. Wow, he must have been scared. I don't think he would have done that if he could avoid it at all. "Thanks. Did Adrian get his coat back?" I sunk a little more into the water.

"He did. Do you wish more hot chocolate?" Ilse asked.

I shook my head. "Kara? This is going to sound odd, but did I see you this afternoon? After lunch?"

Kara looked at me strangely, while Ilse let out a strangled hiss. Kara looked to her, confused, while answering my question. "I don't think so. I never saw you, but that doesn't mean much."

"It happened again, didn't it?" Ilse cut in. "An illusion that led you, where?"

"Basically into the storm. Especially after trudging through the creek, it wasn't much of a stretch that hypothermia would set in." I shook my head, regretting it instantly as slivers of light and pain pierced my brain. "I am so stupid. It didn't even occur to me that it wasn't you. Not until I got to the creek."

Then I had to tell the whole story. It wasn't easy. I had to admit my own stupidity while trying to ignore Kara's sub-vocal growls and Ilse's nails drawing blood as she dug them into her hand.

"We need a way to prevent this from happening again," Ilse said. "There are charms that can be acquired to allow one to see through such illusions."

"Yeah, I've seen them. Not to mention, the prices on them," I said. "Not possible. I'm here on scholarship, and I don't think most of the rest of us could afford them either."

Ilse licked a fang. "I would need to request the funds myself. I doubt I could convince my parents I needed nine of them."

Pride warred with practicality at the thought of accepting a gift that expensive before common sense kicked in saying it wasn't going to happen anyway so shut up already. "Well, if we can't get the charms, we need something else. Maybe a code or something," I suggested.

"But if we used a code every time, someone would hear it and figure it out anyway," Kara said.

"Maybe not, if it was something innocuous and we only used it if we were suspicious. Something like, asking about homework," I said.

"That might work," Ilse said. "Are we reporting it *this* time?" I guess she was still miffed that I hadn't reported it when someone imitating her tried to lead me into a deathtrap.

I didn't have a reason not to report it this time, even if I wasn't sure it would do a lot of good. Of course, if I did tell the faculty this time, Ilse was going to wonder why we didn't tell anyone before. Adrian had saved me last time too, but he made me promise not to tell anyone about his involvement. I had kept my promise, at times against my better judgment. "I'll think about it."

Only Adrian and I knew about his involvement last time and neither of us could be read by telepaths, for the same reason. Even if Taria did read someone's mind, she wouldn't find out. But I did need to ask Adrian why I was keeping it a secret. I had suspicions, but that was all.

Ilse made a sound of frustration, but dropped the subject. The water was cooling so I asked if I could get out now. Ilse and Kara helped me out of the tub and to my room. Both paused at the door because both vampires and werewolves have an ingrained sense of territory. You don't cross into another's territory unless you have permission or are making a challenge. I nodded, too out of it to want to talk. They helped me to bed; someone had warmed up the blankets, then left to let me rest. The cold was making me so sleepy.

***

To make Ilse and Kara feel better, I went to Taria the next day. Unfortunately, she wasn't in her office when I got there. Not terribly surprising, she had to be very busy.

Her office hours were due to start in an hour, so I could come back then. She had a list on the door where students could sign to make an appointment. It gave them priority over walk-ins. I rummaged through my pockets looking for a writing tool.

"Problems?" A voice from behind me made me jump, turning to see Ms. Graz. "My, you are a nervous one, aren't you?"

"Sometimes," I stammered out. "Do you have a pen I could borrow, please?"

"Making an appointment?" The dragon eyed the door. "Taria is a very busy woman. I hope it's important."

"It is." Well, I thought so anyway.

She arched an eye ridge. "Then perhaps I could help. I am a member of the senior faculty, after all."

I couldn't come up with a good reason to refuse. "Okay, I think someone tried to kill me yesterday."

The dragon went very still. "Perhaps you should explain."

I gave a quick run-through, as she frowned, listening.

"Hmm." She exhaled a puff of cold air, making me shiver and try to burrow into my jacket. "While that was undoubtedly a frightening experience, and you did get a nasty chill, I think you are exaggerating a little."

I started to protest, but she continued. "These illusions are sometimes used as practical jokes. A sign of immaturity, true, but not necessarily malicious."

"When they lead someone to freeze to death in a blizzard I count it as malicious." That came out a little harsher than I intended.

"But are you certain it was meant to kill? Perhaps they underestimated your cold tolerance, or your sense of direction. Perhaps they didn't intend for you to go through the creek. Or perhaps you were supposed to get inside in time. You did say you were only about thirty yards from one of the buildings. No, what happened was probably a practical joke. An ill-planned one that could have led to tragedy, but it didn't."

I shut up. There was no way to convince her, and she might even be right. I doubted it, but I probably wasn't the most objective. "Alright. Thank you for listening." I could talk to Taria later. Then again, she might feel the same way.

I wandered back to my dorm, trying to figure out how I felt. What happened yesterday could easily have killed me, but Ms. Graz was acting like I was throwing a hissy fit over a prank. A lot of things had happened since I started school and for the most part the staff hadn't been particularly helpful. In fact, some seemed to think I was the problem. Not a fun situation to be in. But I had to stay. Hyde needed at least one human to stay open.

The room was quiet when I got back. Ilse was still asleep, of course, and I was still more sensitive to cold because of yesterday's events. After cocooning myself in blankets, I wrote a quick email to my family. I mentioned having a quick brush with hypothermia, but not how it happened or how bad it got. Just as I finished sending my email, another one popped up. From Jesse.

Hey, Vi,

Just wanted to let you know I got accepted to Hyde. So plan on my joining you after Christmas. You'll introduce me to your roommate, right?

Jesse

I buried my head in my hands and tried to ignore the feeling that things were about to get worse.

Chapter Six
Holi-Daze

By the next time our oath group gathered, everyone had heard of my mishap with hypothermia, though not everyone knew that I had been deliberately lured away. It was quickly agreed that we did need some safeguards, and possible measures were discussed.

"How is research going?" I asked. Tim, Adrian, and I were still blocked, but hoped others were having more luck.

"We found the code of conduct," Bria said. "We're still looking into the founding of the school and other things, but you want to read this." She pulled out some papers she had printed.

Fortunately the thousand year old creed was not written in English, meaning the translation spell translated it into something more equivalent to modern English.

I swear to maintain discipline, academically, physically, and mentally; to abandon intolerance and embrace understanding. To be loyal to the school and my home, obey my superiors, and defend the school as necessary. I will strive for peace, but prepare for conflict. I will do my best to be my best.

We all read the creed in silence. "Okay, how does this change things?" I asked when it looked like everyone was done. "It looks like we have to make sure we work hard in classes and try to avoid prejudice. That's not surprising."

"It may mean making sure we get the best possible grades we can," Kara said. "I know a few times, I've felt a bit sick when I didn't put all the effort I could into a grade."

Allison nodded. "I think she's right. And it might be worse, now that we know. Physical discipline. I think they mean exercise. Does everyone have an exercise routine?"

Some of us did, some didn't. I had played lacrosse in school, and developed a routine based on that. Some of it still carried over, like my tendency to take a walk around the island in nice weather. Sometimes I used some of the exercise equipment at the gym, or the pool, but not as often as I could. I made a mental note to get back to that. Maybe we'd start an exercise program.

"How about the mental discipline?" Denise asked.

"Probably concentration, making decision based on logic instead of emotion, not letting your mind wander when you need focus," Ilse said dismissively. "Not terribly difficult."

"Not everyone has been trained in that," I pointed out. She looked a little surprised at that. "Though, I think you're right. That's something I'm sure we can all work on. Loyalty to the school and obeying teachers, not a surprise. What's this about defending the school? Do they mean verbally, or…"

"It was written in a time of frequent war," Tim said. "That was probably put in place in case the school was attacked. Now, I believe verbally will be sufficient."

"Quick question, are we disobeying the oath by continuing to look into all this?" I asked. Breaking an oath seemed to be a very bad thing, and I really wanted to avoid that.

"We were never explicitly told to leave it alone," Allison said, looking at the floor, an uneasy note in her voice. "It was implied, but never said."

It would have to do, especially as I wasn't sure we could drop it now.

***

"Hey, Mom. It's Violet. Happy Thanksgiving." If I had timed this right, thanksgiving dinner would have ended about half an hour ago, and everyone would be sitting around wondering if it was worth getting up to lie down.

"Violet! I'm glad you called. Happy Thanksgiving."

"I didn't interrupt dinner, did I?"

"No, of course not. Here, let me put you on speaker."

Soon my sister, Rose, and Dad were wishing me a happy Thanksgiving too. "Why couldn't you come home?" Rose asked.

"Because it's a Canadian school. They don't celebrate American Thanksgiving," I said. "Canadian Thanksgiving is in October. Must not be a big deal here, I didn't even get the day off." The school hadn't celebrated at all, I had no idea how major a holiday it was in Canada proper. "Besides, if I came home for Thanksgiving, I wouldn't be able to come home for Christmas."

"But you will be back for my birthday, right?" Rose continued. She was turning fourteen on the fifteenth.

"Yes, my tickets are for the eleventh."

"So your semester is wrapping up. Finals coming up?" Dad asked.

"Soon. The teachers are starting to make 'subtle' remarks about how much studying we'll need to do. Final papers and projects will be due in a week or two. If I don't procrastinate too much, I should be fine." I heard Mom stifle a laugh at that, and smiled. "My Biology project is almost done, and I've been working on my Lit papers." I needed as much time and help on those as I could get.

"Alright, we won't nag," Mom said. "Is everything okay? You keep sounding… distant."

I bit my lip wondering how to answer that. Things had been tense lately. As a group we spent more time working on our school work to avoid breaking the oath. Ilse had taught us some mental discipline tricks, some of which helped the studying part. Each of us developed an exercise routine, some overlapping to share. For example, twice a week Kara and I used the treadmills at the gym. She was faster and had more stamina than I did, but it wasn't a competition. Adrian turned out to have studied stick fighting, and insisted on teaching me, working with me three times a week, though he was willing to work with others also. He said that he wanted to make sure I wasn't defenseless, and chances were good that I'd be able to find something that resembled a stick in most environments. So we were busy.

Research was stalling out. I had gotten a few more of those mini panic attacks, and several recurring headaches. "It's been a bit stressful. I think I'll be glad of a break."

I could just see Mom shaking her head. "Maybe you shouldn't have gone to a college so far away."

"No, I think this was the right one. I'm learning things here that I wouldn't learn anywhere else. That doesn't mean it's always easy though."

"No, it wouldn't be." Dad sounded like he was smiling. "You are studying hard?"

"Of course." I didn't dare not.

"I've been in your room!" Rose piped up.

"Surprise, surprise. You aren't making a mess, right?"

"Not much."

I shook my head. "Make sure to clean up."

"Or else what?"

"Or I'll leave your birthday present here," I mock-threatened.

I could hear Rose grumbling over the line. Time to change the subject. "Are you going to Uncle Jack and Aunt Laura's house tomorrow?" Dad's brother and his wife had lived in our neighborhood since before I was born. Traditionally we would get together for major holidays, though Thanksgiving and Christmas, it was usually the day after.

"Yeah. Jesse asked if you'd bring home your school handbook so he'd have some idea what the school's like," Rose said.

I winced. Not at all possible. Jesse had to sign a magic contract to not share any of Hyde's secret before I could tell him anything. I was pretty sure that included showing him the handbook. Magic contracts were way too dangerous for me to be willing to risk it. "I'll see what I can do." Now I just had to remember to 'forget' the book at school. "So, it's definite? He's coming to Hyde?"

"Seems to be. Though it's weird. All of his best offers from other schools came after he had been accepted at Hyde." Dad said.

My fingers gripped the phone. That was… interesting. Thinking back, I was pretty sure that most of my best offers came after Hyde also. Could that be one of the reasons why Hyde didn't get many human students? Someone pulled strings to try to get the humans to go other places? "Interesting. But he wants Hyde, huh?"

"I guess so. Hey, can I go to Hyde when I go to college?" Rose asked.

"You can apply if you want to," I said as calmly as I could. It would make my life both easier and more difficult if Rose came to Hyde. Though she had about five years until college, so I wouldn't worry about it too much. Right.

We didn't talk much longer. International calls weren't cheap. Good thing Dad had given me an International phone card before I left. Hanging up the phone, I sunk into the couch. I had been feeling melancholy all day, probably because of Thanksgiving.

I had never been away from home during Thanksgiving. Of course, I had never been away during my birthday before either, but there had been too much going on to think much about it at the time. Today, I just felt down.

This was the longest I had been away from home. I missed everyone. At the same time, I was worried about what would happen when I went home. Things were not going to be easy. I wasn't sure I would be able to talk to my family without sounding like some kind of idiot.

I wondered if this was a holiday for any of my friends. Adrian, Allison, and Denise were from my dimension; but the Chars were Canadian, and Denise was from the Bahamas. Had someone asked me earlier, I wouldn't have said that Thanksgiving was that important to me. Meeting with Uncle Jack and Aunt Laura was something we did often. The time off school was nice, the meal was fun, but that was more or less it. Why did I miss it so much now?

Shivering, I got up to put on a sweater. I still couldn't adapt to the cold. It wasn't as bad as it had been for the week or so after my hypothermia, though. In fact, usually I seemed to deal a little better than I used to. Maybe it was my depression that was making everything worse.

Almost without thinking about it, I turned on the computer and opened my latest email from home. Mom had sent some pictures. I ran through the slideshow twice. If I went through it again, I'd probably end up crying.

It helped some. I got through the rest of the day, even had turkey for dinner. I think Ilse knew something was wrong, but I didn't say anything and she didn't ask.

***

The week before finals was called Dead Week, which felt accurate. It didn't kill anyone, that I know about, but those projects and papers stressed me out more than finals did. It didn't help that we learned; yes, we really did have to do our best in school or face negative consequences. Fortunately, whatever was judging our actions judged our intent, not our actual grades. I had a terrible headache for a day when I didn't put enough effort into a music assignment, but I did get an A on it. While a paper for lit, where I scraped by with a B- didn't cause any problems.

I'm not sure if the prank war between the science department and humanities department helped or hindered the stress. At least the polka dots went away on their own after a day or two. All my books turning completely yellow, including the text, was worse but that was only a couple hours.

Still, the week passed, and so did finals. One more day until the semester ended and we dispersed. Today, we had special plans. But first, I had to get through Adrian's lesson.

"Hold it up! Your staff isn't going to protect you if you have it next to your ankles," Adrian said.

Easier said than done. My arms were getting tired, and he seemed worried about how I'd do at home where I wasn't surrounded by Adrian and the rest, so he was driving me hard. But, I lifted my padded short staff, and eyed him carefully.

"Watch your feet." He danced around me. I followed, with much less grace. I could see that he was going to swing his staff just before he did, and was able to block him. "Good. Now, try to attack me."

Yeah, that part was harder. I was getting fairly good at defense, mostly from watching body language. Offence was still a little beyond me. "Do I have to?"

"Yes."

Sighing, I watched him trying to figure out the best angle of attack. There wasn't a good one. Adrian was a lot more experienced then I was, and his reflexes were amazing. I snapped forward, swinging. He grabbed my wrist, pushing it to the side, leaving me open. "Too impetuous. The speed was good, but I'm faster than you. Most people in this school are. Speed is not going to help you."

Most in this school were faster than me, most were stronger than me. "Then what am I supposed to do?"

"When you can? Run. Somewhere out in the open, where others can see."

"Great advice, Adrian. I'm all warm and fuzzy inside." I looked at my watch. "I promised I'd meet Kara soon. Walk me there? In case I get attacked by faster, stronger beings who aren't afraid of sticks?"

He breathed out a laugh. "Sure. Let's just put things away first." We had reserved a room in the gym. It kept us out of the cold (it was a balmy fifteen degrees today) and gave us a clear spot to move. But it also meant we had to put away anything we pulled out. Which wasn't much, just some padded short staves. We put those away, donned our coats and I headed for the tunnels claiming that it was too cold to walk outside.

I led the way to my dorm, while trying to keep up light conversation. Asking about finals, was he looking forward to next semester, things like that. He answered my questions, but the answers were slower in coming.

"Violet, is something going on?" He finally asked.

"What do you mean?"

"You're acting weird," He said flatly.

We had reached the basement of Price, I walked a little further than turned to face him. "Weird how?"

He was looking at me very suspiciously. "What's going on?"

Paranoid much? "Seriously Adrian, what are you talking about?"

His eyes narrowed. "Violet…"

I smiled. "Trust me." With that, I opened the door to Price 18.

"Surprise!" Several voices cried out. Adrian practically flew to stand between me and the door before he stopped and realized it was just the oath group. "Happy Birthday, Pink Panther," Allison said, coming forward, ignoring his reaction.

I moved to the side so I could see his face. He just stared gob-smacked for a moment as he looked around. "Birthday? You threw me a birthday party?"

"Yup, so come in already," she said. Most of the rest were holding back a little trying to see if he was pleased, but Allison didn't even blink. She walked up to him, grabbed his arm and pulled him inside.

I followed after a moment, allowing me to see that Allison had clearly picked the theme. Only she would have decorated the room with Pink Panther decorations. Most of the rest of the group had only heard of Pink Panther through her. My favorite was the inflatable five-foot tall Pink Panther in the corner, wearing a party hat (also Pink Panther) and holding a sign wishing Adrian a happy birthday. The streamers, the cake, the party hats that everyone was wearing, even the table cloth and a lot of the wrapping paper had Pink Panther designs on them. The plates were pink, as was the punch.

Adrian stared for about another minute before he started laughing. "Thank you. I think." That was Kara's cue to sweep up and put a silly party hat on him and give me one.

"Someday you are going to explain the significance of this 'Pink Panther' to us." Tim said, now that it was evident Adrian wasn't going to throw a fit or run away. "You said it was a cartoon, but I'm afraid I still do not comprehend."

"That's fine. I'll see if I can't bring back some Pink Panther cartoons when I come back next semester."

That could be fun. I didn't think I had ever seen any of them myself. I put the hat on and helped Ilse serve up punch. Someone had even thoughtfully made sure there was a foil packet or two for Ilse. I'm not sure if she could drink the punch or eat the cake or not.

"You were the distraction?" Adrian asked, after we sang and Allison made him blow out candles. Those of us who knew the song and the significance of the candles had to explain it to the others.

"I was. What I want to know was why you immediately thought I might be in danger. You said yourself that I was acting weird, and wouldn't you know if I was actually in danger?"

Adrian gave a one armed shrug as he took a piece of cake. "Danger can come pretty quick. I might not have gotten the warning quickly enough, and was already on edge."

"Presents!" Kara flounced over. "Open them, open them!"

He backed up a step under her enthusiasm, holding his plate up as a shield. "Can I finish my cake first?"

She pouted but backed off to let him eat. I fought off a snicker, and started talking to Kara about how we could communicate over Christmas break. Communication between dimensions is tough unless one of those points is in both dimensions. For example, I couldn't call Ilse directly, but I could email her school account that she would then check from home.

"I have been conferring with my family, and they have invited everyone over for a visit during January's break. They'll be meeting us half-way." Tim surprised us with.

"Where's half-way?" I asked warily. I'm not sure what dimension Tim is from, or what part of the planet he lives at in his dimension, but I was used to stories of yetis coming from the Himalayas.

"The North Pole."

I could feel my jaw drop. "You can do that?"

"In my dimension, certainly. I have spoken to the school and they have agreed to temporarily remove the spell preventing dimensional travel."

I didn't remember what they were celebrating, but there was a four day weekend near the end of January. As scary and cold as such a trip would surely be, it was a once in a lifetime chance. How could I possibly say no? Apparently I wasn't the only one to feel that way. Especially when Tim promised his family was picking up travel and lodging expenses. It didn't feel right to take advantage of them like that, but Tim wouldn't even tell us what the costs were, just saying it was reasonable in his dimension. Of course, since I didn't know anything about the currency in his dimension, I didn't know what counted as reasonable. I decided to thank Tim, and his family, and stop worrying about it.

"What is your family like?" I asked Tim.

He smiled, revealing long canines. "My clan is relatively small, run by my Granddam, my Dam's Dam. It includes my parents, my two sisters, and myself."

I wondered if yeti clans were often matriarchal, but it didn't seem polite to ask. I could look it up sometime. "You are going to see them for Ch… whatever the break is for you, right?"

"First Winter's Night. Yes, it is a major holiday for us. The beginning of a new year and the start of the Festival of Ice."

I nodded as if I knew what he was talking about.

"Have fun," Kara said. "I know I'm looking forward to going home. I haven't been away from my pack this long, ever."

"What exactly is your 'pack'?" I asked. "Is it immediate family? Extended family? The neighborhood?"

She took a bite of cake as she considered her answer. "Sort of a really large extended family. I'm technically related to all of them, but half the time I'm not sure how. Though I was mostly thinking of my immediate family."

"How big is your family? I remember you mentioning siblings." I suddenly felt bad for not knowing. Kara knew about my sister, why didn't I know about her family?

"Three sisters, and twin brothers. I'm the oldest, the twin terrors are the youngest. Probably with good reason." Kara grinned. "They're five, Lisa's eight, Mina's twelve, and Susan is fifteen."

I smiled back, wondering how one managed in such a large family. Still, Kara seemed happy. Adrian sauntered over, having finally finished his cake. I turned to him. "How about you? Are you looking forward to going home?" I knew he had spent the summer here, so he probably hadn't been home since last Christmas.

"I'm staying here. I signed up for an intensive course in Calculus." He didn't look at any of us, choosing to study the inflatable Pink Panther.

I bit my lip, trying to figure out something to stay. "Um, I didn't know you were interested in Calculus."

"It fit the time slot."

Okay, that just made it worse. What on earth was going on with his family? Both Allison and Adrian had occasionally hinted that things weren't great, but I had trouble imagining deliberately avoiding going home. "Sorry."

Adrian shrugged, but didn't look up. "Allison will come back early, part of her committee stuff. I'm not too worried about it."

Kara, Tim, and I exchanged a look. Tim looked confused and a little concerned, and Kara looked like she was trying not to look horrified. Then she took a deep breath, and smiled. "Okay, time for presents!"

Chapter Seven
Home for the Holidays?

I had forgotten just how much travel wore me out. In my defense, I really only had one other experience with extensive travel. But I was remembering the lesson very clearly as I shuffled through the Newport News Airport. I'd say I was zombie-like, but I've met zombies, and they have more brains than I did at the time.

It's impossible to get seriously lost in the Newport News Airport. It just isn't big enough, and it's built in straight lines. But I made a spirited attempt at it. Dad was waiting for me by baggage claim, and he says I walked right past him. Perhaps I did. I do know I nearly walked into a pole so it's entirely possible. I had been traveling for about ten hours straight. Four airports, three planes, and one of those airports was O'Hare. Thank goodness I hadn't lost all my brain cells by then, or I might still be there.

"Hey there, Purple Girl, no hug for me?" Dad stopped me from nearly walking into a support column again.

I smiled at him. "If I did, I might fall asleep on you."

He laughed. "I know how you feel. C'mon, let's go home. You can eat something and collapse."

"Good idea. Airline food is lousy. Why am I telling you that? You know better than I do." Dad's job as a company vendor took him all over the country. He probably had enough frequent flyer miles to buy a plane.

"True, but Mom's making your favorite."

I grinned and not just at the thought of Mom's hamburger casserole. Whenever any of us was gone for more than a weekend, Mom would insist on making our favorites when we got back. There would probably be apple pie for desert too. Just because that was how Mom did things. "Looking forward to it."

***

Rose had been at choir practice, so I got home before she did. I could tell the instant she walked home. "You're home! How was Hyde? Did you get me anything?"

I laughed. "Sorry, Violet has been replaced by a zombie. A really dumb one. Try again tomorrow."

"Hmph." I still got a hug though. "It isn't even that late."

"You try traveling for ten hours. Good thing there's only two houes time zone difference or I'd spend half of break trying to adjust to that."

"And the same time adjusting when you got back," Dad said. "Now, who's going to set the table?"

Dinner revived me, but it also gave my family the chance to ask more about school. Being vague worked a lot better over email. Yes, I liked my teachers. Mostly. The classes were interesting. I had made friends. What were they like? Well, you know... No, I didn't have all my grades yet. Yes, I had registered for next semester's classes.

"I'm taking Basic Genetics, Bio 2, a government class, a math class, and this required course for all students. It's kind of a practical life skills class." If I remembered correctly, it was called 'Practical Life Applications' on the transcript. Probably because most schools would think something was weird if it said 'Magic for Non-magic Users'. It wasn't the only class to have a different name on the transcripts, but it was one of the most well-known.

"How many of those are required for all students?" Mom asked.

"Most of them. Bio 2 fits my science requirement. Basic Genetics is a requirement for my major, since I'm concentrating in Genetics. It's an upper-level course, but I asked the teacher. He said I could take it if I got an A or better in Bio 1. I already know I got an A+ in that. That's like an A here. The rest are required."

"Good job. So, you like Hyde?" Dad asked.

"I do. I'm learning more than I ever anticipated. I also have some great friends and it's amazing. But there are a lot of adjustments."

"Is it a monster school?" Rose asked excitedly. She had been calling it that since learning the name, probably because her class was reading *Dr. Jekyll and Mr. Hyde* while I was applying.

No one understood why I suddenly started laughing so hard that I fell out of my chair, but Mom declared that it meant I was tired and needed to get some sleep. Since that sounded wonderful, I didn't try to argue.

***

As a senior in high school I had been involved in the Young Scholars Science Competition. My project, which involved breeding fruit flies for particular strains, took me through a few levels of the competition, meaning I kept up the project for months, much to Mom's dismay. It also meant spending an extraordinary amount of time with my biology teacher, trying to figure out how to improve my project and pass the contest. Ms. Green was the one to tell me about Hyde and how much she loved it there. She did not, however, mention anything about how odd it was.

Finding Ms. Green wasn't hard. All her students knew she regularly hung out at the coffee house by the school, willing to answer questions and help with homework. Fortunately there weren't many students today, as she sat sipping her coffee. She glanced up in surprise as I sat down next to her. "I could use some help on my homework."

She brought up her cup a little too slowly to hide her smile. "What kind?"

"What to tell my parents so they don't think I'm insane."

Her smile fled. "That is the hard part."

"Was it for you?" Did your family know ahead of time? Did you know ahead of time? Are you fully human?

She took a small sip. "Perhaps not as much as for you. Do you want to talk about it? Somewhere else?"

"If possible."

"Sure." She looked around. "Doesn't look like I'm needed here right now."

I followed her home, which felt pretty surreal. Sure I knew, intellectually, that just because she was a teacher didn't mean she spent all her time at school. She had a normal life, a house, etc. But actually going to her place was… just not done. But, it was the best place we could talk in privacy.

Ms. Green unlocked her front door, then spun around. "Name three of your professors."

I blinked, before realizing she wanted to make absolutely sure I was in the know. She ran quite a risk if she told me and I wasn't aware. "Professor Shale, Dr. Gronk, and Professor Pod."

She smiled. "My sympathies." Only then did she open the door. It didn't escape my notice that the door shut after me without either of us touching it, or that she turned on the lights with a negligent gesture.

"Magicus?"

"Yes, actually. We're more common than you would expect. About five percent of the population in this dimension."

Interesting. "Mind if I ask you some questions about that later? We're having trouble with a magicus back at school."

She leaned back on a comfortable looking recliner, and waved for me to take a seat. I took a quick look around. The biggest thing to stick out to me was that everything in the room was in shades of green or blue, from the green-blue tweed rug, to the furniture, to the aqua ceiling. Even the woods were painted. "What kind of problems?"

Maybe it wasn't wise, but the chance to fully explain everything was almost my undoing. Before I knew it, we had been there almost an hour and I had told her almost everything. She just stared at me as I finished. After a few minutes the silence was getting to me. "Ms. Green?"

"Linda. I'm not your teacher anymore, and after that, you definitely count as an adult in my book." Linda shook her head. "I knew things were odd lately, but I had no idea. Violet, I swear, had I known you would be in danger, I never would have mentioned the school."

"I had heard of it before. Besides, if I wasn't there, the school might be forced to close."

She started to say something, stopped, then continued slowly. "I'm not sure that the school is worth the risk to your life."

"Honestly? Neither am I. But I can't back down now."

"What can I do to help?" She leaned forward.

"If my parents ask, will you please try to reassure them that I haven't lost my mind?"

Linda snickered at that. "They'll only think you lost your mind if you tell them the truth."

"I don't think my attempts to reassure them are helping any. Now my cousin is going to be coming next semester. Who knows what will happen?"

"No one. Which is why you shouldn't spend your time worrying about it. You'll spend Christmas tied up in knots, and you won't accomplish anything useful."

That surprised a laugh from me. "You're right. I'll try." Her clock, one of those singing bird clocks, chirped the hour. "Wow, is it six already? I better get back before they wonder where I am."

"Okay, but remember to contact me if you need anything. I still check my school inbox, and I know you know my phone number."

***

Two less than pleasant surprises awaited me at home. First, Mom was irritated. "Where have you been? You didn't leave a note or anything."

I automatically glanced at the clock. Yeah, I had been gone about three hours, but it wasn't late, no one had said anything about something I needed to be home for, and I hadn't even taken the car. "I was catching up with some people from high school." I had run into a friend who was a junior last year while heading back. We chatted for a few minutes. Two counted as 'some', right?

Besides, I was nineteen now. I had more freedom than this in high school.

Mom sighed. "We didn't know where you were. Jesse's here. He wants to talk to you about the school."

I had turned to hang up my coat so I had a little time to force my face into a neutral expression. "Is he?" I really didn't want to talk about the school. I didn't have a clue how to do this without giving things away.

"Yes, he is," A familiar voice said as a hand messed up my hair. "So, did you bring the handbook?"

I smiled at him, trying to smooth my hair back in place. "No, sorry. You see, the school has rules about telling non-students too much before they get there. They don't want to scare them away." I felt a painful twinge and decided that was probably a warning about saying too much.

Jesse laughed. "You could just say you forgot."

I shrugged. No, I couldn't say that because I hadn't forgotten. I had left it behind deliberately. "Sorry."

"Well, you can tell me about it, right?"

"Some things. I don't want them tracking me down for violating the confidentiality agreement." Amazing what you could say with a smile. Besides, if I kept this up as a running joke, then maybe everyone would stop asking me about the school. I sat down on the couch, took a breath and waited for the first question.

Jesse sprawled on a chair that was an angle to the couch. "What are the class sizes like? Big or small?

"It depends. I had one class that had almost three hundred students. But most of my classes were about twenty to thirty students. Of course, these were required classes, upper level classes will probably be smaller."

"How big is the campus?"

"It's on an island that's a little over a mile in diameter at the widest. Basically, wherever you are, you aren't too far from anywhere else."

He nodded. "How about the teachers? Are they cool or strict?"

"I had both. Professor Argus was a real grouch, but Professor Shale was cool, and my biology teacher was wonderful." I figured I could get away with 'Argus' and 'Shale', but 'Gronk' was almost certainly pushing it.

Jesse didn't even blink at the names. "Okay, makes sense. How about sports?"

"I haven't gotten involved in any, but there is a thriving sports program. Mostly intramural. What I have seen is pretty intense."

Jesse's brow furrowed. "Why haven't you? You played lacrosse in high school."

First of all, I wasn't sure there was a lacrosse team in Hyde. Secondly, sports were a lot more intense at Hyde than I wanted to deal with. Third, if someone was trying to kill me, a sports 'accident' would be easy to arrange. Besides, I played lacrosse more because my parents encouraged it to round out my resume. I didn't hate it, but it was more a hobby than a passion. "I want to focus on studies at the moment. Besides, lacrosse is a spring sport. There isn't much in the way of spring up there. The lake's frozen until about June."

"Then how do you get off the island?" Jesse asked, puzzled.

"When it isn't frozen, there's a ferry. When it is, usually November to June, we can rent snowmobiles. A friend taught me how to use one." Adrian had been rather kind about it, and I don't think I traumatized him too much. "I suppose you could walk or skate, it's not *that* far."

"Did your roommate teach you?"

I rolled my eyes at his tone. "No, you don't know him."

"Oh-ho, *him*." Jesse waggled his eyebrows. "Do I have to meet him, make sure he's treating you right?"

I threw one of the sofa pillows at him. "No, but I'll introduce you anyway. If you promise not to embarrass me."

"Aw, where's the fun in that?"

I grabbed the other sofa pillow and glared at him. "Any relevant questions?"

Jesse laughed. "Are the classes hard?" He slipped the pillow I had thrown behind his head.

"They aren't easy. The focus is different than I'm used to, and I had to learn a lot of things to keep up."

"More focus on Canadian history, literature, etc.? Makes sense."

There was more Canadian focus than I had gotten in school, but less than Jesse would think. I just smiled, rather than correct him.

"How about the library? Is it big, well stocked? Convenient hours and location?"

"It *is* big. About four floors, and at least one basement, with lots and lots of books, and a homicidal staircase." That won me a laugh. He'd find out later. "The library is actually open twenty-four hours a day. It's not far from the dock, which is close to freshmen housing. Though you probably won't be there. Did you get your room assignment?"

"Yeah, I'm in Shelley. I think it's 408."

"Hmm, okay, you are in the freshmen guy's dorm. I'm in Price. That's within shouting distance." I'd have to ask Tim where he was in Shelley. Maybe they'd be on the same floor. Come to think of it, I didn't even know what dorm Adrian was in. I guess I was a little self-absorbed. I'd have to work on that.

"So, tell me about your friends," Jesse said.

I bit the inside of my lip before I caught myself. What was I supposed to say?

"Dinner!" Mom called from the kitchen. Dinner never sounded so good.

***

"I love it!" Rose held up the stuffed moose I had picked up for her from the general store at Wollaston Lake. "Have you seen any moose? For real?"

I hid my silent sigh of relief. It was so hard to shop for Rose's birthday because it was only ten days before Christmas. I didn't want to shortchange her on either, but I couldn't afford to spend too much. So, for her birthday I had gotten her the moose and a Hyde tee-shirt. I didn't think the shirt would impress her much, but I was afraid she'd decide it offended her newly-fourteen-year old dignity to be given a toy. Then again, she got me a bear for my last birthday. "I have actually. Once. He was on the outskirts of town while I was visiting. He was *huge*."

"What did you do?" Rose leaned in closer.

"I ducked inside the general store as quickly as possible and watched from there. Moose can be dangerous."

Mom nodded in approval. "Good. You don't want to get close to wild animals."

Rose and I exchanged a smile. Mom was definitely not an animal person.

After that we had the cake. We were about halfway through when the phone rang. I didn't pay much attention, figuring it would be one of Rose's friends, probably to wish her a happy birthday. So I was very surprised that Dad said it was for me.

"Hello?"

"Violet? It's Linda Green. I was thinking that today might be a good day to answer a few more of your questions. I've finished the grading until the exams."

"Oh, um, well, it's my sister's birthday. Can I talk to you later?"

"Oh! Of course. I didn't realize that. Well, give me a call when you're ready."

I thanked her and said goodbye before going back to the table. Everyone was looking at me.

"Who was it?" Rose asked, as she turned her spoon upside down to lick off the ice cream.

"Ms. Green. My old biology teacher."

"Why was she calling you?" Mom asked, confused. I don't think she particularly liked Ms. Green. Not since I started breeding fruit flies on her suggestion.

"She's an alumna of Hyde, and I wanted to ask her a few questions. Apparently today's a good day for her." I took another bite of ice cream cake.

"I see." There was more warmth in Wollaston Lake right now than there was in Mom's voice. I looked up in surprise. "So you would leave your sister's birthday party to talk to your former teacher about your school, but you won't tell us anything."

"I said I couldn't talk to her right now. It can wait." Apparently that was the wrong thing to say.

"And why can't you talk about this school, and I don't want to hear your joke about it being classified?" She glowered.

About then, I got mad. I had only been home for four days and I was already getting stressed about not being able to tell anyone anything important. "Because she actually understands."

"How can we understand if you won't tell us anything?" She was practically shouting.

I knew she was right, but was too mad to concede the point. Besides, I couldn't tell her anyway. "I have my reasons."

"Like what?" Rose asked, sounding scared.

I took a deep breath. I had never gotten into a major fight with my parents before and this wasn't the time or place to start. No reason to ruin Rose's birthday. "It's complicated. Please, just trust me."

My calming down seemed to calm Mom a little. Or she just realized the same thing I did. "It isn't that I don't trust you. I'm just worried. And confused. You've never been so secretive before."

I shrugged, not knowing how to answer that. "I really did sign a non-disclosure agreement about some things. Maybe not like I've been joking about, but there are things I can't tell you. Ms. Green signed the same contract. It's easier."

"Why would a college need a non-disclosure agreement?" Dad asked skeptically.

"The science department, for starters. They accomplish some amazing things there," I said.

"You're just a freshman. Why would you know anything valuable?" Dad wondered.

"It's a small school. Secrets travel fast." That ended the conversation. For then.

***

Rose stopped by my room before bed, wearing the tee-shirt I gave her for pajamas. "Is everything alright?"

Since I had almost fled to my room about an hour ago when I felt the start of another mini panic attack, it was a legitimate question. "Yeah, I just have a headache." It wasn't a lie. My head had started throbbing while arguing with Mom and hadn't subsided yet. I was debating on whether or not it was worth going down to find an aspirin or something. I wasn't sure if the headache was a warning from the oaths, stress, or anger. Possibly all of the above.

Rose shook her head. "That was scary."

I gave her a sad smile. "Sorry, Kiddo. Didn't mean to ruin your birthday."

"You didn't. But this isn't going to happen again, is it?"

"I hope not; I'm not entirely sure what happened."

Rose gave me an odd look. "You changed."

I gaped at her. "What?"

"You're different. You don't talk to us about anything important. You stay in your room a lot. You get snappy faster, and you go out talking to others instead of staying home." Rose counted her claims off on her fingers.

I wanted to argue with her, but I wasn't sure how. I did spend a fair amount of time here, writing emails to my friends from Hyde. Stress had made me more short-tempered, so it was just easier being with old friends where I could get them talking about their school experiences rather than talk about mine.

Besides all that, going to Hyde had to have changed me. There's no way an experience like that wouldn't change someone. When Rose referred to one of her classmates as a 'harpy', I asked her what color were her wings before realizing it wasn't literal. I tried passing it off as a joke, but it did get me a few odd looks.

Thankfully, no one had notice the fine line of salt at my 'thresholds', i.e. the door and window. There was no easy way to explain that one. "I'm sorry. I'll try not to be such a grouch."

"It's not that you're grouchy, it's that you're different. You read one of my books for German yesterday. You never took German! I watched you, you were reading, not translating."

Blast it! I had completely forgotten about the language spell. It never occurred to me that some of the books here might not be in English. How did I answer that one? 'That was German?' wasn't going to cut it. "I learned a little at school. I can't hold a conversation in it, but reading it is easier." That was actually almost entirely true. I can't speak German, only understand it.

"Why German?"

"My roommate is from around that area." Actually I was pretty sure Ilse was from close to our Romania, and Romanian is totally different from German. Plus, Ilse had taught me a great many things, but languages weren't one of them. But I didn't have a better explanation.

Rose shook her head. "You're still a lousy liar. Something is going on. Sooner or later, you're going to have to tell us what it is. And it'll probably be sooner." She left before I could say another word.

***

The next few days were *interesting*. I would start the day swearing I would be more involved with my family and try not to be distant. Then someone would say something about the school and I'd get defensive. Sometimes an argument erupted, often it didn't. Mom would try to get more information about the school or my friends, Dad would ask about classes, and Rose kept watching for more evidence of whatever was going on.

I tried to handle it calmly. I would be vague about the school or my friends, with only a little more detail about classes. Making sure the books I read were actually written in English and trying to act appropriately when Rose would start using German conversation was a little harder.

Eventually I would lose my calm, sometimes over something very minor, and would leave for a tme trying to get it back. It was about the fifth time or so that I started wondering if I was more changed than I realized. After all, I wasn't usually prone to anger and I had never had this tense a relationship with my family. So what was going on here? Even *I* didn't like the way I was acting.

In fact, I got so worried about it that I finally asked Linda to check what kind of spells were on me. I didn't tell her what I was wondering about though. She thought it was a strange request, but agreed.

I watched in fascination as she sliced a fern into fine pieces, dropping them and two pieces of amethyst in a silver bowl. Then she poured boiling water over them and stirred with one of my hairs. "Never seen this before?" She asked, noticing my interest.

"No, I've only seen quick, light based spells."

"That's fine for minor things, easy spells you don't need much control over, or for some other magical races. But for a detailed spell like this, I need more." Her hands were glowing as she infused magic into the mixture.

The rocks started glowing in different colors, pulsating with light, before erupting in a bright nova of light. I had to blink back spots. When I looked back at the bowl, there were different color streaks and splotches on the surface and both my hair and the fern were gone.

"Okay, this white one, this prevents you from crossing dimensions. The blue line is the language spell. Notice how it's larger and deeper? That's because it's a permanent spell, unlike the dimension spell which is meant to be temporary. These two splotches that are almost faded look like attack spells. You said you had been attacked by magic twice. They didn't penetrate, leaving a permanent effect, but for now you have evidence of it if anyone tries a ritual like this."

"How long will that be evident?" I asked.

Linda shrugged. "Depends on what they use to test. I'm using your hair. So any spell that either has been put on you or remains part of you while you had that hair is visible. When you have a new set of hair, those splotches won't be there. So, assuming you don't cut your hair or shave it, probably about six to eight months, I'd guess. If I used your blood, it might not be there at all because you probably have a different set of blood cells than you did at the time."

"So it's like a drug test? Hair gives you longer readings than blood?"

"Precisely. Okay, this wide orange one? I've never seen that before, but I suspect that's why you are a closed mind. You see how big it is, and it goes almost to the bottom of the bowl? Whoever cast that wanted to make sure there was no way to undo it. I certainly wouldn't dare try. Don't take anyone else up on the offer either. It looks like the spell is tied to your brain cells. Trying to fiddle with it would probably cause brain damage. You're lucky that didn't happen when it took hold."

I inhaled sharply. "Got it. Don't mess with mind magic."

"Never. It's incredibly risky and very illegal. When they catch who did this, they'll wind up in jail for a very long time."

"We've been trying to help a friend of mine who had something similar happen and some memories blocked. He has a couple pieces of memory and isn't a complete closed mind. Is there anything we can do, or should we leave it alone?"

Linda winced. "Not good. Okay, you aren't using magic or telepathy on him, and it doesn't sound like it was as strong or deep as what they did to you. Be careful though. You probably won't hurt him, but if he's feeling pain, then back off immediately. For the sake of whatever you hold sacred, don't use magic, telepathy, or hypnosis on him to try to break it. Do keep in mind that you probably won't succeed."

I nodded quickly. "Let me write that down." I'd email Adrian tonight. "I wondered why the faculty just dropped the issue, but I never realized they had this good a reason."

"They usually do, believe it or not."

I didn't say anything about that. "What about the rest?"

"Rest? Oh, the spells. Okay, this green is a nutrition/fast recovery spell. Just gives you a little boost to prevent malnutrition and speed up healing. Not by much, but some. It's between the blue and the white. That's because it can be permanent or temporary. When you graduate, they'll ask which you prefer. If you were expelled, it would be removed. I'm not sure what happens in case of a transfer. This one," she pointed to a small silver streak, "is a minor alert spell. That's how the school knows if you're injured, and allows the healers to find you. I think it has a non-specific tracking spell too. For example, it will tell staff that there are students in a building and where, but not who. It only works on the island and gets removed when you leave."

"Can they track me when I'm not injured?"

"No, I'm pretty sure they can't."

"Okay, how about that one?" I pointed to a black streak. It seemed to be competing with the orange one on which was bigger. I thought the orange was a little bit bigger but it was hard to tell.

"That's the spell that prevents you from sharing information with people who aren't supposed to be informed about the dimensions, etc. It's so big because they wanted it to be strong and permanent."

"How did they get all these spells on me without my noticing?"

"Well, other than the mind spell, they all went on as you signed the paperwork in the ferry. Because you agreed to them, probably while tired from traveling, you didn't feel the spell latch hold. Besides, lots of spells aren't actually felt by the enspelled." Linda frowned at the bowl. "I'm a little confused by this." She pointed to an iridescent circle partway through the bowl. "It isn't a spell. More of a … bond?"

The oath. "It's alright. I think I know what that's from."

Linda raised an eyebrow. "Alright, but be careful. Does this answer your question?"

"Actually, I'm not sure." I explained about my difficulties at home.

Linda listened sympathetically. "Sorry to tell you, but that's not magic. It's stress. Even ignoring the whole mess at Hyde, you're trying to live in two worlds. It simply doesn't work. Eventually you will have to make a decision. You can't integrate the worlds, it's just not possible in your situation, so you'll have to choose. One to live in, and the other to visit occasionally."

Chapter Eight
Christmas Quarrels

Linda had left me with a lot to think about, even as she tried to reassure me that there was no need to be hasty. Presuming I stayed at Hyde to finish my bachelors degree, that was at least three and a half years. If I stayed for one of the graduate programs, it could be a lot longer. Of course, that was assuming I could balance things that long.

Did swearing an oath to stay loyal to the school mean I would have to stay if they couldn't find any other humans, even if I was done with my education? Could I remain at peace with my family if I stayed for a masters or even a doctorate?

I shook my head. This wasn't helping anything. Jesse was going to be joining in January, and it was quite possible he wouldn't be the only one. If nothing else, I could ask him for advice on what to do. Worrying about it now was just stressing me out.

Dad was in the living room, reading the newspaper, when I got home. It was kind of odd having Dad home all the time. I was used to him traveling all over the country. But he had taken two weeks off for Christmas. Mom's job as a real estate agent often had her busy too, but she was at least in the same city.

Dad looked up when I walked in. "I thought you went with your Mom and Rose?"

I shrugged my coat off. "I didn't know they went out. I was talking to Ms. Green. Where did they go?"

"Last minute Christmas shopping." Dad put the paper down. "Sit down, Violet."

Puzzled, I did so. "Something wrong?"

"Yes, I think it is. Look, Violet, you know we love you and always will."

I nodded. I had never doubted that.

"So, do you understand why we're worried? You aren't acting like yourself, you won't tell us much of anything. I know some bad things happened at college, but you'll barely mention them. You did say something about a boy who you were concerned might be stalking you, then suddenly you seem to be best friends with him. Now you're rarely home. We don't know what's going on, and every time we try to find out, you get upset."

I winced and stared at the carpet. When was the last time it got vacuumed? "I…"

He sighed. "Okay, just answer a few questions, please?"

"What kinds of questions?"

"Did you do something at school that you don't want us to know about?"

I blinked at that. There was a great deal that I didn't want them to know about, but most of it involved the secrecy oath. "Like what?"

"You aren't on drugs, pregnant, involved in a gang, participating in illegal activities, or anything like that, right?"

I wanted to laugh, but when I looked at him, I could see the fear. "No, I promise. Nothing like that." Well, by the original definition of the word, our oath group could be considered a gang, but that wasn't what he meant.

Dad watched me for a moment before nodding. "Alright, I'll trust you. But please try to take it easy on your mother. She's even more worried than I am."

"I'll try."

"So could you at least explain this Adrian character?"

I took a deep breath. "He's actually a pretty good guy, but he does seem a little scary at first. Actually, well, he isn't good with social skills. So when he was interested in me, he basically followed me around instead of actually trying to talk to me. We've worked through it, and his sister joined one of the alumni committees, so she's helping him with social interactions." That wasn't too far from the truth, and left out things like him being a defender psychic who basically had to protect me whether he wanted to or not.

"His sister's normal, then?"

"Well, she's better with people, at least." Normal was a bit of a stretch for the Char siblings.

Dad stared into space, clearly trying to decide if he was reassured. "Why didn't he pick up social skills?"

I shrugged. "Some people are just worse at it than others. Besides, I get the impression he's never had many friends. He doesn't seem to know how to respond to having them."

"Fine, but if he makes you uncomfortable, I want you to tell him to leave you alone. Okay?"

"Alright, I will." He probably wouldn't actually leave me alone, but if I told him something made me uncomfortable, he'd probably at least try to change it.

The conversation came to a close when Mom and Rose came in carrying bags. "No looking!" Rose said when she saw us in the living room.

With smiles, Dad and I obediently closed our eyes. I didn't open mine until I heard doors close upstairs. Rose came down a few minutes later. "Do you need to do any more Christmas shopping?"

"No, I finished most of it at school, and took care of the last already. Cutting it close this year, aren't you?" Christmas Eve was tomorrow.

Rose shrugged. "I haven't been off for two weeks already."

It wasn't two weeks yet, but close enough. "Just one of the many sacrifices of college."

Rose blew me a raspberry. "Is everything wrapped?"

I winced and she laughed at me. I was a bit notorious in my family for having trouble wrapping presents. Everyone knew that the most awkwardly wrapped presents and the perfectly wrapped presents were usually from me. The perfectly wrapped ones were the ones I had professionally gift wrapped.

Mom came down a few minutes later, on her cell phone, talking to her client. "Yes, it is a little expensive, but do keep in mind that it's in a great area. Good school district, near your work, a nice park, a good neighborhood. Remember, location, location, location."

My eyes widened as I heard the often repeated maxim. "I've got to…" I didn't even finish my sentence as I flew up the stairs, ignoring the stares. I had to ask Ilse, this could explain everything.

At the last moment, I decided to send it through the mailing list I made for our group.

Hey, everyone,

Merry Christmas, or Happy whatever-you-celebrate. Quick question. Is the school based in Wollaston Lake because that spot is in all the dimensions, or is that island in all dimensions because the school is there? The other two nexus points, they aren't owned by anyone, right? What would happen to the land if the school closed? Does anyone have any specific claim to that land? Okay, that's a lot of questions, but I think my point holds. Maybe I'm barking up the wrong tree (meaning I'm on the wrong track, no offence to anyone) but I think this might explain a lot. Hope everyone's having a good vacation.

   Violet

After sending that one, I wrote a quick note to Kara, wishing her an easy transformation and sympathy for transforming the night before a major holiday. I knew she celebrated Christmas, because she had been rather enthusiastic about it.

Kara must have been checking her email because she responded inside of ten minutes.

Good thoughts on the island. I'm no expert, but I'm pretty sure dimensional overlap is a natural occurrence, not something that can be forced. Don't know what would happen to the land. Probably something for the Inter-Dimensional Council to handle.

Thanks for the sympathy, but it's not necessary. In an all Were community, the chances of accidentally hurting someone is minimal, and nothing beats hunting with your pack. The transformation itself is still unpleasant, but this way there's fun afterwards. In fact, this might make Christmas better. Merry Christmas!

   K.

I was finishing reading when Rose barged in. I jumped and shut the email as quickly as possible. "Sheesh, you startled me." I spun to face her.

"What was that?" Rose asked, eyes fixated on the screen.

"Email."

"Why'd you close it so quick?" Of course she would notice.

"It's personal."

"And you can't tell me?" Rose looked at me, hurt in her eyes.

"No, it's… It isn't something I was telling someone else. It was something someone was telling me. No, I can't tell you, because it isn't mine to tell." That made the little email seem a lot more important than it was worth, but technically it was all true.

"Oh." Rose pondered that awhile. "I guess that makes sense. So, why did you run upstairs anyway?"

I fought back a wince. Of course there would be questions about that. "I thought of something suddenly and wanted to make sure I didn't forget." I had done that once or twice before, so it should be believable.

Rose shook her head. "You need to start carrying a notebook of something. So what was your brilliant idea? Clean renewable energy? Perpetual motion? Cold fusion?" She dove belly-first onto the bed, letting it support her torso and elbows as she propped her face in her hands. It didn't escape my notice that this gave her a fantastic view of the computer. Good thing nothing important was up.

"I'm a biologist, not a physicist or a chemist. And no, nothing so earth-shaking." I think. "Just a possible answer to something I've been trying to figure out over last semester."

Rose groaned and rolled over to avoid my playful swipe at her. Now she was flat on the bed, looking up at the ceiling. "Even on vacation, you can't stop thinking about the school. Don't you ever stop?"

"It's not as easy as you think. Before you know it, it absorbs most of your life. Doesn't school take up most of your brain?"

"Not during vacation, and mine isn't even as long as yours."

"Yeah, but I actually live there during the school year. It becomes to me what water is to a fish."

"Maybe I shouldn't go to college if it makes people act weird like you." Rose levered herself off the bed. I knew what she was going to say next. "Of course, you were already–" The door slammed shut just ahead of the pillow I threw.

***

Christmas went better than I expected, and much better than I feared. No fights, no storming off angrily, and no uncomfortable questions. The atmosphere was strained, but absolutely everyone was determined to keep the peace. It may have helped that I was so tired I couldn't gather up the energy to get mad even if I wanted to. Weird, the day before I had been almost hyperactive, then Christmas, I was borderline exhausted, and I had no idea why for either of them.

The next day, we had lunch with Uncle Jack, Aunt Laura, and their kids. In addition to Jesse, they had Charlene, who would only answer to Charlie; she was about Rose's age, and Lesley, a four year old boy they adopted two years ago. Apparently they liked gender neutral names like my parents like flower names.

It didn't take long in the visit that I began to suspect that my parents had confided in them about my reluctance to talk about the school. Uncle Jack and Aunt Laura seemed determined to try to help draw me out. However, because there were a lot more people, there were also a lot more ways to re-direct conversation.

"So, Violet, did you get your grades yet?"

"Yes, Uncle Jack. They were pretty good. How about you, Jesse? How was your semester?"

"What was your favorite class, Violet?"

"Biology, but music was pretty cool too, Aunt Laura. Hey, Charlie, weren't you in the holiday play? Did they do anything new this year?"

That was basically how dinner went. There weren't too many mis-steps in the conversational dance, but I did make a big one.

"Tell my about your roommate. You get along with her, right?"

What was with Jesse's obsession with Ilse? "She's nice. Smart. Her parents are important in her home government, but she doesn't talk about that much. She's studying to become an ambassador."

"Wow." Jesse looked impressed. "Where is she from, exactly? I could tell she had an accent, but not what."

"One of the smaller Slavic countries, I think. She never mentioned which one." I wasn't sure exactly where she was from, but the geography probably wasn't the same anyway.

"I thought you said she was German?" Rose turned to me suddenly.

I panicked a little then. Just a little. My mouth didn't though. "No, I said she was from near Germany. She's fluent in more than one language." That actually was true, even without the spell. "German is a common language in the area."

Fortunately for me, Lesley accidentally knocked over his cup then, and the topic didn't get mentioned again.

***

After two days of relative calm, I was hoping things would stay on that level. Unfortunately, after a brief respite things got even worse. Actually, it scared me just how bad things were getting. Mom and I came close to having shouting matches on more than one occasion. Dad had started traveling again, and Rose seemed to be hiding from the tension. I didn't blame her, but things were smoother when at least one of them was there.

It hurt that things were so tense. Mom and I had always gotten along well, and now we had suspicion, anger, and bitterness poisoning almost every conversation.

I started spending more time with Linda just because I was afraid of what would happen if I was home. Unfortunately, she didn't really have any advice for me. Her parents were magici too, and had known about Hyde before she attended. Interestingly enough, neither of them had actually gone to Hyde. According to Linda, there are a few small exclusive schools in this dimension for non-humans. Others go to normal schools pretending to be normal humans. I had suspected this must be the case, but I hadn't spent too much time thinking about it.

"Everyone has to find their own balance. You will too," Linda assured me as I left. I wasn't sure I believed her, but I had to hope she was right.

Arriving home, I decided, for the nth time, to try to be more understanding and open. This resolution lasted until I got to my room and saw my mom searching through my dresser.

"What are you doing?" I asked in shock.

Mom flushed. "Looking for dirty laundry."

"In my dresser? Besides, I do my own laundry." A nasty suspicion crept into my brain and whispered in my ears. "I don't keep a diary." I had the journal Kara and Denise had given me for my birthday, but despite my best intentions, I had only made two entries. Still, those two were enough for me to leave it at school.

"I know that."

"Then what are you looking for?" I demanded.

"Something that will explain what's wrong with you! What have you been taking?"

"Drugs? You think I'm on drugs?! Do I act like I'm high?"

Mom just looked at me without answering.

Fire and ice raced up and down my spine. "Fine," I snapped before moving over to the dresser. I ran through everything in that drawer before moving to the next, not even caring about the mess I was making. "Where next?"

"Violet…"

"Where. Next?" I ground out.

"The bed." Mom didn't even look at me. Good, she should be embarrassed. I lifted up the pillow, shook it, and stripped off the sheets and blankets before doing my best to move the mattress. Mom helped without a word.

"Next?"

"Closet," She bit out. My ire had started to fade, but hers dumped gasoline on the fire.

I threw open the doors and opened the boxes of summer clothes. The boxes were clear, so I didn't bother doing more than a cursory rummage through. "Are you satisfied now?"

"Your desk."

I stalked over, opened all the drawers, lifted the equipment, and didn't care about the things I tossed to the floor. "Enough?"

"I want to see what's on your computer." Mom didn't meet my eyes.

"No."

Now she looked at me. "What?" I had never truly defied either of my parents before. Not after, say, five.

"No. Out of the question. You've searched my room. There is nothing illegal or immoral in here. You don't get to read my private files and emails. I'm drawing the line."

Mom stared at me, clearly expecting me to back down. Not this time. Even if I could let her read the Hyde emails, there was still the fact that I was just too angry. "Fine."

"Then will you *please* leave my room." I didn't snarl, not quite.

Mom went white, but left. I collapsed on my bed, not even caring that the sheets were on the floor, and stared blindly at the ceiling, trapped in a morass of fury.

It was hours before I came out of it again. I only know that because it was ten o'clock and I had come back before dinner. My head and jaw hurt; I must have been clenching or grinding my teeth. A quick glance at my mirror revealed tear tracks. I hadn't even known I was crying.

I didn't want to go downstairs so I checked my email. One was new. It was from Adrian, asking me if I was alright. Apparently he could tell I was upset even from Canada. I just sent back a quick note telling him I was okay. Hopefully I wasn't lying to him. Then I changed my passwords; the email password became one of the unpronounceable scientists I had learned about in Bio, and I changed the general password to one of the unpronounceable authors from Lit. Neither were from this dimension, so no one here could figure out the passwords. Not easily anyway.

My room was a wreck, I looked horrible, and I was hungry. The room could wait. I took a minute to splash water on my face before heading downstairs to find some food. Only to stop on the stairs. Mom and Dad were in the living room. He must have just gotten back, because Mom was telling him what happened during our altercation. I eavesdropped, trying to figure out if I was hungry enough to deal with this. "Honestly, I don't know what to do with that girl anymore. This isn't acceptable. I still don't know what's going on, and now she's defying me."

"Well, you did push things. A lot."

"Don't I have a right to know what she's doing under our roof?"

I walked in. "In that case, let's remedy that. I can move up my tickets and return to school early."

They stared at me. "Violet, you don't have to–"

I cut Dad off. "Apparently I do." I looked at them and shook my head. "We can try this again in the summer."

Mom sighed, "If that's what you really want."

"I think it would be best."

"Give me your ticket information. I'll see what I can do about getting you on a different flight," Dad offered.

I fetched my ticket and passport before heading to the kitchen. Mom was almost finished heating up a plate she had made up for me earlier. Dad came in while I was still eating to tell me he had gotten me on a flight early tomorrow. He must have used some of his frequent flyer points or something, because I didn't have to pay extra to be bumped.

Telling Rose was the hardest part. Especially since she seemed a little relieved that I would be gone and things would calm down. I went to bed feeling utterly miserable and alone.

Chapter Nine
Back to Hyde

I ate my breakfast while trying to convince myself that everyone was so quiet because it was early. Maybe if I told myself that enough times I'd believe it. Mom was making chocolate chip pancakes, but I could barely eat. Pity that, they were one of my favorites. I did thank her though. No one said anything about the fight before, which I was grateful for. No one was saying much of anything. I threw out the occasional comment about the things Mom usually asked. Yes, I was fully packed. Yes, I stripped the bed. Yes, I had something to do during layovers, money, and a little food. I would call when I got there.

I even threw in a casual mention about how thankful I was for my new coat. Mom had taken me shopping to buy it a few days ago. It was a Christmas present, but we wanted to take advantage of after Christmas sales. I had checked this morning; Wollaston Lake was about five degrees today.

Dad finished his breakfast and started walking me through the schedule for the second time, even though it was practically identical to the one I had going to Hyde in the first place. "Jesse will be arriving on the fifth; it might be nice if you met him at the airport."

I nodded. He'd probably need help getting to the island anyway. Classes started the ninth, but he'd need to come for orientation. It was extremely important for Hyde.

"The school does know you're coming back early? You cleared it?" Dad asked.

"I called last night, making arrangements with my dorm. Some students stay the whole break."

He nodded. Rose had been quiet the whole morning, when she suddenly spoke up. "Are you coming back in the summer?"

"I'm going to try." I certainly wasn't ready to cut ties. Judging from the way some of the tension seemed to leave Mom, I wasn't the only one.

"Alright, we should get going," Dad said, noticing we were done with breakfast.

I was a little surprised that everyone was coming to see me off, but I wasn't complaining either. The ride to the airport was as quiet as the breakfast table had been, but it wasn't too long. Dad had arranged e-tickets for me, because there wasn't time for anything else, but it wasn't a problem at the desk. I had one bag to check, and watched them put the tag on it for Wollaston Lake, which was ZWL. Not sure why there's a 'Z'.

Once my luggage was dealt with, I turned around to my family. They wouldn't be able to follow me any further. Well, Mom and Dad could with proof of ID, but Rose didn't have one, and they couldn't leave her behind. I wouldn't want them to anyway. I tried to smile and was almost knocked over by Rose's enthusiastic hug. When she pulled away, her eyes were teary. "Be careful up there. Watch out for wild moose. And squirrels."

I chuckled even as I promised I would. Then I turned to Dad. His hug wasn't as dangerous, but I was sure it was just as sincere. "Stay alert in the airports, keep your bag with you at all times. If anything happens, anything at all, call us."

"Yes, Dad." I turned to Mom, not sure what I to do. Should I hug her, or not? Before I could hesitate too long, she hugged me. I could feel a tension I didn't even know I had relax.

"Remember, this is still your home. No matter what. And no matter what, I'll always love you. We all do."

"I know, Mom. I love you too." I just couldn't live there. Slinging my backpack over one shoulder, I gave them one last smile and wave, and left to find my gate. I didn't look back.

***

A few centuries later, I got off a plane in Wollaston Lake airport. I wasn't quite as tired this time because I had dozed on a couple of the planes. I blamed that for the streaks on my face. Definitely because of sleep. Of course, I was still tired. The biggest proof of that was that it wasn't until I got to baggage claim that I realized I didn't have a way to get to the school.

When I got here for the fall semester, the postman had given me a ride to the dock, where I caught the ferry. When I was leaving, the town was nice enough to set up a shuttle because they knew the students would be leaving on a certain day. I couldn't count on a ride this time, and the ferry wouldn't be running. I could rent a snowmobile from the school to get to the town, but not from town to get to the school. They would set up vehicles for the students when they were supposed to be back but that was more than a week away.

Before I could get too worked up, I saw my suitcase get snagged just as I was reaching for it. "Is that all you have?"

Surprise turned to pleasure when I spotted Adrian. I must have been out of it not to see him there. Then I was barely able to answer him. "What... How... Yes. That's it."

He nodded. "I've got a ride back to the dock for us."

"Oh, thank you." I forced myself not to laugh when I thought of the way I discovered he frequently came to the mainland to entertain the local children. He still didn't know I knew, but I had a feeling that's how he got a ride.

Sure enough, the driver wouldn't accept payment. Adrian tried to argue with him until he saw me shiver. I was wearing my new coat, and it helped a lot, but five degrees is five degrees. Adrian cut the argument short, thanked him, and led me to the snowmobile he had rented from the school.

I wanted to ask how he had known I would be there, but snowmobiles aren't good places for conversation. Besides, I wasn't sure I wanted to talk right then. What if he wanted to know why I came back so early?

Should have known better. Adrian wasn't the type to try to start emotional conversations. He checked in the vehicle and walked me to my dorm before saying anything. When he did speak, the question wasn't what I expected. "What time did you want dinner?"

At home I usually ate early, but at school I ate late so I could spend some time with Ilse. Of course, Ilse wasn't here. It was six here right now. "How about seven?"

"Sure."

"Everyone else is home, aren't they?"

Adrian shrugged. "Pretty much. Allison's been back and forth. You just missed her; she had to go back after lunch. She's back for good after New Years."

That was still a couple days away. I nodded. "Okay. Oh, Adrian? Thanks. For everything."

He may have blushed a little. Or maybe it was cold. Hard to tell. "Don't mention it." He wasn't going to leave before I went inside, and I didn't want to keep him in the cold too long, so I said goodbye and went in.

Rachael, the second floor RA, was on duty. If memory served correctly, she was a magicus. Maybe we could ask her a few questions. If we could figure out a way to do it without seeming suspicious.

"Back from the holidays already?" She asked as I tried to claim my key.

"Yeah. I did arrange it with the school." Perhaps she hadn't been informed though.

She shrugged. "Here you go, room 613." She gave me a look over. "Everything alright?"

I really didn't want to talk about it, especially not with someone I barely knew. "Yeah, I guess so. Thanks."

"Okay. Grewlizt from fourth floor and I are the only RAs here for the moment, so if you need anything, call one of us."

I nodded, wished her a belated Merry Christmas and went up to my floor. It was very quiet. I was pretty sure I wasn't the only one back, but for a few minutes I felt like it. Even Thylica had a note on her door saying she was away for break, and we could call Rachael or Grewlizt if there were problems. She included both of their numbers and room numbers. I hadn't realized each RA was in room number six on their floor.

The suite felt even stranger. Ilse slept during the day, so most of the time I was in the room I was alone. I hadn't realized it before but even with her asleep, there was almost a presence of her in the room. Now it wasn't there. The room felt cold, still, almost dead. Creepy. Suppressing a shiver, I went to my room and basically dropped my suitcase and backpack on the floor. At least here no one cared if I cried.

***

I was a little late coming down to dinner, but at least I felt a little more human. A quick shower and change of clothes made me look a little less bedraggled, and if my eyes were red, well, what did one expect from traveling all day. Besides, Adrian wouldn't say anything. It wasn't his way.

What was his way was for him to be outside my dorm waiting for me. Which he was. "Nice coat."

"Thanks." I had been saying for a while that I was going to ask for a new coat for Christmas. Adrian knew that. It was a nice coat, two layers that could be worn separately or together. Best of all, it seemed to be nice and windproof. The wind could be piercing on the island.

Dinner was pretty quiet. I doubt there were a hundred people in the cafeteria. Possibly less than fifty. Hard to tell, some were invisible for some reason. Adrian didn't ask me any questions about home, but he wasn't chatty on the best of days. He did talk a little bit about his classes, and thanked me for my warning. I nodded, understanding the need for discretion.

Finally I had to ask. "How did you know I was coming back?"

"Most dimensions have some kind of transportation center near the school. The faculty keeps an eye on who comes through those centers. Allison saw your name on a list. She wanted to come meet you, but had to be somewhere else."

"Well, thanks. I probably would have had a lot of trouble getting to the school without your help." I wasn't entirely pleased at the idea of the school keeping tabs like that, but I wasn't surprised either. Besides, it wasn't Adrian's fault the school seemed to feel entitled to know everything. Just like my parents did. I had to stop thinking like that.

He shrugged. "Wasn't like I had somewhere else to be."

I almost smiled, wondering what it was about Adrian that he was so reluctant to admit to doing something nice for people. "Hey, can I ask a favor? My cousin is due to come to Hyde. He'll be arriving the fifth. I'm worried he'll have trouble adjusting. The school doesn't give anywhere near a decent explanation. Will you help me try to fill him in?" Before he runs away screaming.

"Sure, no big." Adrian acted blasé, but there was an intensity there that surprised me. Before I could ask him about it, he continued. "What's he like?"

"Jesse? Oh, he's a decent guy. Older than me by a couple years. A bit of a tease. Pre-Law. Loves to research. Pretty sure he was reading dictionaries by eight." Of course, I was reading science journals in middle school. "Wants to meet Ilse since he talked to her on the phone."

Adrian choked on his dinner, a hamburger that was rarer than I would trust. "He'll be disappointed then. Odds are good your roommate's got a betrothal contract with someone back home."

I dropped my fork. "She never mentioned anything like that."

He shrugged and took a sip of water. "Maybe she doesn't. But a lot of the vampire aristocracy does. She's not the heir to the family, but she is the only female. The Teps have a high social standing, so she's sure to have offers. For some reason, there are a lot more male vampires than female right now."

She had mentioned that, but never in regards to a betrothal. "So she might not get to choose for herself?"

"Depends. Legally, her parents can decide whether she likes it or not, as long as they have the seat in the council. If her brother had the seat, he could accept a proposal on her behalf, but she has to agree to it. Of course, there is a lot he could do to get that agreement."

"Ilse said she wanted to be an ambassador."

"Then they might be waiting to see if a better match or treaty could be formed. Or maybe they're liberal enough to let her decide. Don't know. Never met them."

I shook my head, dazed. I knew arranged marriages happened sometimes, even in my dimension, but it still seemed a bizarre concept to me. Of course, vampires had a lot of concepts that seemed strange to me. Like the high born families spending time as slaves to learn humility, or that certain metals burned them, but only if they didn't have a right to touch them. Anyway, if I wanted to learn more, I'd have to talk to Ilse. "When are your classes?"

"Ten to twelve, then two through five."

"Okay, I can meet you for lunch."

"Appreciate it." He looked a little hesitant before continuing, "There's less people here right now."

"True." I wondered where he was going with this.

"A lot less. But we don't know who's a threat."

"So don't go wandering around while you're in class?" I raised an eyebrow. Did I have 'Treat me like a child' written on my forehead lately?

"I mean, I think you should be careful. Especially when I'm in class."

I deflated. He did have a point and I didn't have the energy for another argument. "I'll do my best."

"Thank you."

I was fading by then, the last couple days had worn me out. Adrian noticed. "Come on, I'll walk you back to your dorm."

Good idea. Especially since I had promised to call home, and hadn't yet. The walk back was quiet. I think the only thing I said was, "Thank you," when he opened the door for me and "Goodnight."

The only thing he said was, "Night." So I guess he beat me in the quiet department.

Nervous as I was about the call home, it went well. Rose answered. She said she was glad I got there safely, and she'd tell Mom and Dad that I called. She did ask that I call back on New Year's, so we could talk when she was a year ahead of me. I was too tired to laugh, but smiled and agreed. After my third yawn, she told me to go to sleep. Wise girl. I decided not to argue with her.

Maybe tomorrow I'd write to the others, telling them I was back early. Or maybe I wouldn't. Didn't matter much. I had told Linda, so she wouldn't expect me to visit, but was there any need to tell my school friends? They would want to know why I came back early and I really didn't want to get into it. Maybe it would be best not to mention it. Oh well, I could worry about it tomorrow. Me and Scarlett O'Hara.

Chapter Ten
Making Friends

The campus was a ghost town over break. Not literally, as even with everything I learned, there was no evidence to prove the existence of ghosts. But the student body was usually about two or three thousand, and I suspected we were at less than a tenth of that. On my floor, only three girls had stayed. Phyna, the dragon who lived next door to Kara and Denise; Cal, the wind elemental from the other end of the floor; and Gradune, a gargoyle who roomed with Cal. I didn't know any of them that well, but I did know Phyna better than the others, probably because I saw her more often. Both Phyna and Cal had occasionally helped play interference when Adrian was considered a stalker. Honestly, I'm not sure what they were told afterwards. Gradune, I wouldn't swear to ever having a conversation with.

It wasn't that they were unfriendly, we just hadn't talked. At least in Gradune's case, she didn't seem to talk much to anyone. Tim's roommate, Slate, was the same way as far as I could tell. Maybe it was a gargoyle thing. Cal was nice enough when I was around, but she was friends with Arie, so we didn't hang out frequently. They were part of the same synchronized flying team. I had seen a performance once, and was extremely impressed.

Phyna and Gradune could fly too, making me the only one on the floor who couldn't at the moment. I had thought about the coincidence before realizing it probably wasn't a coincidence at all. Room services did their best to put everyone in their 'comfort zones'. For example, flyers were usually put on the top floor or floors of a dorm so they could have roof access. Beings with earth or plant based powers, unicorn, or centaurs tended to be on the first floor or below ground, or in the forest. Willow, the dryad at the end of the hall was an exception. I didn't know her story, except that staying on the top floor of a tall building supposedly required stubbornness.

Beings with water based powers tended to stay near the edges of the campus or in one of the dorms the creek ran through. Sometimes they stayed in underwater caves. I hadn't seen them, but I'd been assured they're there. Personally, I'm glad I didn't have to design the college. It must have been a nightmare!

I hadn't signed up for any classes because I wasn't supposed to be here, and it was too late to sign up now. So my schedule was empty and wide open. Which was a little creepy and very boring. I didn't want to wander the school alone, and other than Adrian, I barely knew anyone.

So, not having any better ideas, I spent my time trying to get to know the other girls on the floor. Phyna was related to Ms. Grazletz and spent loads of time in the library. I went with her a few times to do research and she taught me a few tricks. I especially appreciated the self-updating map so I could always find the elevator. I was right, the library did rearrange when no one was looking. She tried to explain the library cataloging system, but we couldn't come up with enough common ground that I could understand it. Instead she taught me how to fine tune the catalog spell so I could find what I was looking for.

Cal had Professor Argus for Foundations of Literature next semester and wanted to know what to expect. I offered to loan her my text books for the semester so she didn't have to buy her own copies. Since Cal *wasn't* given a full scholarship and would have to buy her own textbooks, she was quick to accept. She was also a model plane enthusiast. I might not know much about model planes, but I had gone through a stage where I was an avid paper plane flyer. We compared notes, made planes, and flew them off the balcony. Since she was a wind elemental, she made them do all kinds of tricks that wouldn't normally be possible. Once we got Phyna and Gradune involved, and had the 'Paper Plane Olympics'. We each made and decorated a plane and flew them. Of course, since we all knew Cal was controlling them, it wasn't much of an Olympics. I won 'Most Loops', which Cal swears she had nothing to do with. Phyna had 'Best Decorated', Gradune won 'Highest Assent', and Cal had 'Most Colorful Tail'.

Gradune never exactly opened up, we didn't have heart to hearts or anything, but we did talk a few times. Gradune turned out to be from a shade dimension. That seemed weird to me, but it really shouldn't have. I had been told there were lots of students from shade dimensions. Apparently one of her parents had come to Hyde, but hadn't said a word to warn her, or even told her other parent anything about it. I suspected she was holding a bit of grudge.

That was a scary thought. It had never occurred to me that I wouldn't even be able to tell my children about my college years. I might not even be able to tell my husband. I should have realized, but I hadn't. Not a pleasant thought to think about.

It wasn't only the girls on my floor I made friends with. Since there were about twenty or thirty girls in the dorm, the RAs were usually bored, and I often struck up conversations with them. Grewlizt, the goblin from fourth floor, didn't like daylight so she usually took the later shift. I talked to her about Goblin celebrations and culture. That was interesting enough for its' own sake, but what I really wanted was information from Rachael.

Rachael usually had desk duty during the day, and since she was seldom busy, she didn't mind talking. When I found out she was a Political Science major, I quickly took advantage of it, by mentioning I had Prominent Forms of Government next semester.

"With Dr. Kraes? Oh, you'll like it. It's a good teacher," Rachael said when I mentioned the class. She was doing that trick of walking a pencil across her fingers.

"It?"

"Dr. Kraes is a Solurt."

I nodded. I hadn't actually talked to any Solurts yet, but I had seen them around. Ilse said they don't make gender distinctions. Considering they look like walking beams of light, perhaps that isn't surprising. "What's Dr. Kraes like?"

"A little strict, but open to questions. The syllabus has a few pages of material that isn't required reading, but can be very helpful. Especially if you are having trouble with a concept or person. You'll often see it in the library and it loves to help students who ask questions. It has students re-enact important political talks from different dimensions, and is sponsor of the debate club. All students must take part in at least one debate." She smirked at the look on my face. "Most students do their debate in class, but some debate in open forums."

Public speaking. Oh, lovely. "Huh. Do all the political science teachers do that?"

Rachael laughed. "Don't worry, it isn't too hard. And you'll learn more from Dr. Kraes than you would from most."

I sighed but dropped the subject. Now, could I segue this subtly enough? "I'm not much for public speaking, but I can handle a class debate. Probably. I'm a little more concerned about the magic class. After all, I've studied governments before, but I know next to nothing about magic."

Rachael cocked her eyebrows. Drat, not subtle enough. "I wouldn't worry too much. It's not like you have to actually *perform* magic. It's more of learning what magic is capable of doing. Basic rules, like magic always leaves traces, magic always has a cost, how different types of magic are done. Plus how to tell if someone casts a spell on you and what is and isn't legal. It's really more memorization than anything." As she spoke she stopped messing with the pencil and started fiddling with her necklace, a large emerald on a gold chain, making it go from one end to the other.

"Well, memorization at least, I can do. Usually."

"Now, my classes in magic? I have to prove capable of doing different kinds of magic. That's a lot harder." Swish, swish went the emerald.

I stopped watching before I accidentally hypnotized myself. "I'd believe it. So you have magic classes, too?"

"All beings with magic have to prove capable of using magic without hurting themselves or someone else. Most of us have been training before hand, so some can test out and only take a class on the rules and regulation on magic in different situations and areas. There are classes on advanced techniques, but those are optional."

"Kind of like getting a driver's license? Just about everyone needs a basic one, but there are other kinds that are optional?" That I could relate to.

"A lot like that."

"So what makes a magicus different from any other magic user?"

Rachael started twirling the necklace. Must be one of those people who has to fiddle with things to think. "Mostly the type of magic being done. Lots of beings have certain kinds of magic they can do. Thylica is a wood elf, so she has magic that's mostly related to plants. Any spell she does has to be based on something a plant, that she's familiar with, can do. If she understands a plant that can poison people, she can use a spell to replicate that. If she knows a plant that can block pain or heal, she can do that. But she has to *understand* the plant. Not just know it exists, she has to know its limits, its growing cycle, etc. before she can use it for a spell. Don't know why it's so important, but for her it is." Rachael shrugged. "Now take Risa. She's a fire elemental, and not a magic user, but that's a little like having fire based magic, but only fire based magic. Control fires, put them out, build them up, etc. Following so far?"

I nodded.

"Magici, in general, are less limited in what they can do. Thylica can't do Risa's 'magic' or vice versa. Some magici, myself included, could easily do anything the both of them together can do. We have specialties, of course. Some are good at elemental type magic, usually with a specialization in one type, others are better at illusions, transformations, or certain kinds of rituals. Some are good at enchanting, or strengthening magic in a potion or the like. There's more, but those are some of the most common."

"So, is there a way to find out what someone specializes in?" Most of the problems we had been facing were the result of illusions. Not all, but certainly a lot. If we could limit our search to the ones who were good at illusions, it would be a huge help.

Apparently that was a suspicious question. I could almost see shutters close across her face. "Well, you could ask, but that's considered rude. Most won't answer either. Whatever our strength is, there's always a corresponding weakness."

I winced. Once again, I was looking suspicious. "I didn't know that."

Rachael shrugged. "Didn't think you did. Well, I'm pretty good at elemental magic, so I can answer your questions on that. If you want to know more about one of the other types, there are clubs." She rooted around in the desk for a minute before pulling out a pamphlet. "Here we are. I knew I had this. This is a list of different magic clubs on campus, updated to show when the next meeting is. I doubt you could actually attend, not without permission at least, but the leaders are good people to ask questions from. They love to talk about magic."

"Thanks! This should be very helpful." My smile was so big it hurt.

"Really interested in magic, are you?"

"Well, I had no exposure to it before I got to Hyde. I didn't even believe in it. Now there's this whole world out there I know nothing about, and I'm curious." I shrugged. "Besides, I've heard there's work to integrate the laws of magic with the laws of science. It sounds fascinating."

Rachael laughed and shook her head. "There's a couple every year." Necklace in hand, she pointed the emerald to the door. "Is he looking for you?"

I turned and saw Adrian standing just outside. We had agreed to meet for dinner but I hadn't realized it was so late. "Yes, I'm supposed to meet him. Wow, that was quick. Thank you for your help. Good night."

"You're welcome." Her voice followed me out the door, but I barely heard it. I had to fill in Adrian. This was going to be such a big help.

***

Adrian was reading the list, for what I'm pretty sure was at least the second or third time. "I *took* Magic for Non Magic Users, and I never found out some of that." Finally he put it down. "Probably shouldn't check out the illusion club alone."

Even knowing he had a point, I found myself getting irritated, but I forced it down. I had already gotten in a big fight with my family and couldn't go home for a while, I couldn't get in a big fight here and storm off. I had nowhere else to go. "You're probably right. In fact I don't think anyone should go by themselves. At least two or three people would be better."

Adrian murmured something that might be agreements as he took a sip of coffee. He drained the cup then looked at it regretfully as if it was somehow the cup's fault it was empty. "Do you have plans tonight?" He didn't look up, but I was pretty sure he wasn't talking to the cup.

My fork paused on the way to my mouth. "Well, my sister wanted me to call at some point between midnight there and midnight here, so she'd be a year older, but other than that, no. Does the school do anything for New Year's?"

"Yeah. There are some fireworks, mostly illusion, though the fire elementals help too. Then the cafeteria does what they call the 'Start of the Year Feast'." I could tell that the last part wasn't English, but I wasn't sure what it was. "It's free." Worth noting, because I had trouble making arrangements for a meal plan during the semester break. The school arranged something, but it was coming out of my scholarship. Adrian had swiped me in a few times, but I didn't want to leave him without meals he'd need later. "Then there are the games. Some believe that if you stay up all night, you'll have good luck the next year."

I snickered. "Pity I don't believe that. I could use some luck."

The shifter shrugged. "I did it last year."

I bit my lip before I could say something like, 'if that was good luck, I'd hate to see bad'. "So you don't plan to this year?"

"I might. My luck got better." The look he gave me was so intense that I found myself staring at my food just to avoid it. How did he put more emotion in one glance than I could by shouting at the top of my lungs?

"Well, I promised Rose I'd call her. Can I meet up with you after that?"

"Sure. Eleven-thirty? Your dorm?"

"Fine." It wasn't until I got back to my room that I wondered if this might count as a date. No, I was just reading too much into it. Probably.

***

I found a news streaming site that let me watch the ball drop in Times Square, then called Rose almost immediately after. It wasn't a long phone call. Mostly Rose bragging that they were a year ahead of me, and exchanging New Year's wishes. I mentioned watching the ball drop, but not any plans for tonight. It wouldn't make sense for a school with less than three hundred people currently in residence to put on fireworks, and mentioning a college party would probably make my parents assume alcohol was involved. Come to think of it, I hadn't seen any signs of alcohol on campus at all, and the school never mentioned a 'No Alcohol' policy. Weird.

When it was time to go, I pulled on my warmest sweater and made sure I was wearing several layers. According to local weather, it was about ten degrees at Wollaston Lake. The campus might be a little warmer, but that meant it might get as high as seventeen degrees. Not knowing how long I'd be outside, I wanted to dress warm. I just had time for that and brushing my hair before running down so Adrian wasn't waiting.

Grewlizt was on desk duty. She waved a spindly green-blue hand and smiled with needle-like teeth as I wished her a Happy Mid-Year's Night. Goblin New Year was in June. They used a calendar based around constellations in their home dimension. We had discussed it a few days ago.

To my surprise, Adrian wasn't there when I left my dorm. I burrowed into my coat and debated about waiting inside or outside. After almost ten minutes, I decided to go back inside and call him when a black panther raced up to me before changing to a familiar face. "Allison called, wouldn't get off the phone."

I nodded. "Okay, I was just about to try calling you."

Adrian stared at the ground looking sheepish. "Sorry." I was pretty sure that was the first time he had directly apologized to me.

"It's fine. Where are the fireworks?"

"Near the infirmary. That way it isn't far to the cafeteria. Come on, I know where we can get a good spot."

I followed him to the cafeteria building, but he bypassed the cafeteria proper, leading to the roof. Evidently he had been up earlier, because the snow had been moved so there was a clear spot to sit and there was a backpack loaded with blankets. He put two on the clear spot, and a couple others on the snow behind it so we could lean back while sitting.

"What a good idea. When did you have time for this?"

He shrugged. "Didn't take long. Though we might not be the only ones with this idea."

I took that as an implied 'Sit' and did so. "This is comfortable."

"Won't stay warm for long though." He sat next to me, pulling the last blanket over us.

"We won't stay here all night, and I dressed warm." I could see other people assembling, mostly on the ground, though sometimes on balconies or at windows. It was still early, but I could understand wanting a good spot.

Adrian was right. As the clock ticked closer to midnight, a few others congregated to the roof. Only five others, so it wasn't crowded. I think some might have been jealous of our blankets though. If I hadn't been on the verge of shivering, I might have offered to share, but the cold was making me selfish. Sitting still, even with blankets, was not a good way to keep warm.

"One minute to Midnight." The announcement came from nowhere, like all school announcements.

I straightened up, looking through puffs of my breath, trying to figure out where the fireworks would come from.

"Thirty seconds to Midnight." I shivered and tried to read my watch in the dim lighting.

"Twenty seconds to Midnight." Adrian put an arm around my shoulders, probably trying to warm me.

"Ten. Nine. Eight. Seven. Six. Five. Four. Three. Two. One!" There was a flourish of some instrument I didn't recognize.

I turned to Adrian to wish him a Happy New Year. The words died on my lips as he leaned in, lips gently touching mine. What? Adrian was kissing me?! Then came the fireworks.

Chapter Eleven
Happy New Year

The kiss was short. Too short for me to regain my mental balance. When he wished me a happy New Year, I responded in a daze. I ended up mostly ignoring the fireworks while trying to figure out what just happened.

Then I almost smacked myself. What an idiot. It was New Year's. New Year's kisses at midnight were a tradition in the U. S. and probably Canada. Not a tradition I had ever bothered with, but I had never been out on New Year's either. This didn't mean anything. Maybe.

I came out of my musing in time to watch fireworks of a dragon and a phoenix perform what might have been a fight or might have been a dance, while more normal fireworks went on in the background.

"Are phoenixes real?" I whispered to Adrian. Fortunately, illusionary fireworks are a lot quieter than normal ones. Probably more environmentally sound too.

"They're real, but more like really intelligent animals than people, so there aren't any here as students or faculty. Maybe a few to study, but they are protected so there are strict rules on that."

I nodded, watching the aerial ballet as they eventually burst in a rain of glowing sparks. Apparently that was the finale. Pity I had missed so much.

Adrian stood up. "Better hurry down before the crowd gets there."

Not wanting to wait in line outside the cafeteria, I hurried to help Adrian gather the blankets and stuff them back in the backpack. He took the backpack with him this time. We weren't the first to arrive but apparently most had further to go than we did, so the line wasn't too bad.

The Start of the Year Feast was good, though I ended up trying a lot of things I normally wouldn't touch. Different foods were supposed to influence your luck for the next year. Eating the blue flowers with green sauce from dimension 7d gave you wisdom for the year. The stew, fish, I think, from dimension 9b meant it would be a good year financially. The honey cakes, which were really good, from 15c was supposed to improve your love life, while this repulsive smelling fruit that grew in colors I didn't have names for, was supposed to improve your luck. Adrian cajoled me into trying it, because I really wanted to avoid it. It didn't taste as bad as it smelled, which might not have been possible, but I was still only able to try a few bites. Of course, it was from dimension 1b. The further a dimension is from your home dimension the less likely you'll be able to digest the food. Then again, Adrian was eating it, and he was from my dimension. Though he did have to hold his nose.

"Anything else interesting tonight?" I asked, after drinking copious amounts of water to wash the fruit taste away. Maybe I should have some more of the honey cake. That was delicious. Then again, the server seemed to think it strange I took seconds of it, so maybe not.

"A few pick up Durchy games; a concert or two, but I don't think you like Trwliterz music." I winced as I remembered the screeching, discordant music that I had been introduced to in music class. "That's what I thought. There's bound to be a party or two, but you probably won't know most of the partygoers." Not my style. Didn't seem to be Adrian's either. "Doctor Gronk does a talent show, but he sometimes calls out random audience members to make them demonstrate a talent."

"Doctor Gronk?" I thought about my favorite teacher. "Yeah, I think I could see him doing that."

"Want to see it? It starts in about an hour."

"Could be interesting. I just hope I don't get called on."

"I've heard he's quite the tap-dancer," Adrian said.

I raised an eyebrow thinking of the large, bright orange troll; tried to imagine him tap-dancing, and failed miserably. "That I have to see."

"Okay, we'll do that then." He took a bite of the blue flower medley. "What would you do if you got called on?"

"Faint. I don't have any performing talents, and I can't perform in front of a crowd." I shook my head, trying to suppress a shudder.

Adrian pondered the ceiling. "I don't know. Fainting on command counts as a talent. I guess."

I was about to argue with him when I saw his smirk, so I scrunched up my napkin and tossed it at him. "What about you? What hidden talents do you have?"

"If I told you…"

"They wouldn't be hidden!" We finished in semi-unison.

***

For someone built as solid as a house, Dr. Gronk was amazingly light on his feet. Fortunately, the stage was re-enforced, because it breaking under him would have taken away some of the awe. After him, Taria came up and performed a 'puppet' show using her wings to form the figures she wanted while Dean Clixot provided voices. The unicorn had a wider vocal range than anyone I had ever heard.

Then some students I didn't know put on a skit about a poor hounded dragon who constantly had to defend himself from mean, vicious knights and warriors. At last, the dragon drove the king and his knights out of the kingdom, which had originally belonged to the dragon anyway. I thought it was an interesting role reversal, but to some, that was how the tale was supposed to go.

There was a magic show, involving two magici performing illusions. Professor Shale sang, causing her snakes to dance a frenzied dance. A giant centipede juggled with multiple sets of arms. Then Dr. Gronk called someone from the audience. The student looked human but I suspected he was a vampire. He came up and hypnotized a few volunteers. Definitely vampire.

A few shifters shifted into their animal forms and did tricks. A morpher, someone who could shift into looking like different people, changed into different teachers to do impressions. Some of those were fantastic. Then Dr. Gronk came forward again. "Let's see, we need another 'volunteer'. How about you?" He pointed straight at us.

I almost choked. Did he mean me? I couldn't perform. I couldn't do anything like what they were doing. I had only been joking about fainting, but for a second I was truly afraid I would.

Maybe he wasn't pointing at me. Maybe Adrian was afraid I'd pass out. Or maybe he actually wanted to do something, but Adrian stood up and started making his way to the front. Relief and guilt swept through me in a flood, as I leaned forward to whisper to him, "Break a leg." It was only after that I realized he might not be familiar with that stage tradition. He gave a quick almost smile, so I guess he did understand.

As he had for all the other, Dr. Gronk had Adrian introduce himself. "My name is Adrian Char."

"Okay, Adrian. What are you going to be doing to entertain these fine beings in the audience?"

Even from a distance, I could swear I saw him smirk before getting control of it. "I'll sing."

"So you can sing?"

"I never said that. Either way, you'll be entertained. Or annoyed."

Dr. Gronk laughed. "Very well, take it away."

I had never heard Adrian sing, so I leaned forward to hear better. Adrian had a rich baritone when talking, I could only imagine him singing. The first lines took my breath away.

"There's no time for us. There's no place for us."

"*Who wants to live forever*," I breathed. It was one of my favorites. By the time he was halfway through, I was tearing up. Unless I was mistaken, I wasn't the only one.

"Thank you, Adrian Char," Dr. Gronk said, sounding a little moved himself when he finished.

When Adrian got back to me, I was barely able to whisper to him, "That was beautiful."

He shrugged, looking like he was fighting off a blush. "Allison is better."

"Maybe, but she isn't here. You were, and you did a wonderful job."

The talent show continued until four in the morning. I was barely awake by then, but Adrian seemed to think it was a good idea to stay awake at least until six. I wouldn't have taken Adrian for the superstitious type, but he kept pushing me towards all these good luck traditions. Maybe it wasn't superstition, maybe it was tradition. Or maybe he was a night person.

I was always skeptical about the idea of certain things giving you luck, good or bad. Then again, my boundaries of reality were constantly being expanded. If magic was real, maybe some of these really did work. Besides, I could definitely use some improvement in my 'luck'.

Still, I was struggling to stay awake as it was, I didn't have energy for anything too intense. No snowball fights, no sports, and I'd probably fall asleep if I sat still much longer. Finally we compromised.

"Roll it, like this," Adrian instructed. "Haven't you ever done this before?"

"Not really. Virginia doesn't get snow every year, and when we do get snow, there isn't a lot and it's usually gone in a day or two. Sometimes a week." I followed his instructions. "Is this big enough?"

"Not even close. About twice that size."

I looked up from the snow I was working on. "How big is this going to be?"

"Big," Adrian said, in a matter of fact tone. "The first snowman of the year should be big. Besides, it's your first time."

I had no idea Adrian was a snowman aficionado. Still it was easier to humor him. "How's this?"

He nodded and helped me put it on the ball he had been making. "You've seriously never made a snowman before?"

"Well, never a big one. A few years ago Rose and I made some mini ones, but someone came tromping through and knocked them all down. Then Jesse thought they were snowballs for a snowball fight." I smiled remembering. "Rose and I thought he knocked down our snowmen, so we tackled him and dropped snow down his back."

Adrian shook his head, but I could see his shoulders shaking. "You two close?"

"Rose and I? Pretty close, especially when you consider the age difference. I'm not sure if five years apart helped or hurt the relationship."

"I meant you and your cousin."

"Oh." I frowned at the snowball that would be the snowman's head. "Not very. I mean, we live within a few blocks of each other, so he's always been there. When we were younger, he was a terrible tease; always acting like I was a little kid while he was a responsible grownup. Sure, Jesse was pretty mature for his age, teasing excluded, but so was I, and I hated being treated like a child." I shrugged. "Things got a little better when I was in high school. He was two years ahead of me, and already thinking about college, teasing younger relatives wasn't as big a priority.

I also suspected that Jesse was the reason I never dated seriously in high school. I know for a fact that he scared at least one guy away from talking to me. Of course, considering what I had heard about that particular guy, I was better off with him avoiding me. Then again, I knew better than to listen to rumors.

"So what happens when he gets here?"

For a moment I almost had to ask Adrian who he was referring to, but I caught myself. "No idea. But I know this, if he plans to try running my life, he's got another think coming."

Adrian gave me a raised eyebrow.

"Sorry, it's been a long..." I trailed off, not knowing how to end it. A long day? Week? Month? Semester? Year? All were true.

He let it slide. "Is that a habit of his?"

"Sort of. When he thinks he knows better. Then again, I really haven't seen him much since he left for college."

"I'm sure you've both changed since then."

"Yeah, you're right." I certainly had. "Snowman looks good."

It did look good. We might not have had coal or carrots, but Adrian and I scrounged up some pebbles for eyes and mouth, a twig for a nose, and branches for arms. I wrapped my scarf around him, and Adrian draped his duster around it long enough to take some pictures. Adrian was sure that his camera could handle it despite being so dark.

"So, what now?" I asked. It was almost five, and I was so ready to get some sleep, but I could last another hour. Probably.

He gave me a measuring look. "Now we get you warmed up."

"I'm not that bad!" I rolled my eyes and tried not to shiver.

"Good. Now let's get some coffee."

"How about hot chocolate? I would like to sleep at some point."

"Fair enough. As long as it's after six."

I trailed after him. "Bossy."

"Hey, I'm buying you hot chocolate, aren't I?" If I wasn't mistaken, there was a note of laughter in his voice.

"I have money. You don't need to buy mine."

"That's nice. But Allison would kill me if I let you buy your own drink." I stared at him, so he clarified, "after all, I'm the one insisting you stay awake. Besides, she keeps thinking she can turn me into a gentleman." He shook his head, as if pondering the futility of such a measure. "Optimist."

I was inclined to agree. It wasn't that I didn't like Adrian, I did; but I was forced to admit that he didn't always 'get' the social graces. He had started opening doors for me recently, and he helped me carry my books, but that was more of an inside joke. He didn't think to make small talk, tended to answer questions simply, and rarely encouraged conversation. His intensity could border on, and at times, cross into rudeness. Not to mention, he almost never addressed anyone by name. I knew he meant well, and I wasn't exactly Miss Manners myself, so I rarely said anything. Besides, when he felt like it, he could be surprisingly charming. I was my usual awkward self all the time.

"Well, put that way, I suppose I could accept a free hot chocolate if it meant preventing sibling strife." I smiled to let him know I was teasing.

The café was pretty full as more and more were starting to lag, and a few were starting to wake up. It was too noisy for a decent conversation, and even the hot drink was only partially effective at keeping me awake. I had pulled all-nighters before, but usually I wasn't so worn during the time leading up to it.

It was five-thirty as Adrian led me back to my dorm, finally recognizing that I was going to collapse soon. "Try to stay awake until six."

"I'll try," I promised, not sure I could make it. "Happy New Year."

"You too." Adrian looked at me for a minute. I was about to ask him what was wrong when he leaned in and kissed me.

My eyes flew open in surprise, but it was over and he was leaving, with only a, "Goodnight," on the wind behind him.

"'Night," My shaky voice responded without my telling it to. I ended up in my room, not sure precisely how I got there, staring up at the ceiling while trying to make sense of everything.

Adrian had kissed me. Twice now. The first time might have been a fluke. New Year's traditions and all. The second time, unless it was a tradition I wasn't aware of, was entirely his choice.

He kissed me. No warning, no declaration of feelings, not even asking for a date. Why? Probably at least in part because I didn't say or do anything about the first kiss. Was it a message? Was it a way of proclaiming his feelings? Was it an impulse?

I groaned as I realized that one way or another, Adrian and I were going to have to talk about this. I couldn't imagine he'd be happy about it, and I wasn't exactly thrilled myself. But I seriously wanted to know what was going on!

Whether he intended it or not, Adrian managed to get me to stay awake. It was hours before I fell asleep.

***

I might have spent some time avoiding Adrian. He may or may not have been avoiding me. Whichever the case, I really didn't see him during the rest of the first or the second day of the year. Once I caught up on sleep, I spent most of that time studying. I had a lot of research to do, and not many other demands on my time.

I figured as long as I stayed with Phyna, it should be safe enough. She was working on a major project and was glad to have company. If she thought anything was odd about the topic I was researching, she didn't say anything. Her project was going well. Good for her. My research was leading to more questions than answers and I was getting frustrated.

"Anything interesting?" I looked up to see Allison standing there, looking a bit nervous.

"Back already?" I wasn't willing to ask my questions in front of Phyna. The poor dragon was looking back and forth between us, curiosity painted on her scales.

"Of course. I couldn't stay away too long. Who knows what kind of trouble Pink Panther could get into if left alone?"

I gave a quick smile but didn't say anything.

Phyna gave another look around. "I think I need to get another book... over that way." She pointed at a direction that I'd bet a semester's tuition was picked at random.

"Actually, I have to go. See you later, Phyna. Good luck with your project." I didn't say anything to Allison because I was sure she would follow me.

While I was scooping up my books to put them away, Phyna extended her neck so she could whisper in my ear. "Say the word and I'll hit her with my tail."

Biting my lip, I shook my head. "I'm not mad, but I do need to talk to her," I whispered back, even though Allison could probably hear us.

"Be careful."

I nodded as I walked away. Allison helped me re-shelve the books before suggesting we go to her room. Since she was an alumna, she didn't have a roommate, but it was alright for me to go to her quarters. Deciding that was a good place to not be overheard, I agreed; after making sure it really was Allison.

Her room was in a squat dorm, one of the few co-ed housing buildings. Apparently it was for alumni and married students. Her room was on the third floor, which was the top. It didn't look very different from my room, except smaller, clearly not meant for two people. From the looks of it, she had to share the bathroom with whoever lived next to her.

I sat down on a neon pink canvas chair, while Allison plopped down on the bed. Releasing a breath, she broke the silence first. "So, you've been looking up defender psychics? There isn't much in the Hyde library, but it can give you a foundation. I've done a lot more research." Her words were quicker than usual, sliding into each other. What had Adrian told her?

"Good. Because I have a lot of questions." Okay, that came out colder than I planned.

"Right, what do you want to know first?"

Alright, if that's the way she wanted to play it. "I want to know why you never told me that defender psychics almost always marry their primary bonded protectorate."

Chapter Twelve
Destiny and Dates

Allison winced, before trying to cover it with a smile. It didn't work. "Violet–"

"There are records of twelve thousand, three hundred, twenty-one defender psychics in the past seven hundred years. Eleven thousand, nine hundred, seventy-three married their primary bounded. Of those that didn't, approximately half had one or the other die before they could be married, or circumstances interfered. The other half remained together for life, but chose not to marry or were unable to. Only in three instances did they not stay together. This is not a coincidence, and I had the right to know," I ground out. How could she keep something like this from me?

"Well–"

"Does everyone else know about this? Were you planning on informing me, or were you just planning the wedding and decided I'd figure it out eventually?"

"That's–"

"Adrian's never said a word. Does he plan–"

"I don't think Adrian knows." Allison's calm voice caused my brain to crash into silence. When she was sure I was actually going to let her talk, she continued, "I never mentioned the statistics to him. He probably knows, vaguely, that most defender psychics marry their bonded, but telling him that fate says one thing is the best way to get him to run in the opposite direction."

"Fate?" I was almost surprised that sarcasm didn't literally drip on Allison's carpet.

She sighed. "You're a scientist. Or aiming to be one, anyway. What do the statistics tell you?"

"So Adrian and I will marry and have no choice over the matter?" I tried not to growl. I was nineteen and a freshman in college. I wasn't ready to think about marriage, and wanted to make my own choices when I was ready.

Allison stood up and moved to her coffee maker. "That's why I didn't tell either of you. So you could have as much choice as possible. If neither of you knew about the odds, then you'd be able to have a relationship on your terms. Not because one or both of you felt that fate said so."

"I don't think I believe in fate."

Allison shrugged and rummaged around for two clean mugs. She held one up, silently asking me if I wanted coffee. I nodded. She turned to collect condiments for it. "Someone once said that the existence of psychics may be the biggest single proof that some form of intelligence guides our steps."

I took the offered cup and busied myself with fixing my coffee while trying to think about what she said. "You mean someone shows you what you see?"

"Someone or something. Think about it. You've seen a few of my predictions. How important are they in the grand scheme of things?"

I took a sip. Too hot still. "I suppose if you get large enough, the only really important thing would be the death of the universe."

That shocked a laugh out of her. "I hadn't thought of that. But even if you just focus on this planet, what do I get? I tell Adrian he'll meet you, or tell you that you need to stay at Hyde. How big is that, really?"

"So, there's something, or someone out there." I tried to think about it rationally.

"Probably. I don't want to get into a theological argument with you, so we won't discuss the nature of that intelligence, but I believe there is one."

Interesting as this was, it was pulling us away from my main topic of conversation. "Okay, we'll leave that for now. But I'm still a little confused about psychics in general, and why they exist. From a genetic standpoint, they wouldn't continue unless there were advantages. But from my research, psychics seem to tend towards insanity, especially the more powerful ones." I had discovered that yesterday, and spent most of last night thinking about it.

Allison nodded. "You're right, it can be difficult to deal with. Now, many parents take steps to damp down their child's psychic abilities when they show up. I was given injections twice a year from the time I was ten to the time I was twenty to keep my powers in check. If they hadn't, I'd probably be about twice as strong psychically. But I'd also be more likely to go insane." Was it my imagination, or did Allison sound just slightly bitter about the whole thing.

I forced my bottom jaw back in place. "Did they do that to Adrian, too?"

She shook her head. "They still don't know he's a defender psychic. After all, his bond to me is a weak one, so there was little proof until he met you. We both knew he was, but neither of us told them."

"Was that risky? I mean, if you needed those steps…" I shut up before I dug myself deeper.

Allison pursed her lips. "I think our parents were unnecessarily aggressive in their steps to protect me. There were other routes they could have taken, to make things safer for me, but not damp down as much of my ability. Trying to do that to Adrian might have been a case of the cure being worse than the curse. Besides, defender psychics tend to be very stable mentally as long as they have someone to protect."

I took another sip of coffee and tried to think this over. "So what are the genetic advantages to being a psychic?"

"In general? Usually a psychic will know when a situation will turn dangerous so they can avoid it. Before there were steps to protect a developing psychic, when one developed the ability, it was common to quickly arrange a marriage in the hopes of producing children who would also be 'Seers'. A defender psychic usually has slightly faster reflexes, and a little extra strength. And, as you pointed out, they almost always marry their primary bonded, it increases the chances that their DNA will continue to the next generation."

"So, why didn't you tell your parents about Adrian? I mean, you don't have to answer if you don't want to, but…"

Allison stared into her coffee. "They weren't pleased that I was psychic, and I had a feeling it might be best not to."

I could tell there was more than was being said, but decided to leave it alone. "How exactly does the bond work? Why does a defender psychic latch on to a specific person?"

"That's why they record every instance they can find. No one really knows. If you go with the divine intelligence theory, some account for it by claiming that the two are soul mates. For those that don't believe in soul mates, Ratcherd's theory is popular."

"I read about that, but I'm not sure I get it. Something about the defender psychic having a particular type of vibration to the aura, and looking for the one that matches out of multiple possibilities?"

"Think of it like a very picky Hydrogen atom, looking for another atom to form a bond with. When it finds one, it bonds hard, like carbon bonds. No matter how many others may come that it could bond with, the atom is bonded to stay. Slightly mixing my metaphor, but I'm not a chemist."

I nodded, picturing it. "You don't seem to agree with that theory."

"Oh, I admit it does explain a few questions, like how every single defender psychic finds their bonded, or even why the distance between the two grows as the possibility of travel opens up. Three hundred years ago, the largest distance between the birth of a defender psychic and his bonded was about seventy kilometers. Now it can be on the other side of the world, as long as they come in contact at some point. But it raises other questions. For example, ages. Did you know the average age gap between a defender psychic and his bonded is about two or three years? The record, the largest age gap in the *history* of defender psychics is seven years."

I shook my head. I hadn't been looking at that information. "That does seem odd if it's mostly random chance."

"Also, the rare female defender psychic. There were three hundred eight of them. Three hundred bonded to a man. So it can't be that males have one type of vibration and females another."

"I read that. So what does the bond do exactly?"

"Good question." Allison grabbed a piece of paper and drew a line down the middle. "Okay, he has a minor bond to me, so let me explain what that means. When we're physically close, say within one hundred kilometers, he can tell a little bit about my emotional state, mostly knowing if I'm upset or afraid. He'd know if I felt threatened, or if I was in imminent danger, even if I didn't know about it. The last part has a wider radius. If I were in serious danger, and knew about it, I suspect he would know from pretty much anywhere on this continent. Perhaps further. He probably wouldn't be able to do anything about it, but he'd know. Kinda sad when you think about it. As long as we're both in this dimension, he can point in my general direction if he chooses to find me. He may be able to estimate a distance, or maybe not."

She was writing all this down on paper. "This is a *minor* bond?" I asked.

"Exactly. Now, you are his primary bonded. I don't know of any method that could hide your location from him if he tries to find you. Doesn't matter if you're both in the same dimension or even the same planet. Well, if you left the solar system, he might have trouble. Anyway, he'll know where you are, and the distance, probably to the centimeter. Of course, he doesn't know this instinctively, only when he tries to find you."

"So he doesn't know we're talking right now?"

"Oh, he knows. I told him we were going to."

I nodded. It wasn't like it was a secret. "Okay, so he *can* know where I am, but usually doesn't?"

"Right. He also knows when you're in trouble, no matter where you are, and is emotionally compelled to do something. Because he's *psychic* not just a defender, he also usually has some sense on what the best way to help is. When he stops to think, anyway."

"And this is forever, isn't it?"

She nodded.

"No wonder they always marry! Who else could possibly understand?" I burst out.

Allison laughed. "It would be a difficult thing to explain to a spouse. 'Sorry, dear, I can't stay for our anniversary dinner. I have to go save this other woman again.' Can't you imagine?"

"It would be worse than being married to Superman!" We laughed a little more than the situation warranted. Finally, I stopped and got serious. "I think, maybe, that on some level I expected something like this."

"I think Adrian's at the same stage. I do know everyone else expects it."

I winced. "Maybe, but…"

"Look, forget the statistics. Forget 'fate'. Whatever happens, you and Adrian have to find your own way. Decide for yourself the right path. Just remember, this bond is for life. So, please, try to get along?"

"I'll try, but you tell Adrian that this bond doesn't mean he can get away with taking me for granted. I like to actually know if and when I'm dating someone."

Allison stared at the carpet, cheeks reddening. "He's sorry if he upset you, but isn't sure how to talk about it. I don't know all the details but I can guess."

I sighed. Was I ready to handle this? Did I have a choice? "I'll talk to him, and I won't even mention the statistics if you want. But we do have to straighten things out."

"Good. I can arrange something, somewhere quiet you can meet. Please, be patient with him. I'm pretty sure he's never really dated anyone before."

"I'm not particularly experienced at it myself," I said with a shrug. "Besides, even if I was, this would be different, wouldn't it?"

"More than likely." Allison collected my empty mug. "One way or another, it will work out, you'll see."

"Do you hope that, or 'see' that?" I asked, curious.

Allison tilted her head to the side. "Little of both. I've dreamt about it, once or twice. But I'm not sure if that's my sight, my hopes, or just a dream."

Okay, that wasn't the least bit creepy or unsettling. "Even if Adrian and I do get together, that doesn't mean it will be smooth or easy. We'll still disagree and fight sometimes," I warned her.

"Of course. But since your bond is forever, it's kind of stupid for you to go around refusing to talk to each other for long periods of time. So you'll have to work things out."

I nodded. I still had questions and things to think about, but most of all, I had to talk to Adrian.

***

The next day, Adrian asked me out. An actual date, to the diner on the mainland. I knew it was probably Allison's prompting, but it wasn't worth arguing over. I accepted his invitation, then spent twenty minutes or more in a dither trying to figure out what to wear. Even at the time, I knew it was silly since he'd mostly be seeing my coat.

I almost went with my deep blue sweater. It was a favorite of mine, and I had been told that it was a good color for me. But I wore that when I went on a blind date with Tim. I wanted something different this time. So I pulled out my purple sweater. The amethyst necklace Ilse gave me for my birthday worked well for an accent. I brushed my hair, knowing it would get ruined on the trip, and tried to figure out what to do with it. It was about shoulder length, so it was too short for anything elaborate, but a ponytail just wouldn't do. Finally, I left it loose, but made sure I had a comb in my pocket.

I don't usually wear make-up, but I do own some. Again, anything I did could get ruined on the trip across the ice. I finally settled on a little eye-shadow, to emphasize my blue eyes, and a little lipstick so my lips weren't colorless.

Kara probably wouldn't have let me leave without mascara, blush, and possibly other things I didn't know about, but she wasn't here. Though, considering how nice I looked when Kara and Ilse did my make-up for my date with Tim, maybe I should ask them for advice. Or maybe not. I shuddered as I remembered just how apprehensive I had been as Kara forced a make-over on me.

I wasn't even sure why I was spending all this time trying to make myself pretty. Adrian knew what I looked like. He had seen me at close to my worst; a little make-up wouldn't change anything.

Still this *was* a date. Our first official date. New Year's might count as an unofficial date. I hadn't thought of it as one, but Adrian may have. I should make an effort to look nice.

Adrian was waiting for me at the docks, where he had already rented one of the snowmobiles. While I could use a snowmobile, I wasn't good at it, so we shared one. Riding a noisy snowmobile is not a good time or place to talk, so other than greetings, we didn't really talk before getting to the mainland.

I had never been in Mama Rose's diner, but Adrian had recommended it before. As such, I let him take the lead in ordering. My favorite part was probably watching Mama Rose, a plump Italian woman, probably my grandmother's age, come out and fuss at him. Then she turned to me. "Now, introduce me to your lady friend. You are treating her right?"

Adrian looked like he was trying to force down a blush. "This is Violet. My friend from campus. She hasn't tried your soup yet, so we have to fix that."

"Yes, we do." Mama Rose nodded seriously. "Don't worry; we'll have you warmed up in no time. You just wait."

I turned to Adrian as the woman bustled away. "Do I look that cold?"

Adrian shrugged. "A little. But she also thinks most people 'without enough meat on their bones' suffer from the cold. She's always trying to fatten me up, too."

I bit down a smirk. "Well, you do have a very *feline* physique."

"Ha ha, very funny." He looked around to make sure no one was paying too much attention to us. I wasn't sure what he was worried about. It was a simple enough statement. Even as a human, he had a tall, lean look, and he moved a lot like a cat. Actually, I'm a little surprised I didn't figure out he was a panther shifter earlier.

The soup came quickly, and was as good as I had been told, but when it did, neither of us knew what to say. We couldn't talk about the school, not more than the vaguest basics, anyway. Adrian shied away from talking about family, which was a topic I was a little sensitive to at the moment. So if we couldn't talk about those, what did that leave?

"What do you want to do after school?" I asked. If our futures were entwined, it would probably be a good idea to figure out ways to make them complementary.

Adrian looked up, startled, before shrugging. "Not sure. I'm a Chemistry major. I like studying chemistry, but I don't know what to do with it. I don't want to teach, and working in a lab is only fun when *I* decide what I'm working on. Research scientist might work. I'd love to invent something new. How about you?"

"I came to Hyde wanting to be a geneticist. I daydreamed about joining the Human Genome project before it closed. Now, I think it's changed. I'd love to track DNA to learn more about…" I trailed off realizing I couldn't speak about it in public.

He nodded, understanding why I stopped, even if he wasn't quite sure exactly where I was headed. "There are some interesting options open. Though for some of the more unique options, you may have to stay close to Hyde or someplace like that."

Maybe coming to the mainland was a bad idea. I had already learned how hard it was to communicate without being able to talk openly. I wasn't sure what Adrian was hinting at, and I couldn't ask him here. "Do you plan on getting an advanced degree in chemistry?"

"I might. Hopefully by then I'll know what I want to do with it. You?"

I took another bite of the soup, a cream-based chowder. Corn, I think. "To get anywhere in the field of genetics, I would pretty much have to have at least a masters. A doctorate would be better. As you say, Hyde is probably my best option to pursue some of the more *esoteric* areas." I just had to survive people trying to kill me or drive me away. Though things had been quiet lately. Maybe they left or got scared off.

Adrian nodded, and I could just see him mentally adding more time at Hyde to his future plans. On one hand, it didn't seem fair to have one person have to rearrange their plans based on what the other wanted. On the other, I wasn't sure I could make it through Hyde without him, and it didn't seem to be something he was against. Besides, all relationships are based on compromise; we would just have to make sure it was balanced. I didn't say anything, though. I could be wrong, and this wasn't the time.

"Your cousin is coming in a couple days. Are you looking forward to that?"

I shrugged. "I'm not sure. I know he's heard at least some of what happened before I left. He's sent some emails asking if I'm okay. Then there's his reaction when he gets to the school. Though, it might be nice not to be the ignorant newbie for a change." I smiled at the thought. "I figured I'd meet him at the airport. He's never left Virginia, so I'm sure he doesn't know how to use a snowmobile. Of course, I won't be able to explain anything until we get to the island." Not until after he signed the contracts.

"Might be best if you let his RA explain the basics."

"I don't know. He'll want an explanation right away, and I'll be there. Besides, I know I would have preferred to have someone I know explain."

Adrian gave what might have been a shrug. "You know him, I don't. I'll go with you to the airport. You'll need another snowmobile for luggage." Not to mention someone to back me up when Jesse didn't believe me.

I gave a shaky smile, realizing that this was going to be harder than I thought. "Thanks."

We finished our meal, and Adrian insisted on paying. I eventually got him to let me leave the tip. Mama Rose came out and ordered both of us to bundle up warm and come back soon so she could ensure we were eating properly.

I thought we'd go back to the campus, but instead he led me to what seemed to be the center of town, not far from the general store. Curious, I gave him a look, wondering about his sheepish looking posture.

"Do you like kids?" He asked.

Suddenly having an idea what this was about, I hid a smile, giving what I hoped looked like a confused nod.

"Good. Can you blow up balloons?"

I was right. The kids were already on their way as I took a handful of balloons from his hand. Early last semester, I had seen Adrian make balloon animals for the local kids, then perform a skit using the balloons as props. One of the locals, Paul Rutchkin, said it was a weekly tradition for him. I had never mentioned what I saw, and I'm pretty sure Adrian didn't know I knew.

Practice, and possibly a stronger lung capacity, meant that Adrian was faster blowing up balloons than I was. But he was also taking the time to make balloon sculptures with them, so I was able to help. Once each of the approximately thirty children had a balloon, they started calling for a story.

"A story?" Adrian asked, sounding like no one had ever asked such a ridiculous request from him. "You want a story?"

Amidst lots of laughter, there were scattered shouts of, "Yes!"

"Okay, but I need some help." He turned to me. "Miss Violet, will you help me tell a story?"

Before I could respond, the kids turned to me. "Please, Miss Violet?"

I let out the deepest sigh I could manage. "I suppose." I gave him a quick hidden smile so he knew I wasn't mad. "What do I do?"

Adrian borrowed a couple of props so I was wearing a balloon crown and holding a giraffe, before having me sit on the post office steps. "Okay, Miss Violet is the lovely princess with her magical pet giraffe."

Biting my lip to keep from laughing, I sat there, trying to look princess-like while petting the giraffe.

"Now the princess had a problem. She was very lonely, with her giraffe as her only friend."

"Oh, Stretchy," I pretended to cry. "You are my only friend." The giraffe 'licked' my face.

Now Adrian was trying not to laugh as he mouthed 'Stretchy?' at me, before turning back to the kids. "The reason the princess had no friends was because an evil," he borrowed another animal, looked at it, shook his head and continued, "poodle had kidnapped her and Stretchy, forcing them to stay at the poodle's lair."

Somehow I managed not to burst out laughing. The kids didn't bother holding back. In time, a troupe of animals, led by the Brave Knight (Adrian, of course), fought the evil poodle, with Stretchy's help. They almost defeated the poodle, before the evil poodle ran and grabbed the princess to escape with her. So the lovely princess pushed the evil poodle out a window. That was the end of the evil poodle, and Stretchy led everyone home.

Adrian made sure everyone got their balloons back, and I helped him pass out some candy. By then, most of the parents had come, encouraging their kids to come in out of the cold.

I stepped back to watch as the little kids left. Adrian got more than a couple hugs, and a lot of the kids called him Uncle Adrian. He looked embarrassed, but he handled it well. After everyone left, he thanked me for helping with the story.

"It was fun. Sorry I'm not much of an actress."

"You were fine. But seriously, 'Stretchy'?"

"Well, what would you name a giraffe?"

He thought for a moment. "Spots?"

Personally, I thought Stretchy better than that, but it wasn't worth an argument. "So, the lovely princess, huh?"

He shrugged. "It worked. Didn't you like being the lovely princess?"

I was still trying to get the static out of my hair from that crown. "Well, at least I got to partially save myself instead of just waiting to be rescued."

Adrian smiled. "You aren't the type to just wait to be rescued."

I sighed. "Maybe, but I haven't been doing too great on my own. I feel like I've constantly needed rescuing."

"Not constantly. Besides, you don't just sit back waiting for help when trouble does come. You try to get out on your own." He leaned closer. "Just don't forget, I'll always come when you need me. It may take me a while, but I will come."

There was nothing really to say to that. The ride home was silent.

Chapter Thirteen
Welcome to Hyde

"Hey, Jesse! Over here!" I probably didn't have to speak up so loudly. There were only about fifty people in the airport, but Jesse looked as tired as I felt when making the trip.

"Hey, Squirt." He gave me a quick hug, before eyeing Adrian warily. Adrian met his look and raised an eyebrow. I looked at the two of them before deciding that whatever was going on, it might be best to break it up.

"Jesse, this is Adrian. Adrian, my cousin, Jesse. Adrian came with me so we'd have two snowmobiles for your luggage."

"Oh, okay. Thanks." Jesse offered his hand for a handshake. Adrian took it after a brief hesitation. I'm not sure Jesse noticed.

"Baggage claim is this way," Adrian said, turning to lead the way.

Jesse trailed behind. "Real charmer, your friend."

I winced. There was no way Adrian didn't hear that. "He has his moments. Anyway, I appreciate the help."

Jesse had packed light, which was good because we'd have to double up on the snowmobiles. We took a taxi to the dock, and loaded up the bags. They all fit on one snowmobile.

"You ever use a snowmobile?" Adrian asked Jesse.

"No. Not much opportunity in Virginia." Jesse was trying not to show that the cold was affecting him at all. Since it was about seven degrees, he was less than successful.

Adrian nodded. "That's what Violet keeps saying. We'll have to double up. I taught Violet how to use one, but I'm definitely better at it. Do you want to ride with me or her?"

"You're the one who taught her?" Jesse sounded surprised. I didn't know why, I had told him a friend taught me. What else had I said? He turned to me. "How good are you?"

"Well, I don't think I traumatized Adrian too much, and I haven't been in any accidents, but most of the way there isn't much to hit." People played on snowmobiles or went ice skating near mainland or the campus, but most of the trip was open space.

Jesse frowned before telling Adrian that perhaps he should ride with him. I nodded, feeling a bit relieved. Maneuvering was my weakest part and having two people on a machine just makes it worse.

Adrian didn't say anything as he took the vehicle that didn't have luggage and passed Jesse the spare helmet. Once everyone was ready, he motioned for me to go first. Probably so he could keep an eye on me.

I found the area that looked the emptiest and started leading the way. The snowmobiles had a GPS to find the school or mainland, activated by the school ID. At least I didn't have to worry about getting lost. I still preferred the ferry, even if the ferryman was probably the creepiest part of the school. Considering the school, that says a lot.

Soon we were in sight of the island. Good, I truly wasn't comfortable on these machines. There were people playing close to the school, so I had to pay attention to make sure I didn't hit anything or anyone.

I thought I was doing pretty well when a different snowmobile suddenly swung in front of me. I was going too fast to stop, so I tried to swerve to the side, slowing down as much as I could. That would probably have been more successful if the other snowmobile hadn't headed straight for me. We didn't collide, but the other rider and I were close enough that I might have been able to lift up his or her helmet.

I was leaning away when the other rider's hand grabbed my arm, trying to make me let go of the machine. I was only surprised for a few seconds, but those seconds were costly, as my snagged arm let go, and my other hand couldn't hold on by itself. I tried to bring my one arm back to grab the controls but I was losing. A shout reminded me that Adrian was on his way, but he couldn't possibly get here in time.

My grip gave out, and I hit the ice, hard. My coat and helmet provided protection, but it was definitely a good thing I wasn't going too fast. My snowmobile raced on without a rider and the other snowmobile was bearing down on me.

I rolled out of the way, knowing the machine wouldn't be able to maneuver easily to come back and hit me. Sure enough, I was able to avoid the crazy rider this time, but before I could stand, they were turning around for another try.

The ground was ice. Standing would take too long and running would be near or completely impossible. My best odds were to stay on the ground. As much as I wanted to move, I forced myself to stay put. Not until there were almost on top of me did I roll closer to the island.

I was showered with ice shards as the machine roared past. Wiping my eyes, I searched for the crazy rider, braced for another go. But Adrian was almost there, and we had attracted attention. The phantom rider rode off as a crowd began to gather. One or two tried to stop the crazy rider, but he or she got away.

Adrian helped me up while a shaking Jesse checked me over. Twice. He had taken off his helmet, and his face was almost as white as the ice. "What was that about? Are you alright? What was that crazy person doing? What…" He trailed off as he started to really look at the people surrounding us. He blinked a few times. "Violet? Did I hit my head?"

"I doubt it," I answered before turning to the hydra who had caught my runaway snowmobile. "Thanks. It didn't hit anyone, right?"

"No, I managed to stop it first," He said.

"Thanks."

"Um, Violet? What's going on? What… um, who is this? What is he saying?"

I winced and turned to Jesse. "Welcome to Hyde. This is your last chance to back down. I can't explain anything until you sign a few things, and once you do, you can't talk about Hyde to anyone who doesn't know. Ever."

"Actually, I'm not sure he can leave now," Adrian said. "At very least, they'll want to make sure he can't tell anyone what he saw."

From the looks of it, Jesse wasn't listening. Probably a good thing. "Jesse?" I waited for him to look at me. "Are you ready? I really can't tell you anything here."

He slowly nodded, and got back on the snowmobile with Adrian. I turned to the crowd that appeared to be starting to get bored. "Thank you all for your help. I'm glad no one got hurt." After that, I climbed on my snowmobile and waited for everyone to disperse. It didn't take long, and Adrian made sure not to stray more than a few feet from me as we rode slowly to the school.

The security guard on the dock had seen what happened, and collected our reports of it quickly. Unfortunately, the snowmobile had been a rented one, and none of us could give any distinguishing characteristics of the machine or the rider. Perhaps an illusion to keep us from noticing anything specific?

Adrian and I discussed it while Jesse filled out the paperwork. I was shocked to find myself wanting to scream at him not to sign the papers, just go. I knew how much trouble I had gotten into because of those papers, those spells. What right did I have to stand quietly and watch someone else have their life irrevocably changed without warning?

I must not have been subtle enough, because Adrian started rubbing my arm. "He already has more warning than you did. This is his choice," He murmured in my ear.

"He doesn't know what he's getting himself into."

"You can't tell him, and you know it."

"But–"

"Are you alright?" He cut me off.

"What?"

"You fell. Are you alright?"

It was probably just a distraction, but I answered anyway. "I'm fine. Probably get some interesting bruises, but that's it." I shook my head ruefully. "I'm not even in shock." Which probably said more about last semester then it did about me.

Adrian frowned. "We'll get you, both of you, some coffee or something while we find someplace safe to explain everything."

"How about the library? He'll probably want to see some of those books, and it should be pretty quiet." Like when I first arrived, he probably wouldn't be able to register until tomorrow, but we could buy some sandwiches from the café or something for dinner, and getting his room key shouldn't be too hard.

"Library works," Jesse said as he signed the last paper. "I can't *wait* to hear this."

"Okay, you said you were in Shelley?" I asked, not bothering to wait for confirmation. "That's Shelly right there." I pointed to one of the dark stone buildings close to the dock, then pointed to the other. "That's Price, across the way. My dorm. The library is this way."

Adrian led the way, while Jesse tried to ask questions. I didn't answer him, wanting to get somewhere private first. The library was close by, and we slipped past studying students on our way to one of the study rooms. It wasn't until I spotted Ms. Graz that I realized I had been looking for her. Fortunately, she was talking to a student; Rachael. Good, it meant we got past with nothing more than a harsh glare.

Jesse sounded like he was hyperventilating, so I used the map to find the first empty study room. Of course, pulling up the map, much like the catalog, was enough to make Jesse even more shocked.

Finally we got to the room. I made Jesse sit down and tried to figure out how to start. I looked to Adrian hoping for some help, when the panther shifter excused himself to get some coffee. Thanks a lot, Adrian.

By the time Adrian returned, I had explained the basics of dimensions; the three places that were in all dimensions: the school, the market in the Bermuda Triangle, and the Library of Alexandria; and the spells that had been placed on him.

"This is a joke, right?" I don't think he actually believed that, but it was easier and more palatable than the truth.

"Jesse, you saw the dragon librarian, the hydra who caught my snowmobile, and fairies downstairs. You probably saw more than that too. How could I possibly pull off a joke this elaborate?"

He shook his head before meeting my eyes. "This is what you couldn't tell us at home?"

I nodded. "You wouldn't have believed me. Besides, one of the forms you signed is a magical contract that takes effect if you try to tell someone who doesn't know about Hyde. I don't know what the consequences are for breaking it, but they are bound to be unpleasant."

"Why didn't you warn me?"

I inhaled sharply at Jesse's accusation. "I…"

"She did warn you. As much as she could without breaking the contract herself." Adrian swished his coffee around in its' cup without looking up at either of us.

"I wasn't asking your opinion." Jesse turned back to me. "Violet, you should have–"

"Should have what? Told you my roommate is a vampire? Told you that Adrian is a shifter? That before you got here, I was the only human on campus? Even if I could tell you, you would never have believed me. Not until you got here and saw it for yourself!"

Jesse steadily got whiter and whiter. "The only human?"

I sighed and sat down. "Yeah, and there are several who don't think I should be here. You'll probably have the same problem." I looked at Adrian debating on whether I should tell Jesse or not. Finally I decided he needed to know. "We didn't find this out for a while, but apparently part of the founding agreement for the school requires there to be at least one human, one vampire, one elemental, one Were, and Taria. You'll meet her later. If the school doesn't have at least one of each, it is considered in violation of oath, and might be forced to close. We think someone is trying to close the school."

"What makes you say that?"

"Because last semester there were several attempts to get me to leave, frame me for something so I got expelled," *or arrested*, "or even injured." *Possibly killed.*

"What?!" Jesse stood up so fast, his chair fell over backwards. "Then why are you still here?"

"And let them win?" It wasn't my real reason, but he could understand it. "Besides there are a lot of good reasons to stay. Give it time." Maybe I shouldn't have told him the worst already, but he needed to know. Needed to watch his back. If someone was trying to drive away humans, Jesse would be a target too.

Jesse shook his head. "None of this makes sense."

"I know. I was in your shoes last semester. You'd be surprised how fast you get used to it."

That one earned me a look that had me wondering if I had somehow turned orange or something. Considering stranger things had happened, I snuck a quick look at my hand. Nope, still normal.

"Get used to it?"

Oh, that's what he was reacting to. "Yeah, coming in early helps, and remember, about a quarter of the school comes from shade dimensions and are in the same boat you are. When you've had some time to adjust, I'll tell you some of weirder things I've been through."

Jesse stared at me, eyebrows practically in his hairline. "What about the 'someone trying to hurt you' part?"

I decided that throwing defender psychics at him right then would probably be a bad idea. "I've been pretty lucky so far, but be careful, and stick with friends or in groups as often as possible. That's been one of my biggest advantages."

Adrian raised an eyebrow, but didn't say anything. Jesse was too dazed to notice when I carefully put my left hand over the right and slowly slid it down my fingers. We, the oath group, had carefully invented a couple hand signs. Nothing too elaborate, but something to pass on a quick message inconspicuously. This one meant '*Follow my lead.*'

Adrian scratched at his ear twice. *Message received.*

Jesse hadn't noticed a thing. "This is crazy."

"This is *real*," Adrian countered. "If you can't adjust, you aren't going to make it very long. The school wouldn't have accepted you if they didn't think you could handle it."

Jesse shot Adrian a glare, but he seemed more composed. I took a relieved breath. "The reason they bring you in so early is so that you can get used to all the differences and learn how to react to others from different dimensions. You may be able to understand what they say, and vice versa, but you still need to learn things like phrases, gestures, etc. to avoid around others. Things like that. There are more involved explanations than I can give you, I can tell you what books helped me, and I'm still asking my friends questions."

Jesse didn't say anything.

"Come on. Why don't we get you to your dorm? You can settle a little and we'll get some sandwiches. You can't register until tomorrow anyway," I suggested.

Jesse agreed, but I don't think he really believed me about adjusting. I wasn't completely sure he really believed me about the school. But he would. Anyway, jetlag wasn't helping anything.

Shelley was only a brief walk, and the RA let us in. He was a mountain elf, recognizable by the grey skin, white hair, pointed ears, and glowing black eyes. We were allowed in the lobby since we were there with Jesse, but the RA asked me not to go upstairs. Adrian could, with a visitor's pass, but they had strict rules about opposite gender visits.

The RA, Widam, turned out to be Jesse's RA. Widam was relieved to find that Jesse had gotten a basic explanation to the school, and offered to give a more in-depth explanation anytime Jesse was ready, especially if he was willing to sit in the lobby for it. Like Price, there were only a couple RAs on duty during break.

Widam gave Jesse the phone number to his room, and I gave him mine. We agreed to meet back here in an hour for dinner. Adrian volunteered to pick up something from the café, so Jesse wouldn't have to be exposed to too many more new things today. Neither of us said that was why, but I think Jesse knew anyway. Besides, he didn't have his meal plan settled yet, and mine was a mess. I had been imposing too much on Adrian as it was, it wasn't fair to ask him to let Jesse impose on him too. I did have enough money to help with sandwiches.

Jesse went up, and Adrian and I left. He was quiet until we were outside. "There was a lot you didn't tell him."

"No reason to overwhelm him. I'm pretty sure finding out about you would push him over the edge."

"You may be right."

***

One plus to Jesse coming was that he now knew that I wasn't crazy, on drugs, or anything like that. He also understood why I couldn't tell anyone. I had no idea what he was telling everyone back home, but my parents seemed a little more relaxed with Jesse there. Perhaps they thought he was keeping an eye on me. He could barely take care of himself.

It was nice not to be the clueless newbie for a change, but I admit I was worried about how Jesse was adjusting. Within twenty-four hours of my first arrival, I had become, perhaps 'desensitized' would be the best word. But I was accepting things that I would have thought ridiculous and unbelievable two days earlier. Yes, I still ended up shocked at times, but by the time classes started, I thought I was adjusting well. Maybe I wasn't very objective about myself, but Jesse didn't seem to be handling things anywhere near as well.

Then again, everyone adjusted at their own rate. I decided to just wait and see. Provided I could keep Jesse from getting killed because he accidentally offended someone.

Classes started tomorrow, and everyone was back. I had managed to explain to my friends, mainly by email, what I had and hadn't told Jesse, and they agreed to let me handle my cousin. Because we were all here and classes hadn't started yet, we made it a point to meet at the cafeteria for dinner. We weren't the only ones with that idea, meaning the cafeteria was lot more crowded than usual. It was especially jarring after the ghost town it had been.

This wasn't Jesse's first time in the cafeteria, but he had never seen it this crowded before. I had only seen it this full a few times. Getting across was difficult enough, but Jesse kept stopping and staring at everything and everyone.

"Did you see that? It looks like–"

I cut Jesse off before he could say anything about the live maggots in the clearly spoiled meat. "That's a delicacy for harpies. You've seen it before. Keep moving."

"But… Whoa, look at him!"

"Her. Keep your voice down. Don't stare." I moved as close as I could. "Mealtimes go a lot smoother in here if you restrain your curiosity. I try not to pay a lot of attention to what others are eating."

I should have expected this. There had only been about three hundred people on the island until yesterday. Now there were closer to two thousand. He was bound to be seeing things he hadn't seen before. But he was also making people uncomfortable, and some seemed insulted. Jesse might not have been the only new person staring, but he was the only one I was responsible for.

We were the last to arrive, probably because Jesse kept stopping. It wasn't until we got to the table that I realized the only people he had met before were the Chars. Ilse, Kara, and Denise all looked human, mostly. The Ice Twins could pass if you either ignored the inhumanly blue eyes and blue tint to their blonde hair, or assumed they were wearing contacts and dyed their hair. But I really should have warned him about Tim. Fortunately, Arie wasn't there. It was way too early to introduce Jesse to the harpy.

There were two empty spaces, one next to Tim, and one next to Adrian. Jesse and Adrian were very tense around each other, but Jesse was staring agog at Tim.

Trying to stifle a sigh, I sat next to Tim and hoped for the best. Adrian had shown some jealousy toward Tim in the past, and Tim still didn't completely trust Adrian. Now we were adding Jesse to the mix. Maybe I should have stayed home.

Tim was uncomfortably trying to ignore being stared at, so I asked him about his break, hoping to distract him. "How was your 'Festival of Ice'? What is that anyway?"

It was the right thing to ask. He brightened instantly and gave me a long in-depth explanation. Apparently the Festival of Ice is a five day festival just after First Winter's Night. In their territory, winter is when the ice will support the weight of a full grown yeti. There are some guesses on when that will be, but no one truly knew when that day would come.

This year, it was later than usual, with the festival ending just two days before Tim came back to the school. Tim mentioned some of the activities of the festival, like the building of the snow cave, wrestling competitions, and my personal favorite, snow cone day. Sounded interesting.

Now everyone started talking about what they did over break. Everyone knew I had come back early, but I hadn't said why. Then Kara asked. "So why did you come back early? I thought you were looking forward to seeing your family."

"I thought so too," Jesse said bitterly.

I gave him a questioning look, before trying to find an answer for Kara. "It got too complicated. Not being able to explain what was going on, not being able to tell them why I changed. We started arguing, and it just got easier to leave early. Hopefully summer will go better."

"They were only worried about you," Jesse said.

"I know that. But they wanted answers I couldn't give." I turned to Ilse. "So, did you manage to visit with your brother? I remember you saying you were afraid he'd be away the whole time."

Ilse opened her mouth, but Jesse cut in, "You're changing the subject."

"We're done on that one." I turned back to Ilse.

"No, we aren't. Why couldn't you tell them? Why couldn't you tell me?"

Adrian cut in, "She told you. The contracts."

"And what right does the school have to say who you can tell what?"

I just gaped at him for a minute. Before I could answer him, Ilse spoke up, "It isn't the school; it's inter-dimensional law that dictates what can and cannot be told to residents of shade dimensions. The school is simply following that law."

Jesse scoffed and studied he plate. "This whole thing is crazy."

"Jesse…" I sighed. "You're pre-law. I'm sure you can find where the laws came from and why. In the meantime, it isn't the fault of anyone here."

He shook his head. "Fine. I'll drop it, for now."

Dinner continued, tense and quiet. When we separated, Jesse volunteered to walk me back to my dorm. Since it was on the way to his, I agreed. Adrian didn't say anything, but I had a feeling he'd follow from a distance. A few others at the table seemed relieved to see us go. I tried to hide how that hurt.

"Violet?"

I pulled myself from my thoughts. "Yes?"

"Why do you trust them so much?" At least Jesse didn't sound angry anymore. He seemed more curious than anything else.

"Last semester was pretty intense. We've been through more than a little together."

"Why haven't you told me about it?" I could hear him trying to hide a strain of hurt.

"Because you're still adjusting to the normal things here. Why throw in the extraordinary? I'll explain more later." I wondered if I really would be able to.

"I'm your cousin. We've known each other for our whole lives. You can't explain to your family what's going on, but you can to people who were strangers to you six months ago?"

I winced at the accusation. "Jesse, you don't understand."

He shook his head. "No, I don't. Because you won't explain." He left before I could say anything else.

I walked up to my dorm room, feeling like the ground under me was sand washing away. How many more people was I going to alienate?

Chapter Fourteen
First Day Conflicts

My first class of the new semester was Magic for Non-magic users. As soon as I got my syllabus, I could tell that I would like this class. The class was divided into units, each specializing in different areas of magic. Each unit was clearly and concisely titled so we knew what that unit was about. Each unit also had a subtitle. The first unit was 'The Basics of Magic' or 'Why can't *I* change reality with a snap?' Next came 'Offensive Magic' or 'Sticks and Stones can break bones, but words can blow stuff up'. Ritual Magic was subtitled 'Where do I even find powdered hen's teeth?' There was also 'Illusionary Magic: Why you should never trust your eyes again.'; 'Elemental Magic: The power of nature at your finger tips'; 'Charms and Defensive Magic: Fighting power with power'; 'Transforming Magic: If it looks like a duck, and quacks like a duck, it may still be an elephant instead'; and my personal favorite, 'Safety Rules and Regulations: Why you *probably* won't get turned into a newt.'

The oddest thing was that the magicus teaching the class, Professor Collins, was probably around sixty and looked like he had never smiled a day in his life. His face was etched in lines like someone took a chisel to him, and his scowl was so set that I almost wondered if his face would crack if he did smile. Even when he read the syllabus out loud, there wasn't so much as a twitch to hint he found anything funny at all. He also would randomly make quick zingers that went over the head of anyone who wasn't paying attention. This was bound to be an interesting class, but it would definitely keep me on my toes.

Immediately after that class, I had to hurry to Bio II with Dr. Gronk. I could have taken the class with a different teacher, there were two other options, but I liked Dr. Gronk. Fortunately, the classes were in the same building. I wasn't sure why magic classes were in the science building, but since it meant that I could get from one class to another in three minutes or less, I wasn't complaining.

Bio II wasn't in the same class room as Bio I but it was built in a similar style. The biggest difference I spotted was an enclosed porch for flyers. That particular area wasn't well insulated, so I would have to sit closer to the front to stay warm. Which wouldn't be such a big deal if it wasn't for the fact that students near the front were more likely to get caught in the practical jokes that ran rampant through the Science department. Oh, well.

Magic for Non-magic users was at ten, with Bio II at eleven. I had made it a point to try avoiding early classes this semester. Tuesdays and Thursdays, my earliest class was at twelve-thirty. Of course, on Mondays, Wednesdays, and Fridays I was finished after Bio II so I had time to work on my studies.

I went to lunch after Bio II, but I didn't see any of my usual friends there. We'd have to compare schedules later. Unfortunately, that didn't help me find a seat now. Just as I was getting frustrated, someone got my attention.

It was Phyna. She was sharing a table with a human looking girl that I didn't know. "Need a seat?" Phyna asked.

"Thanks." I sat down gratefully. "I had forgotten how full this place can get at lunch."

Phyna smiled, allowing me to notice how sharp and needle-like her teeth were. They might even be a little scarier than Tim's. I pushed the thought away and turned to Phyna's friend. About my height, I'd guess, with long, curly brown hair and grey eyes. "Hi, I'm Violet."

The girl raised a velvety eyebrow and gave a dismissive sniff. "Morgan."

Grand, another from the anti-human crowd. What fun. Either that or I was incredibly boring and/or dismissible at first glance. Maybe that was my problem.

Phyna was quick to pick up the problem and started asking what class we had taken today. Morgan had apparently only taken one so far, Applied Psychology, which I was pretty sure was an upper level course. Phyna had music, with Professor Shale, so we were able to compare notes a little. Then it was my turn.

"I've had Magic for Non-Magic Users, and Bio II."

Morgan snorted. "Who's teaching the No-Ma class?"

I looked at her in confusion for a moment.

"Morgan, that's not nice," Phyna said in a gentle voice. "It's a way of saying 'No Magic'." Judging from her reaction it wasn't a particularly polite term. "Morgan is a magicus."

Now wasn't that interesting? I nodded, and pretended she was only showing polite interest. "I have Professor Collins. He seems interesting. He looks like he has no sense of humor, but that's obviously not true. The syllabus alone gives it away."

This caused the magicus to snicker loudly. "That's one way to put it. The old professor look?"

"Yes." I answered, the word emerging a letter at a time.

Morgan laughed some more. It was Phyna who filled me in. "Professor Collins is an illusionary magicus. The humorless old professor is one of her favorite looks. Yes, her. She likes tricking the students during the first class. In fact, don't be surprised if she doesn't look the same way twice. She's so good that only the faculty and those who can see through illusions know what she really looks like."

I could feel my face heating. "Oh. Well, I couldn't tell."

"Obviously," Morgan drawled out, before taking a bite of her salad.

"I can only partially see through it myself," Phyna admitted. "Maybe in another couple hundred years I'll be about to see through someone of that skill level, but now it's mostly just seeing that she is under an illusion." She turned to Morgan. "I know you're good at illusions, but you can't see through her either, can you?"

Morgan just gave a negligent wave of her hand. That could have meant anything.

I was more interested in the illusions part. "You're good at illusions?"

The magicus looked at me as if trying to sense a trap. "Why?"

"I'm interested in illusionary magic. I was here over New Year's and saw the fireworks. Weren't those mostly illusions? It seems like a fascinating field." And a very frightening one. Odd that Morgan didn't want to confirm or deny her skill in it. Or maybe not. I suddenly remembered what Rachael had said about strengths and weaknesses. My asking about her specialty could be construed as suspicious. If I was lucky, my explanation would seem innocuous enough.

Morgan studied me, like she was trying to read my DNA. "You can't do magic, you know."

"I know that."

"Every year, every single year. There's a few, not an erg of magical power, but they want it. Badly. And they make things worse for everyone." Whatever she was looking for, she wasn't entirely pleased with her results.

"I know I can't do magic. I don't plan to try." I met her eyes evenly.

"Good. Best case scenario, nothing happens. Worst case, it blows up on you. Sometimes blowing you up with it," Phyna said before making a blatant attempt to change the subject. We let her.

For the rest of lunch, Morgan and I didn't say a single word directly to each other, leaving Phyna to play peacekeeper. I felt bad for her, since I had been in that position and it drove me crazy. But I wasn't sure what to do. I left when she did, not having any wish to share a table with Morgan. I also had two new possibilities to investigate for our mysterious Morgana. Though if Morgan turned out to be Morgana, I would have to see if there was any way that Allison or someone else could check to see if I had a scrap of seer in me.

***

My classes were done for the day, so I had the afternoon free for homework, study, investigating, exercise, and anything else I needed. Of course, since school had just started, I didn't have much in the way of homework yet. I read the first chapter in the magic textbook, *Practical Rules and Uses of Magic*, and answered the review questions in back of the chapter. They hadn't been assigned, but it would help me remember the information later. I was halfway through the first chapter in the Biology text book when I decided to take a break.

I wanted to talk to Jesse, see what classes he had and how he was adjusting. I had seen his schedule, and while I had forgotten most of it, I did remember he had a two o'clock class in Inter-Dimensional History. While I had no idea what class room he would be in, I knew it was in Stevenson, so it wasn't hard to be waiting outside close to when the class would end.

It was a nice day, by January in Saskatchewan standards. It might have been as high as twenty, possibly twenty-five degrees, feeling a little warmer in the sun. I was almost enjoying being out in the sun for a bit when he came out, surprised to see me. To my dismay, his look darkened quickly. "Checking up on me now?" He demanded angrily.

I stepped back into a tree. There was a shake of branches and some snow fell. Had I hit the tree any harder, I probably would have knocked snow on us both. "No! I just… Well, maybe a little. I just wanted to know how your first day went."

He calmed down, probably because he could see he scared me. "Sorry, V. It's just been rough."

I laughed, with little humor in my voice. "Tell me about it. And don't call me 'V'." The smile he gave me did not reassure me, so I changed the subject. "So, do you have Taria for history?"

"Purple lady, weird wings?"

I nodded. "She's also your advisor. Mine too. Telepathic as well, so be sure you only think good thoughts about her."

Jesse gave me an alarmed look. "You're kidding, right?"

"Not in the slightest."

He paled despite the wind. "I'll keep that in mind."

I laughed. "There are clubs to learn how to shield your mind and practice it. I used to go to one that met in Barker about once a week."

"Used to? You don't anymore? You learned how to defend against telepathy?"

"Um, well. Actually, last semester someone cast a spell on me. It made me what's called a closed mind. I can't be read by telepaths, empaths, and possibly aura readers. We haven't tried the last one yet."

Jesse looked at me, confused. I wasn't sure he understood half of that sentence. "Why? Did you ask them too?"

"No, I didn't find out until later. It was an attempt to frame me. For a while it looked like I might be responsible for..." I couldn't say it, "an incident. With me being a closed mind, they couldn't read my mind to prove my innocence. It got complicated."

"You didn't get in trouble, did you?"

"No, they didn't have enough evidence to declare me guilty, so they just kept an eye on me until they found out who was really responsible." Close enough. Plus, Jesse would be less likely to try and drag me home.

"I'm not sure that's legal." Jesse frowned.

"Inter-dimensional law is different from U. S. Law," I pointed out.

"True. I–" Jesse cut off as Adrian came running up.

"Violet, are you alright?"

I blinked at him, confused. "Fine. Why?"

"You were afraid." He looked me over, presumably looking for some injury I was trying to hide.

It took me a minute to realize what he must have felt. "Oh, that. I'm fine. I was just uneasy for a minute. It's fine now."

"What are you talking about?" Jesse looked back and forth from Adrian to me and back again. "How could you possibly know what she felt? You weren't anywhere near her."

I winced. I had really been hoping to get the two of them to warm up to each other before mentioning this. A quick look around showed no one close enough to be listening or paying attention to us. It should be safe if we talked quietly. "Adrian and I have some kind of bond," I spoke as low as I could. "He knows if I'm afraid, hurt, angry, or in danger. It seems to be completely one-sided though." Which didn't seem entirely fair, but there wasn't anything to be done about it.

"What do you mean, 'a bond'?" Jesse was angrier than I had anticipated, glaring at Adrian as if trying to mentally set him on fire.

I shushed him. "Not so loud. It's kind of a secret. I can explain all the details later, but Adrian's a type of psychic–" I didn't get any further than that.

"Did you scare her?" Adrian asked.

"What?" Jesse stared at him trying to get him to back down.

Adrian didn't move a centimeter. In fact, he was simmering with anger himself. "You've clearly been talking for a while. Are you the one who scared her?" The last sentence came slowly, every word bit off.

"You've been stalking my cousin, feeding her some kind of bull about a 'bond', and now you're accusing me of threatening her?" Jesse took an angry step closer to the panther shifter.

I forced myself between them at once. "Adrian, he didn't mean to scare me. Jesse, the bond is real. Please, both of you, calm down. We can discuss this–"

Jesse moved me to the side. "He's taking advantage of you, Violet. I'm not going to let him."

Adrian growled at that. "I'm not taking advantage of anything. In fact, I think you're a bigger threat to her than I am."

I grabbed Jesse's arm as he raised a fist. "Stop it. Just stop it! Now!" Jesse pulled away, causing me to lose my balance and fall in the snow with a surprised cry.

Jesse went pale and turned to me. "Are you–"

Before he could finish, there was a growl and a black blur.

"*Adrian!*"

Chapter Fifteen
Explosive Conflicts

The strangled scream hadn't even left my throat before Jesse was pinned by a black panther. I was still on the ground, giving me a better than desired view of the snarling panther face with large, frightening fangs, and Jesse staring up in horror.

"Adrian, get off him! I swear, he didn't mean to do that. Get off before you hurt him." Adrian wasn't listening, and no matter how I tugged I couldn't get the paw nearest me to budge. "Adrian, *please*."

I think it was the 'please' that did it. Either that or the fact I was starting to cry. The panther looked at me, shifted back to Adrian, and slowly stood up. Once upright, he awkwardly offered Jesse a hand up as well. "I wasn't going to hurt him."

The half apologetic, half surly response drove me over the edge. I burst into tears; not caring that we were in public, that I was still sitting in the snow, that we were attracting all kinds of attention, or even that both of them were glaring at each other as if saying it was all the other person's fault.

Both of them offered me a hand up, but I ignored them, curling into my knee instead. I could hear them shifting nervously, trying to figure out what to do. I'm not sure who said it, but there was a mutter about, "If you hadn't–" I didn't give them a chance to finish.

"Shut up! Just shut up, both of you! I can't believe you, you… you morons! How could you do that?" I glared at Jesse. "What gives you any right to decide who I can and can't be friends with? Do you think I'm some kind of idiot who falls for any scam that goes around? Or some kind of delicate flower that needs protecting? I can manage without your help. I can't believe you tried to hit him!"

I turned to Adrian. To my somewhat vicious glee he took a couple steps back at my glare. "And you! That was even worse! He had stopped. He wasn't even facing you, and you attacked him? Are you crazy?" I lowered my voice. "Aren't you already on disciplinary probation? Do you *want* to get expelled?"

Both were looking at the ground now. I shook my head in disgust and tried to force my shaky legs to stand up. My ankle gave under me when I was almost up, knocking me back in the snow. Adrian and Jesse tried to help me, but I knocked their hands away. "Don't touch me! When you two are done acting like testosterone-laden morons, then you can come find me."

"Security. Everything okay here?" A, presumably male, figure asked. He was about two and a half feet tall, looking like a starry night sky. I had seen a couple of them around campus; I was pretty sure they were called Kaytes. There was one thing I was sure of.

"You're a teleporter, right?" I asked, getting a nod from the uniformed guard. "I hurt my ankle. Would you please help me to the infirmary?"

"Sure, not a problem." He looked at the other two, and apparently decided to drop the issue, at least for now. "I can take someone with you, if you like?"

Both Adrian and Jesse started to say something, but I spoke first, "No, I'm fine. Thank you."

The Kayte took my hand, and reality shifted on me. Pressure surrounded my inner organs, while my outside felt weightless; then it switched. My eyelids fluttered madly as I found myself seated on a bed in the infirmary.

"This is the non-emergency section, so someone will be with you as soon as convenient." The security guard looked around before studying me carefully. "So, want to tell me about that fight?"

"Not really?" It was more of a question than an answer.

He shook his head. "Do you believe anyone was in true danger?"

I bit my lip. Yes, Adrian could have seriously injured, possibly even killed, Jesse by pouncing on him as a panther. But he hadn't, and it wouldn't surprise me to find that he had been careful to avoid hurting him. Besides, if Adrian was still on disciplinary probation, being involved in this might be enough to get him expelled. Jesse was acting like an idiot, but I doubt he could have hurt Adrian too much even if he wanted to. "I don't think anyone was *trying* to hurt anyone else. Tempers were just running high. I'm sure it won't happen again."

His ears rotated, which I seemed to recall reading was their equivalent to a sigh. "I'll let it slide this time, but only because it was over before I got there. If I come across any of you three actively fighting…"

"I understand." I tried to say something else, but I made the mistake of moving. Everything shifted on me, nearly causing me to black out.

"Easy there. First time teleporting? Yeah, that's normal. Don't worry, after a few times, you get used to it.

Before I could accidentally insult him by saying I wasn't sure I wanted to get used to it, Nurse Persephone came in. The tall blue humanoid woman came up to me, magenta hair flying loose in her wake. "Alright, what seems to be the problem?"

"I lost my balance in the snow. When I tried to stand, my ankle gave under me again. I figured it would be best to have it checked out." I had to work at keeping my mouth shut about the rest. This was the second time I had been treated by this woman, and both times I was trying to hide something, but found it hard to keep my mouth shut around her. Again I wondered if it was her or me.

Nurse Persephone stared at my feet with glowing white eyes, before the glow dimmed. "Right ankle?"

"Yeah."

"Slight sprain." She put her hands on either side of the limb, causing me to gasp as something tingled before feeling hard. "There, magical brace. It will last twenty-four hours before dissipating, hopefully preventing you from making it worse. The brace will help speed up your healing, but I don't want you walking on that more than you have to. Keep your foot elevated when you can, especially today. Don't bother icing it; the brace will be more effective without ice. You can take your normal over-the-counter painkiller or ask for some at the front desk. Try not to stress your ankle for the next couple days, and come back immediately if you have another fall, especially inside a week."

I nodded, knowing most of this from first aid classes. The magic brace was cool though. I thanked them both before carefully climbing off the bench.

"I can teleport you back to your dorm, if you like?"

"I think I'm–" I tried to politely turn him down. It had *finally* occurred to me that letting a complete stranger teleport me places might be a bad idea. Especially when at least one or more people on the island wanted me gone or dead.

"Good idea," Nurse Persephone cut in.

"No problem. What dorm?" The guard looked at me.

I forced a smile. Well, at least Nurse Persephone knew where I was supposed to be going and who I was going with. Unless they both wanted me gone or dead. "Price Hall."

"What floor?"

"Sixth."

The guard nodded and took my arm. More alternating feelings of pressure and weightlessness, plus much fluttering of muscles and eyelids later, I was on one of the couches in the floor lounge. After a moment, I realized he had all but pushed me down when we got here. Probably to prevent me from falling or fainting. "Alright there?"

Moving my head didn't cause too much dizziness and all my limbs were still attached. That was a good start. "I think so."

He smiled. "Like I said, you get used to it. Anyway, you change your mind about earlier, or you need anything, just call security and ask for Jostop."

I nodded. "Thank you for your help."

"Not a problem. Be careful out there." He teleported away as I got up to go to my room. What a day.

***

I tried to stay in my room after that, to rest my ankle. That left little to do. I did the first homework assignment for Bio II, and read the next two chapters for M for N, then leafed through the textbooks for the other classes. I would have done that during break, but my scholarship funds didn't kick in until a couple days ago, and I couldn't buy my textbooks until they did.

It was quiet in the room, since Ilse slept during the day, but the rooms felt, well, occupied. As if just knowing someone else was around was enough to make the place less empty, less creepy. Plus, the quiet meant I could get a lot of studying done.

We had arranged to have a meeting tonight to discuss what we learned over break, but when asked, I decided not to tell Jesse. If he found out, he'd probably be upset, but he wasn't part of this yet. Personally, I was glad that I didn't have to deal with both him and Adrian in close quarters at the same time.

Adrian had class at nine, and Ilse had class at eleven, so we were meeting at ten. Ilse wanted to have dinner at nine tonight, which was a little earlier than her usual. I wasn't going to complain, I was starved. Normally, I tried to have something around four or five to tide me over, but I was trying not to walk, especially outside. There wasn't much food in my room, and I had been depleting what there was to avoid using meal allowances.

I was sitting on the couch, keeping my foot on one of the chairs, and reading my magic textbook when Ilse got up. She took one look at me, especially the elevated limb and shook her head. "What happened this time?"

"I slipped in the snow."

She gave me a pointed look. "How did you happen to slip?"

"The ground was uneven?" She was not impressed. "And because I was trying to break up a fight between a couple of idiots."

"That was your mistake, there." Ilse smirked. "Always let the idiots fight it out. Then they aren't paying attention to you and your gains."

I wasn't sure if she was serious, but decided to assume it was a joke. "That might work in the vampire council, but I was trying to prevent these idiots from hurting each other."

"Ah, I see. Do I know these 'idiots'?"

"Yup."

Ilse raised and lowered her shoulders quickly. A vampire sigh. "Why were they fighting?"

"Testosterone. Let's eat. I'm starved." I hobbled less than gracefully to my feet.

"Very well." Ilse nodded, a silent agreement to drop it. At least for now. It wouldn't surprise me if she made an effort to find out what happened later, but she wouldn't interrogate me here and now.

We took the tunnels to the cafeteria, at my request. The cafeteria wasn't too crowded, but it was full enough to require quick maneuvering. My ankle was not happy with me. I really should have taken something before coming down. Maybe there would be some time before the meeting.

It was a typical meal. We talked about classes. Ilse had three tonight, but naturally she hadn't had any yet. She tried asking me how Jesse was settling in, but I was less than communicative about it. For one thing, I wasn't entirely sure, especially considering how badly our last encounter had gone. Secondly, I didn't want to talk about Jesse. Or Adrian. Or my ankle. I did want to tell her about Morgan, and maybe Professor Collins but I didn't want to talk about it in public. Oh, well, I could mention it at the meeting and tell everyone at the same time.

When we finished, Ilse volunteered to get my first aid kit, so I didn't have to keep going up and down. I gratefully accepted her offer, and found myself the first one in the room in the dorm basement. Not for the first time, I wondered what these rooms were for originally. Probably not so a bunch of students could plot on how to save the school without being overheard.

After about a minute or so, I started to get unnerved. I didn't spend much time truly alone anymore. When I was alone, I was usually in my room or the lounge. When I was out in the school proper, I was usually either in public or with friends. Here, I was alone and out of immediate sight.

Stifling a shiver, I told myself I'd be fine. Someone would be there soon. There, see, footsteps. I looked to the door to see who was coming. There was hesitation. Then the sound of someone running away. I blinked before shakily standing.

Before I could get to the door, I heard a different set of footsteps, the knob turned, and the door exploded. I shrieked, hands covering my mouth as wood shards shot in both directions. Tim jumped back, hurriedly smothering tiny flames in his fur.

We looked at each other in shock. "Are you hurt?" I asked, seeing splinters caught in the hair. It didn't look like any penetrated to the skin but I wanted to be sure.

"No. Are you?"

"No. It all fell short of me." An alarm went off. "We need to leave. Someone will be here soon. Go back, call Adrian and Allison. I warn the other girls."

"We aren't doing anything wrong," Tim protested.

"Do you really think it matters?" I asked, limping towards him before eyeing the door. How was I going to get past that?

Tim took two steps forward and literally lifted me over the smoldering door. He started to set me down, before we looked at the elevator and drew the same conclusion. They would make the connection if I took the elevator here. He scooped me up again and sprinted to the library.

We went above ground there and separated. He went to his dorm, while I stopped at one of the public school phones to call Ilse. I didn't want her going down and getting caught in everything.

It wasn't until she picked up that it occurred to me that the school might well monitor the phone lines. At least she picked up; I was worried I hadn't gotten her in time. "Hey, Ilse? Change of plans. Can you let the others know? I'll be up soon."

Ilse was better at this secret stuff than I was, so she answered smoothly. "Certainly. I shall see you soon."

The trip between the library and Price Hall wasn't long, but I was walking slower than usual to make sure I didn't slip again. I was about half-way when I got intercepted.

"Violet!" A familiar voice, that I didn't want to hear, came from behind me. I did not want to talk to Adrian right now, but I turned around anyway. The naked fear on his face stole a lot of my anger. "You... Are you hurt? I could feel it. You were in danger. But I was in class. I couldn't get there."

I sighed, releasing most of the rest of my anger. "I didn't get hurt this time. No one did. But I'm not sure we should admit that we were going to be there." I gave an abbreviated explanation about the door.

Adrian nodded. "I think you're right."

"We'll find a new place, and a new time. I've got to go." I started to walk away.

"Violet." He didn't continue until I looked at him. "I didn't mean for you to get hurt. I didn't want to hurt your cousin. I just…"

I didn't say anything, waiting.

He shook his head. "I'm sorry. Really sorry."

"I can't always be the peacemaker, Adrian. I'm not that good at it, and it frustrates me. A lot." I swallowed hard thinking about how often I needed someone to play peacekeeper for me lately. "You aren't going to get along with everyone, and that's fine. No one does. But could you please try not to attack my friends and family? Especially when they aren't a current threat? Please?"

He scuffed at the snow with his foot. "Not my proudest moment, I admit. I was tense, then you got hurt. I just saw red."

"What happened after I left?"

"We talked. I told him he should talk to Allison. She's better at explaining things."

"Good idea." Allison was less confrontational than Adrian. Though, she was also protective of her brother. "Did you settle things?"

Adrian shrugged. "We agreed that we didn't want you or anyone else getting hurt because we were being, how did you put it? 'Testosterone-laden morons'?" He smiled, just a little, at that.

"I'd apologize, but quite frankly, I still think you were acting like that."

He nodded. "Allison said something pretty similar. Also said I should grovel. A lot."

I started laughing. All the adrenaline, the fear, the anger, of the day just exploded out in a fit of hysterical giggles. The fight, my ankle, the door, the tightrope of my family versus my friends, it just overflowed. It would be back later, but for now, I couldn't stop giggling.

"Um, should I be getting you back to your dorm?" Adrian sounded puzzled.

I laughed harder, but managed to nod. A warm arm snaked around me while my arm was moved over his shoulders. Useful, since I couldn't stand up straight at the moment. Soon I was at the doors of the dorm.

"Be careful. Really careful. I don't know what happened, but you were in danger tonight."

The giggles died instantly. "You're right. I think Tim may have been singed at bit." The lights of the dorm allowed me a better look at Adrian. "Are you alright? You look… not great." He was pale, and his face looked haggard.

He shrugged. "I was sick for a while this afternoon."

"You're okay now?"

"Yeah, it was just a few hours. Brief but intense."

I frowned. How odd. "How intense?"

"My roommate threatened to call the infirmary if I didn't stop throwing up."

"How long did this last?"

"About three hours."

"Did you eat anything unusual?" Food poisoning was the only thing I could think of to react like this.

"No. It wasn't food poisoning." Adrian said, sounding unconcerned.

"Then what was it? Viruses last longer and anything I could think of would have a gradual start and gradual finish."

His brows furrowed. "No, it came without warning and stopped without warning." He shrugged. "Karmic punishment for fighting?"

I gasped in horror. "'I will strive for peace'. That was most definitely not striving for peace."

He let out a breath through his teeth. "You may be right. If so I probably got off lucky."

I shook my head. "Alright. Priorities. You're fine now. Drink fluids, like water, juices, and something with electrolytes. You're probably dehydrated. I *need* to go up and explain before Ilse or someone throws a fit. Talk to you tomorrow."

"Right, we'll figure out a plan then."

I agreed and dashed inside. It was later than I realized. Ilse would have to go to class soon, and she'd probably be about ready to tear her hair out if she didn't find out what happened first. Actually, she never showed frustration that much, but I was sure she was feeling it.

As soon as the elevator stopped on my floor, I was ambushed by a hyper, worried werewolf. "Good, you're finally here. Come on, everyone's in my room."

"Okay, sorry I'm late," I said, nodding to Phyna as she left the lounge.

"What? Oh, right." Kara realized what I had, about not wanting to talk in public as Tatiana, the pixie on the other end of the hall, went to knock on the RA's door.

I was practically dragged down the hall to Kara and Denise's room. All eyes were on me as soon as the door opened. Trying not to wince or blush, I took a seat in the large purple beanbag near the computer chair. "Sorry, I got delayed."

"What happened? Why do you smell like smoke?" Kara asked.

Should have figured she would notice. "Well, the door kind of exploded. No one was hurt!" I said in a rush as the ice elementals gasped, Kara leaned in, Ilse moved closer, brandishing my first aid kit, and Denise dropped the bag of chips in her hand.

Knowing there was no way around it, I explained everything, trying to ignore my friend's reactions. Some were easier than others. I briefly mentioned Adrian stopping me, wanting an explanation, but didn't mention the rest. I would have to at some point. If he really had gotten that sick as a result of the oath, the others had to be warned. But I didn't want to go into it now.

"I'm glad no one got hurt, but why are we hiding?" Kara asked. "We aren't doing anything wrong. There are no rules about students being down there. I mean, okay, maybe we shouldn't have the guys there, but I'm pretty sure that isn't a big deal either."

How to put this without sounding paranoid? "If you saw the same person at the center of several different incidents, what would you think about that person?"

"She's right," Ilse backed me up. "Too many of the faculty still harbor suspicions after last semester. They are unable to prove guilt or innocence, and most are uncomfortable with a true closed mind."

"Besides," Krystal said, "We were all but told to drop the whole thing, and we haven't. They'd want to know what we were doing there."

"The rooms were initially built to allow students to from different dorms to study together or spend time together," Ilse said, staring into space. "We could, if necessary, claim we were going to study, or perhaps play a game. However, they would want to read minds."

So that's what they were for. "We need a new place to meet."

"Probably the library would be best. We could get a study room," Denise answered. "As long as we are quiet and don't destroy anything, we'd be left alone."

I didn't like the idea, but I could see the advantages. She was probably right. I just didn't want Ms. Graz breathing down my neck.

"Why make the door explode? Did they know we were meeting? Was someone supposed to get hurt? Was this an attempt to stop us from meeting, or perhaps limit where we could meet?" Bria mused.

"Or to discredit us, make it look like we blew up the door?" I suggested.

We speculated several different possibilities, but didn't come up with anything. Then Ilse had to leave, breaking up the gathering. We would meet at the library the next night.

I was exhausted. The day had been too long, too busy, and too emotional. I crawled into bed, hoping to fall asleep quickly. Not happening. I had a very restless night, where I would almost drift off then suddenly wake up. Or catch a snatch of sleep, before waking again. My thoughts drifted in strange patterns that made perfect sense when almost asleep, only to have me wondering what on earth that had been all about when I woke up.

Then one thought actually woke me. 'Why doesn't Adrian know about my panic attacks?'

Chapter Sixteen
More Questions Asked

It didn't make sense. How could he tell Jesse made me uneasy, a weak feeling that I had felt for about twenty to thirty seconds; but not that I had panic attacks that were intense enough to interfere with my breathing and sense of balance for almost a minute? Yes, they were short-lived, but so was my problem with Jesse. But Adrian had never once mentioned my panic attacks, checked on me to make sure I was okay, or asked me about them later. True, I never mentioned them either, to anyone, but I didn't have time to mention half the things I went through to Adrian before he found out about them.

Either he was keeping his mouth shut about it, possibly to keep me from feeling embarrassed or because I was obviously fine, or he didn't know. Somehow I didn't think he was keeping quiet out of tact, he was too blunt for that. He was also too on edge to ignore something that sharp. He ought to have at least said something or asked me if I was alright, even if he asked indirectly. So, perhaps he had no idea. But why not?

Okay, time to be rational about this. He knew when someone vandalized my door, though that may have been partly through rumors because he seemed confused about the whole thing. He knew when I was in danger in a training room. He knew when I was angry enough to leave home. I don't know if he knew about the arguments or not. Probably. He hadn't seemed surprised that things escalated that badly. He knew when I was nervous around Jesse, or before a test.

He didn't say anything about when Krystal got hurt in front of me though it wasn't a serious injury. When Denise was attacked, he didn't say much about it, except to try to reassure me that everything would work out. Of course, I wouldn't be surprised if everyone in the school heard about Denise. The problem with trying to figure out what he knew was trying to figure out what he knew but didn't bother to say anything about.

Eventually I came to the reluctant conclusion that the only way I would find out if he knew about the panic attacks would be to ask him. Not something I wanted to do. I didn't want to talk to anyone about them. I was having enough problems without earning the label of emotionally unstable. Though there might be some accuracy to that, sad as I was to admit.

None of this was helping right now. I had to get some sleep. I might not have any early classes, but I did have class the next day, and they would be brand new classes. It took time, but eventually I slept.

***

My first class of the day was Prominent Forms of Government. It was in a large classroom, and each of the chairs had a small partial table attached that could be used as a desk. My preference with those chairs was to sit by myself so I could use the table next to me as well as my own. But I had to wait until class started to make sure no one was going to sit there. To my surprise, as I was waiting, Jesse came and sat down next to me.

"Hi. I didn't know you had this class?" I hoped I didn't sound too strange. I had seen his schedule, shouldn't I have noticed that we shared a class?

"When I was at registration, they said my class was awfully full, would I mind switching. Apparently they knew you were my cousin and that you'd be in this class. So I agreed."

I took a deep breath, trying to fight back fear. "That's odd. Who did your registration?" Why would a student volunteer know my class schedule or that Jesse and I were related? Yes, we had the same last name and were from the same city, but that didn't prove anything, and my schedule shouldn't have been in question at all.

"I think she said her name was Rachael."

I relaxed instantly. We had discussed this class, and I must have mentioned Jesse coming. I couldn't remember doing so, but it wouldn't surprise me. Of course she would draw the connection. Jesse was giving me an odd look. I opened my mouth to say something, though I wasn't sure what, when I saw white fur out of the corner of my eye. "Hi, Tim."

"Good day to you both. May I have this seat?" He indicated the seat next to me. It was one of the larger chairs because I had tried to find an out of the way spot.

"Certainly," I said. Jesse gave him an awkward looking smile and nod. Apparently he was still intimidated by the yeti. He'd learn that Tim was, as Denise put it, "Warm and cuddly. Like fabric softener."

I was trying to fight back my smile at the thought when Arie came by, forcing all my humor away. She eyed the seat next to Tim, before looking around as if she was unsure of what to do. I forced myself not to react to her 'subtle' non-verbal request for an invitation.

Tim, of course, brightened and immediately offered her the seat next to him. Arie hesitated, requiring a second invitation.

I swallowed my irritation like a bitter pill. Or maybe a spider that kept trying to crawl back up my throat. No, that was really gross. Pill it was then. Change of subject. "Arie, this is my cousin, Jesse. Jesse, this is

Arie. She lives on my floor." She wouldn't be interested, but that was no reason to be rude.

Jesse swallowed hard. "Nice to meet you," He said, clearly trying, and failing, not to stare.

"Likewise," Arie responded in a dry voice.

Much to my relief, the teacher began then. As I had been warned, Doctor Kraes was a Solurt, meaning it looked like a walking beam of light. I quickly whispered to Jesse that Solurts either didn't have genders or at least didn't recognize the distinction between genders. Or both. Dr. Kraes didn't recognize gender among the students either. As promised, we were informed that all students would participate in at least one debate, worth a tenth of our grade.

"Sign-up sheets will be on my desk. All students will have until a week from Thursday to choose a debate topic. Each student will be graded on its' research, speaking style, and argument. Winning is not necessary, but it must have a convincing argument. Make me believe you believe it, even if you don't."

A list of approved topics was given with the syllabus so we could ponder our choices. I looked over the recommended reading list and made a mental note to start reading them today. I didn't understand half the terms on the syllabus.

Dr. Kraes finished a few minutes early, which I was grateful for. I had Genetics next, and the Victor Science building was on the other side of campus from the Stevenson Humanities building.

Since Intro to Genetics was an upper-level class, and a specialty one at that; the class size was smaller than most of my other classes. At a casual glance, I would estimate there were about fifteen, maybe twenty students. Perhaps the most interesting was the camel in the front row. Presumably a shifter, possibly one who was temporarily stuck. That, or Dr. Gronk didn't care if animals attended his class. I did feel a little sorry for the camel student because camels can't take notes. Fortunately, it looked like the Chulthu-like being next to the camel was taking two sets of notes. Apparently the facial tentacles were fully prehensile. Learn something new every day.

I had leafed through the textbook enough to know that the first month or two would probably be mostly review but that was alright. That meant I'd have more time for some of the other classes. Besides, I hadn't had biology since ninth grade, and could probably use the review. It was nice to know that some things were still the same. DNA was DNA regardless of what dimension you were from, even if there were genetic differences between each of the different beings.

After genetics, I had two hours before Calculus. This gave me time to drop off my textbooks and spend time in the library looking for some of those recommended reading books. Pity I wasn't the only one, or even the first one to have that idea. But, I managed to find two of the books I was looking for. One was a history of the Inter-dimensional council, and the other was on the history of democracy, what it was, where it was practiced, who could vote, etc. It was interesting, some of the variations. My favorite was the country in 7D where children could vote to elect their leaders, but adults couldn't. I checked them out, and headed to Calc.

I didn't have Professor Pod again, instead choosing Professor Selvis who was, well, a plant. Literally. We met on the outskirts of the forest, because she was a talking tree, and couldn't move. I wondered if she was a dryad even if she didn't look anything like

Willow, but no, apparently she was just an intelligent tree.

There were permanent spells on the area to make it warm enough to stand there for an hour for class, thankfully. We weren't allowed to use paper in that class. Instead we had electronic tablets that had a copy of the textbook, a calculator, etc. We 'emailed' our work to the teacher, who manipulated her pad with flowering vines. I have no idea how she could be flowering in January. Maybe it was an effect of the magic.

Adrian was waiting for me after class. It was a slight jolt to realize I hadn't seen him all day. Odd. Even odder, he had a box of chocolates from the mainland in hand.

"Here." He all but forced the box into my hands, managing to look at everything but me.

"Um, thanks. What's this for?"

He shrugged, feet shuffling. "Isn't this a standard part of groveling?"

I managed not to laugh. As in, biting my lip so it didn't escape. "Don't know. I've never groveled before." I traced my right eyebrow and ran my hand down the side of my face. *Are you being coerced?*

Adrian finally looked me in the eye, before giving a crooked smile. "Only by Allison telling me I'm an idiot if I don't. So, what do I do next?" He must have been able to tell that I wasn't that mad anymore. Honestly, I didn't have the energy.

"Oh, no! It doesn't count if I tell you to do it. Just ask Allison or Kara." I became serious then. "I would like you to apologize to Jesse, though. I'll talk to him, hopefully get him to apologize as well, but you did attack him."

He winced a little but agreed. "You're right. I shouldn't have done that. I'll… try."

Best I was going to get. Besides, what good was a forced apology? "Feeling better?" He looked a little better.

"Yes, you were right. I was dehydrated." He let some air out through his teeth. "I'm definitely going to remember that next time I'm tempted to start a fight."

"Good. So, what are you up to?"

"Five-eleven," He smirked.

It took me a minute to get it, before I shook my head groaning. Well, now I knew his height. "For that, I'm leaving."

He followed me, like I knew he would. Moving close, he murmured in my ear, "We're meeting in the library, fourth floor. Ten tonight."

I nodded, trying to cover the motion by moving some hair behind my ear. Good. We really needed to discuss things.

***

To avoid suspicion, we didn't want to all arrive at the same time. Ilse and I went to the library directly after dinner, making us almost half an hour early. We were the first, so we claimed a study room and started working on homework. I elevated my ankle, even though it didn't hurt, because it was still swollen. The brace had dissolved or dissipated or whatever magical braces do, shortly before Calc.

"If you require assistance, I have had extensive training of various forms of government." Ilse said, noticing I was reading the book on democracy I had checked out earlier.

That made sense; she was training to be an ambassador and was part of vampire aristocracy. She might even be a political science major. I didn't think so, though. "Thanks, I'll probably need it. At the moment, I'm just finding out what's out there. I'm sure it will get more confusing later."

Ilse smiled. "I believe I have my notes about who rules where and how. I shall see if I can find them."

Crib sheets. Cool. It was then I noticed the small red velvet bag Ilse had. "Is that your fortune stone set?"

I had been surprised to find that Ilse was superstitious. She believed that she could tell the future or answer questions by thinking about what she wanted to know, shaking up the bag, and dropping two stones into her hand. Each stone corresponded with a different element from vampire mythology: earth, air, water, fire, metal, or blood, with another for balance. Each supposedly had a different meaning. I found the whole thing too vague to be useful even if it did work, which I hadn't seen any evidence to suggest. Then again, if the Chars were psychic, and I *had* seen evidence to back that up, then perhaps this worked as well. In any case, Ilse definitely believed it, and I didn't want to offend her.

Interestingly enough, Ilse was disdainful of the thought that anyone believed the future could be told by looking at stars, not that I believed that either. Then she found out I was a Libra and decided her balance stone meant me. At least sometimes.

Ilse didn't look directly at me. "I thought it could possibly be of use."

I was saved from making a response when the Ice Twins came in, carrying a few of their books. By the time we were done exchanging greetings, Allison showed up.

Within ten minutes, everyone was there, with some books spread around as camouflage.

Everyone looked around, trying to see who would take charge. Finally, I spoke up, "Did anyone figure out about the island? Is the school here because it's a dimensional nexus or vice versa?"

Ilse answered, "The school chose this location because it is as natural dimension nexus. In most dimensions, the land was unclaimed, but there were a few instances where they had to negotiate for the land. In 3C, a colony of frost sprites lived here. On 5A, the Frostfire dragon clan had settled the area. 8D was mostly underwater, and the island was considered a resort for mers to experiment on dry land. 16E had a yeti colony."

"So, if for some reason the school had to close, those groups might be able to try to claim the land?" Kara asked.

"Not all of them," Tim said. "The yetis, for example, have moved eastward following the migration of our primary prey animals. I do not believe any primarily live close to this area anymore."

It was possible that would change if the school closed, but there was no need to antagonize Tim for something that wasn't his fault. "So perhaps we need to figure out who might want the land back."

"Maybe. But what would they do with it?" Krystal asked.

"Many things are possible," Ilse said. We tossed around ideas for a little while, such as using the land as a platform for trade, tourism, or war.

When the ideas ran down, I spoke up again. "There's something else. I came back to school early, and spent time talking to Rachael, the second floor RA? She's a magicus, and was able to give me some information, like the different clubs on magici specialties. There's an illusion club. I think a few of us should check it out."

"Are you sure Rachael is trustworthy?" Tim asked.

"The faculty tested the magical signature of every magicus in the dorm when the doors were vandalized. Rachael would have been included in that." Ilse steepled her fingers.

"Besides, most of our problems have been with illusions. Rachael says she specializes in elemental magic."

"All the same," Allison said, "You have been careful about what you say around her?"

"Of course. Oh, and I have two possible leads." I explained about my encounters with Morgan and Professor Collins.

"I don't know about a teacher being involved," Bria said. "What would they get out of it?"

"Maybe she hates teaching and wants to retire," Denise suggested.

"Not the usual method, but I suppose it's a possibility," I said, trying not to smile.

The only other discussion was how to restore Adrian's memories. Unfortunately, we were back to square one on that. None of what we knew was safe or possible for us to do.

About eleven-thirty, we decided to break it up. Ilse had class at midnight, and some people had early morning classes. "I just wish to remind everyone of the visit to the North Pole, meeting my family. In two weeks," Tim said. "Violet, do invite your cousin. Perhaps it will make him more comfortable with the rest of us."

I stifled a grimace and nodded. Somehow, I doubted that would go over well. I wanted to ask if he invited Arie, but didn't dare. Fortunately, Kara did.

"I have issued the invitation, but she has not yet given me her answer."

Now I really had to school my reaction. This was going to be fun.

"Before we depart to our separate ways, I thought this might help." Ilse pulled out her fortune stone set. Shaking up the bag, she poured a clear stone followed by an orange stone into her waiting hand. "Balance is the major stone, and fire the minor. The balance is in danger." She took a deep unnecessary breath. "Or Violet is in danger."

Chapter Seventeen
Culture, Clubs, and Cousins

I don't believe in fortune stones to tell the future, my life has been in danger since I arrived, and this might not refer to me at all. Still had to stifle a chill running up my spine. I forced a smile anyway. "Well, what else is new?"

No one said anything to that. There wasn't anything to say. I was completely right, even if no one wanted to admit it. The silence dragged on, becoming louder and louder until it was shouting.

"We'll have to be careful," Tim said, words being swallowed by the vicious quiet. There were a few nods and muttered agreements before we dispersed. Ilse went straight to class, with Allison, because her room was that direction. Adrian walked them over since the rest of us were heading in back to the dorms together.

Tim split off when we got to his dorm, and the rest of us went to our floor. Kara invited me to join her and Denise, but I said no. I was still trying to do my reading for various classes, and wanted to try to make it an early night. Well, semi-early. It was already approaching midnight.

What I hadn't anticipated was just how skittish I felt once I was locked alone in my room. It was both silly and justified. My room had been relatively safe considering how much time I had spent in it, but I had been attacked here before. We also knew, or at least strongly suspected, that someone had been in here before. But it wasn't like I had never been here alone before, or even been here alone recently. This was silly. But silly didn't help me sleep.

***

The first few weeks of the new semester felt like a sink or swim experience. If so, then there were times I was floundering. New things to learn, more investigating to do, trying to get Jesse integrated into the school, making sure I did the best I could on classes and exercising to fulfill the oath we had sworn, etc. Problem was, if I was floundering, Jesse was drowning.

He was in upper-level classes because he had been in college for two years already, but advanced classes expected you to have taken the basics here at Hyde. Jesse was a very intelligent guy and he knew it. He was used to being one of the smarter people in a group. Here there was so much to catch up on, so much more than he was expecting, and he wasn't taking it well. He also didn't seem to quite be adjusting to the shift in reality. I kept having to interfere when he accidentally offended someone, or stop him from staring too much.

Like the time he called Ilse a 'leech'. I dropped my cup, staring at him. I hadn't actually heard that, had I? Ilse was staring at him too, growing white. I had.

I stood up and started apologizing profusely, before grabbing Jesse and dragging him away, out of the cafeteria. Good thing he was still wearing his coat. I should have thought to grab mine.

"What was that about?" Jesse rubbed his arm, sounding indignant.

"What? Are you.... You called her... Do you know how serious an insult that is to a vampire?"

He seemed puzzled, "Is it? I was just kidding."

"Yes! Didn't you pay attention during orientation? I'm sure they gave you a booklet on words, phrases, and gestures to avoid. Don't you remember?"

"Vaguely. I don't think I finished reading it."

I winced and rubbed the bridge of my nose. "Find it. Find it and memorize it. Read it every single day. Before you say or do something that gets you beat up or worse. I found one of the books in the library extremely useful. Um, 'The Dimension Jumper's Guide to Emergency Survival and Etiquette'. I think that was the title."

"Oh, come on, it's not that big a deal," Jesse said.

"There are some who would challenge you to a duel for an insult more minor than that. It's a huge deal. Think about it, Jesse. Even if you traveled to different countries in our dimension, the rules aren't always the same. A friendly gesture in one country can be a terrible insult in another. It's the same here. I know you don't want to go around insulting people."

"Have you checked your email lately?"

The complete non-sequitur threw me for a loop. "What?"

"Have you?" He looked at me as if I should be in trouble.

"Not in the past few days. What does that have to do with anything?"

"Your parents wrote me. They're worried because they haven't heard from you in, oh, about two weeks. I've told them that I've seen you and you're fine. Busy, but fine."

I winced. "Okay, I'll write to them. But I repeat, what does that have to do with anything?"

"You're so worried about being rude to strangers, but you don't care about your family? You couldn't even stay the whole break. Couldn't wait to get back here." There was venom in his voice.

I more than matched it. "Stop right there, Jesse Clyde Peters. I left early because I couldn't tell them about Hyde and they couldn't accept that. Don't you have trouble writing home?"

Jesse turned away from me and took a few steps, before turning back and leaning on a tree trunk. "This place just separates us from home. There are times I almost think it's a cult."

"It's not a cult, and surely you understand why we can't tell them." It was a lame statement, but it was all I could think of.

"I understand, but I don't like it." There was silence for a while. "I'm not coming back after this semester." I blinked at him in shock. "I'm not completely sure I'll finish this one."

"Jesse?"

"I know, I know. It's just… It's too much. I can see what will happen if I stay. I'll become more and more separated from everything I knew before, from everyone I know. Then I'll have to spend the rest of my life pretending this place never happened. One semester, it's a wonder, a novelty. Almost a dream. Years? That's a lot more difficult."

I bit my lip. "Are you sure about this?"

"Pretty sure. I just haven't filled out any paperwork yet." He scuffed at the snow before capturing me with his eyes. "Come with me. Find another school. You can tell your parents you got involved in some weird stuff here, but you're better now. You can fix things with them. You can be normal again."

"If I leave, the school will close."

"So what?" He shouted at me. I stepped back a few paces. "Sorry. But really, is it your responsibility to take care of their problems? Your job to make sure the school fulfills its' quota? Why do you have to be the sacrificial lamb?"

"Because there isn't anyone else." As far as I could tell, Jesse was the only other human here. If he was leaving, than it was up to me.

Jesse grabbed a fistful of snow, letting it fall a little at a time. "Then maybe the school *should* be closed. If it can't manage to get students on its own, then why should it stay open?"

"I'm not going to argue with you. You don't see my side, and I'm having trouble seeing yours. But I'm not leaving, Jess."

"Fine, I'll drop it. For now. But promise me two things, V." I wanted to snap at him for calling me 'V', but technically I started it by calling him 'Jess'. Besides, he didn't give me time. "One, that you'll write to your parents. Today." He waited for my nod. "And two, Violet, promise me you aren't going to be some martyr for the school."

"Jes–"

"Promise me," He cut me off, sounding as serious as I've ever heard him.

"I'll certainly do my best." Wasn't like I *wanted* to die. For the school or anything else.

"Good enough, I guess," He sighed. "Tell your roommate I'm sorry." Jesse turned and started walking back to his dorm.

With a sigh, I took a seat on the steps. I couldn't go back in the cafeteria without swiping my card again, so I had to wait outside for Ilse. Unfortunately, I had been outside for at least five, maybe ten minutes, without my coat. The stone steps sucked any remaining warmth out of me. I shivered, wishing I had thought things out more.

Hopefully Ilse would be out soon. I was sure she'd bring my coat.

I jumped as something was suddenly draped on me.

"You should pay more attention to your surroundings," Adrian said, amusement and worry in his voice. He wasn't wearing his duster, which I belatedly realized was now on my shoulders.

"Yeah, I should. Um, don't you need this?" I shook the corner of the coat at him.

"You need it more. Put it on."

"Really…"

"Put it on, Violet."

I might have argued more, but my teeth were chattering. So I stood long enough to slip it on, and held it closed. "So, what are you doing here?"

Adrian shrugged, taking the seat next to me. It didn't escape my notice that he was paying much more attention to people walking by than I had been. "You were upset." He hesitated. "Want to talk about it?" He sounded like he'd rather be dragged through a mile of nails and broken glass.

I snickered at the tone, and gave him a quick peck on the cheek. "No. But thank you for offering." We had gotten a little more affectionate, but we hadn't really kissed since New Years.

Adrian actually blushed, but he smiled. He had a nice smile. "Oh, there's a meeting of the illusionist club tomorrow. I managed to get an invitation for myself and a few friends. Interested?"

"Very. What time?"

"Two o'clock."

"Great, I'm free." Tomorrow would be Wednesday, so my afternoon was free. Thursday afternoon would be the start of the long weekend, and we were leaving that night for dimension 15D and the North Pole there. "You said a few friends, who do you think we should ask to come?"

Adrian shifted closer, either to prevent being overheard or to conserve warmth. He had to be pretty cold without his coat. "Actually, if he's free, I was thinking the yeti."

I raised an eyebrow. They weren't fighting anymore, but Tim and Adrian were still not in any way able to be mistaken for friends. "Oh, why Tim?"

"Less likely anyone will try anything. Besides, yetis are magic resistant."

I couldn't argue with that. "Works for me. Would you like me to ask him?"

"Probably best."

Ilse came out then, fortunately with my coat. A few shuffles later, everyone was wearing their proper winter wear.

"Thanks, Ilse. Jesse says he's sorry. He didn't know how big a *faux pas* that was."

Ilse was never easy to read, but judging from the sharp lines of her face, she was still upset. However, she wasn't willing to take it out on me, my cousin or not. "Very well. Tell him his apology is accepted."

I nodded. "I told him to study more about the differences between the dimensions and how not to insult people."

That got a tiny smile. "I hope he listens."

"You and me both." Jesse was going to get seriously hurt if he didn't. I didn't understand. This was so out of character for him. He was usually much more careful about other people's cultures. Maybe he just hadn't had enough time to adjust to so many differences at once. Or maybe he was unhappy here, and taking it out on people. But that wasn't like him either.

Adrian told Ilse about the illusion meeting, and she agreed that Tim would make a good choice. When I called to ask him, he was amenable. Ilse didn't have class for over an hour, and normally we would have stayed up to talk. Tonight, for some reason I was feeling snappish and irritable. I decided it was best to go to bed before I said something mean too.

Sleep. I needed to sleep so I could be sharp and alert at the meeting tomorrow. Maybe we would get some answers. Finally.

***

Since Adrian was the only one who knew where the meeting was being held, we agreed to meet at the cafeteria. I was there first, with Tim joining me in minutes.

"Hey, Tim. How did you do on your math test?"

He gave me a quick look. "Not too bad. I hope to do better on the next."

I nodded. "Good to hear it."

"Indeed, thank you for asking."

I smiled. At least he wasn't offended. Adrian arrived then. "Ready to go?"

"I believe we are," Tim said, causing me to follow his lead.

The club turned out to be held in Barker Central building. The room was the same one registration had been in, but with less desks and tables in the way, there was easily room enough for three hundred people to move around easily. Five hundred could probably fit in a pinch. It seemed unnecessarily large for the group of thirty currently here.

It was a student run club, led by a grad student named Cory. Adrian introduced us to the tall red-headed man, who was apparently a friend of Adrian's roommate.

"Thank you for letting us come," I said, shaking his hand.

"Not a problem." He smiled, looking slightly puzzled at Tim's presence, but shook his hand as well. "If you have any questions, don't hesitate to ask. We're not very formal. We'll go over the minutes, make a few announcements, then spend most of the time hanging out and showing off."

"It should be a most enlightening experience," Tim said.

"I hope it is." Cory sent an undecipherable look to Adrian before suggesting we sit down before he started the meeting.

"What was that all about?" I whispered to Adrian as we found seats.

"Nothing." He studied the carpet. It was the same carpet found in every building in the school as far as I could tell.

"If there is something we need to know…" Tim muttered.

"I told Restlo that I wanted the invitation because you were interested in magic." He was still staring at the carpet, and possibly my shoes. Considering they were the same sneakers I had been wearing pretty much every single time he had seen me, I doubted they were that interesting. "Restlo figured I was trying to score some points with you, and I didn't bother to correct him. I didn't think he'd tell Cory that, though."

I bit my lip, guessing where it had gone from there. If Cory assumed that I had been invited so Adrian could impress me, I could only imagine what he thought Tim's presence meant. This was not the place to laugh, this was not the time to laugh, but it was funny!

Fortunately the meeting began soon after, allowing me time to regain my composure. There wasn't much to the meeting portion. Last meeting's minutes were read. Those who participated in the fireworks display were congratulated. Tee-shirts had been designed last semester and were now available for three Hydeonians a piece, about fifteen U. S. dollars. They were green with shiny black letters that said 'You only think you're reading this'. Cory demonstrated a 'simple' spell to make the colors of the ink change while the shirt was being worn, but warned that using it for a whole day was exhausting to most. There was talk of the spring exhibition where magici could showcase their talents. The time of the next meeting was announced and the meeting was adjourned.

Parts of the meeting went over my head, but that was fine. I wasn't a magicus or part of their club. I spent my time looking around at the different people there. Morgan was there, seeming a little surprised to see us. Or perhaps she was surprised to see Tim. After all, magici look human. Tim didn't. At all. Because of that, we had attracted a fair bit of attention.

I didn't know anyone else by name, but there were a few people I could say I had seen around. No one that I had seen a lot of, or at times that would be odd, though. After the meeting, we were given the chance to mingle. I didn't have a clue what to do.

I'm not the outgoing type, and the only people I knew here were the ones who didn't know anyone.

Maybe we should have brought Kara; she'd have everyone's history in an hour. But, she wasn't here, and we were, and we had come here to meet people; something we wouldn't do by standing around in a little cluster. With a deep breath, I smiled and introduced myself to the nearest magicus, a blond guy named Mark.

"I've not seen you here before," Mark probed.

"No, I'm a visitor. My name is Violet."

Mark raised his eyebrows. "You're the human? Wow, pretty gutsy coming here."

"I'm sorry?" He couldn't possibly know why I was here, could he?

"Humans aren't the most popular beings among the magicus population," He explained.

Well, he didn't seem angry with me, so I decided to push it. "I've noticed, but I'm not sure why."

Mark snorted. "They probably haven't told you. Okay, look at it this way. You're from a shade dimension, right?"

"Yeah, it's making it hard to reassure my parents that everything's okay." Blast it, I had completely forgotten about emailing them. I'd have to do that when I got back.

That got a little sympathy. "First gen, huh?"

"First generation? Yes, I'm the first in my family to attend Hyde."

He nodded. "It's tough talking to them, but you don't have to actually hide who you are, right?"

"No, I guess not."

"Now, as a magicus, I have to hide my abilities from non-magici, right?" He waved, making a life size impression of a tiger that made me have to steady my heart rate.

"Wow, that's amazing!" If I hadn't seen him do that, I'd probably be panicking. "Yes, I suppose you're right."

"Thank you. Anyway, it's against inter-dimensional law to reveal my abilities to those who aren't in the know. No matter what."

"I'm sorry?" Surely there was some kind of extenuating circumstances.

"Seriously. Even to save a life. Even to save your own life. It's illegal with stiff penalties."

I slowly let out a breath. "That's really harsh."

Mark nodded. "Because I signed the contract when I enrolled in Hyde, if I performed magic, say, in front of your parents? Magic itself could declare me in violation of my oath. I could die."

I choked. "Die?"

Mark shrugged. "Alright, probably not. But it is a possibility. Magic has weird ways to judge what it considers a violation. It determines your motivation, your act, etc. Also, it's in line with what the school decided when they framed the contract."

"Could I die if I told my parents about Hyde?"

"Don't know. Maybe." He waved the tiger away, causing it to change to an elephant. A slightly small one to fit below the ceiling but still an elephant.

"I will definitely keep that in mind," I said in a daze.

"Good plan," Mark said with a smirk, before getting called into another conversation.

Shaking my head, I decided to try talking to someone else. Except everyone seemed to be busy talking to others. I found myself looking at a display of pictures from the club. Most of them were from last year or earlier, but they were still interesting.

My favorites were the ones of last year's Spring Illusion Exhibition. The winner was a junior named Simon Nicols. He demonstrated an entire three-ring circus for twenty minutes. That was impressive. Hm, if he was a junior last year, than he should be a senior this year. I took a look around to see if he was here. He wasn't. Second and third place winners were, but no Simon. Maybe he was sick or had class or something.

"Looking at last year's pictures?"

I jumped about six inches in the air, before turning to see Morgan there. Hanging around illusionists was bad for my health. "You startled me. Anyway, yes, they're fascinating."

She smirked. "You're jumpy. What are you doing here, anyway?"

"I told you, I'm interested. I got an invitation to come today."

Morgan ignored me, coming over to see the pictures. "It was an exhibition to remember. Guess that just makes it more tragic."

"Makes what more tragic?" I asked, confused.

"Simon. He was my mentor last year, supposed to guide me on the 'way to illusion'," Morgan made air quotes. Visible, purple ones. "Then about a week after the exhibition, he just disappeared."

"Disappeared?" I certainly hadn't heard about this.

"Didn't get much talk, what with your boyfriend's scandal happening days later. But he dropped off the map. Officially, he dropped out." Morgan sneered, both at Adrian and the 'official' stance. I decided correcting her about Adrian wouldn't help.

"You don't buy that?"

She gave me a long look. I had given up on getting an answer when she continued. "His grades were good. He was a model student. No family problems. There was no reason for him to just leave." She went back to staring at the picture. "He didn't even say goodbye." The words were soft, with a hint of tears. I doubted I was meant to hear them. I left quietly, unwilling to intrude on her memories.

Chapter Eighteen
Travel to the North

The biggest success of the meeting was the list of club members. I set that aside to give to Ilse, then sat down and checked my email. Sure enough, there was a letter from my parents. Two actually, but one was just a note saying to write immediately. The other was a little more problematic.

Dear Violet,

What is this I hear about you going away for a long weekend with a boy? Are you sure this is wise? Your cousin seems very skeptical about this whole matter. We're worried, Violet. Are you involved with this boy? You know you can tell us anything. How is your ankle? Did it heal by now? Please, talk to us. We haven't heard from you in so long. Write to us, Violet. Call us. Something.

I love you,
Mom

I groaned. What on earth had Jesse told them? I could only imagine how many previous drafts there had been where Mom had been railing at the situation before she wrote this. I did appreciate the restraint though. Time to do some damage control.

Dear Mom,

I'm not exactly sure what Jesse told you, but I think he may have given you the wrong impression. My friend Tim, who I have told you about, invited a group of us, including Jesse, to visit his family. Jesse wasn't interested because he doesn't know the others well; and I didn't push. It's my roommate, five other girls from my dorm, three guys, the sister of one of the guys, and myself. Hopefully that makes you feel a little better.

I'm sorry I haven't written in a while. It's been pretty chaotic here. I'm studying hard, and even participating in social activities! I attended a student interest club today. I'm not eligible to join, but they let me watch. They're illusionists. (I started to get a headache at that.) *I'm fine. My ankle healed quickly, and it doesn't bother me anymore.*

Hope you are all well. Don't you have a three day weekend coming up too? Any special plans? Do you have a video of Rose's concert? Can you send me a copy? I'd appreciate it.

I love you,
Violet

Jesse had some questions to answer. Either there was some accidental miscommunication or he had deliberately tried to misrepresent what was going on. My money wasn't on it being an accident. He should be out of class, so I called him.

His roommate, a Kayte, according to Jesse, picked up. "Cotyew."

"Um, hi. Is Jesse there? This is his cousin, Violet."

"Oh, of course. Here you go." I could hear the phone being passed over.

"Jesse Peters."

"Hello, Jesse," I drawled out slowly. "I wrote to my parents, and found out something very interesting. Care to guess what?"

"What did you find?" I couldn't tell if he was nervous or not.

"That Mom was apparently of the belief that I was going on some weekend trip with a guy, just the two of us. Considering I never mentioned Tim's invitation, can you think of how this happened?"

"Why didn't you mention it?" Point for him; try to put me on the defensive so I couldn't yell at him.

Because I knew she'd get the wrong impression. "I just didn't. What did you tell her?"

"You don't think she has the right to know that you're leaving school grounds, with a guy?"

"Technically, I do that every time I go to the mainland with Adrian. Besides, it's not just me, there's a whole group. And even if it was just the two of us, it's not any of your business! I'm nineteen. I don't need your permission or your blessing." I winced at the volume, and made it a point to lower my voice. I didn't want to wake up Ilse.

"I'm just concerned."

"Then you could have come. I know you were invited. I even reminded you about it. And one more thing, Jesse Peters. You have a problem with my choices, fine, tell me. But ultimately, they are *my* choices. *My* decisions. You are not going to change my mind by going behind my back and tattling to my parents. Especially if you're going to misrepresent everything." I slammed the phone down before I could say something I might regret later, like calling him a lying, sneaking tattletale. That would really impress him with my maturity.

The phone started ringing seconds later. I picked it up long enough to know it was Jesse and hung up. Then I turned off the ringer so it didn't wake Ilse. I didn't want to talk to Jesse right now, and if I said anything else to him, he wouldn't want to talk to me either.

No, I'd be more productive by finishing my packing or doing last minute touches on my paper for government. That was a much better plan than sulking. I wondered if I'd do it.

***

Somehow everything got done. Ilse helped me with the government paper, but when I handed it in at class the next day, I was pleased that I could mostly understand the class on my own. Arie had fewer chances to sneer down her beak at me, at any rate. We still all sat together, to the dismay of probably everyone with the possible exception of Tim.

Jesse wasn't willing to sit with anyone else, and Tim liked sitting with me, even if it meant putting up with Jesse. Arie wanted to sit with Tim, even if it meant sitting with us. Though in all fairness, she behaved for the most part.

This Thursday wasn't an exception, though Jesse did leave a chair between us, and never spoke or even looked at me. Probably for the best, as it was taking most of my self-control not to snap at him, even knowing what happened to Adrian when he fought Jesse. Though, I hadn't noticed problems from verbal fights. Needless to say, it was a long class. But it ended, eventually, and I made my way to Genetics with a vague, "See you later," that could have included any or all of them.

The other two classes dragged slowly, but finally the day ended and the group of us were at Barker Central building. The spell preventing dimensional travel was lifted, though the dragon doing the lifting seemed reluctant. Then we were given a free teleport to the mainland. Fortunately, Tim was not from a shade dimension. There were a lot of natural jumpers here.

Mainland on 15d was very, very different from 13a. It didn't even have the same name. Here it was Nanooktiw. The buildings were mainly made of stone, though some were made of some white metal I couldn't identify. The town was bigger than Wollaston Lake, and had a much larger selection of inhabitants. Some looked mostly human, some were yetis, some were frost giants, etc. Then there were the clearly domesticated polar bears, tethered to lamp posts and street poles.

I hadn't seen polar bears, except in zoos, but I knew they were the most dangerous bears, and on the list of the most dangerous animals. So, I was more than a touch apprehensive about walking past the large animals. Didn't help that a couple of them growled at us.

Tim ignored them and led us to the transportation center. Finding an open counter, held by a frost sprite, he walked up. "Eleven student tickets for the North Pole Express, please."

The sprite looked at him and then at our group. "Eleven? Are you sure?" He asked slowly. "Raise your hands if you are traveling with him."

We raised our hands, letting him count us while Tim stood there simmering.

"I guess there are eleven," The sprite muttered under his breath. "Alright, eleven tickets. The Express is over there." He pointed. "Your tickets are for the last car. Just ask the conductor if you have any trouble." Every word was slow and loud as if he didn't think we knew the language, or had the intellect of a cabbage.

"My thanks," Tim ground out, all but snatching the tickets from the sprite's hand. "I am most certain we shall manage with ease." He turned and started ushering us away.

What was that clerk's problem? I wanted to ask Tim, but he was upset enough. It wasn't until the conductor tried acting the same way that I made the connection.

When Tim and I first met, he told me that yetis were considered lacking in brains. Like a desert is lacking in rain. I hadn't seen any reason for that belief, but Tim was the only yeti I knew. Nor had I seen anyone treat Tim like an idiot while we were at Hyde.

I wasn't the only one to realize what was going on, either. The second time the conductor came back, to make sure we were all buckled up, he gave an explanation of how we would travel (through vacuum tubes), that seemed more geared to three-year olds than adults. We were the only group he bothered to explain anything to. "Does everyone understand?" He asked, eyeing Tim.

"We understand," Arie cut in before anyone else could. "We understand that you are a complete wormbrain who can't understand that 'Student Tickets' refers to college students, not fledglings. Mind sending a conductor who is brighter than a tree stump next time?"

The conductor turned a fascinating shade of purple, sort of a mix between fuchsia and maroon, before flapping away on green furry wings. He didn't come back during the entire trip, and for a few minutes I wondered why I disliked Arie so much.

Tim had been wilting under the condescending manner, but now he was fighting laughter. We all were. With the conductor gone, Tim started explaining more about what things would be like where we were going.

The North Pole was a popular tourist spot here, including several hotels close by. By law, no one was allowed to build within a mile of the pole itself. Tim would be staying with his family in snow caves, but there were rooms reserved for us in a more traditional hotel, since we couldn't take the cold. There would be several of us per room, but for a few days we could manage.

Tim told us about his two sisters; one older, one younger. Their full names would be hard for most of us to pronounce, just as Tim's full name was apparently Timroyjoughyxwer. But, like Tim, they went by nicknames; Clya and Ren. Yeti societies are made up of small individual clans that are generally matriarchal, but those clans gathered together several times a year. Tim freely admitted to be a bit of an odd one out in the family, but he wouldn't say what that meant.

Because the North Pole was such a popular destination, the express went straight there in about forty minutes. I think the only reason it took that long was because the 'train' traveled through tubes on elevated platforms, and the rise and decent from those platforms had to be slow and careful. The rest of the time we were traveling so fast that the scenery blurred beyond recognition. There was a lot of white.

Then we landed and disembarked from the strange train. There were lots of yetis around, as apparently this spot is particularly popular for them, but Tim quickly led us to his parents.

His Granddam was standing a little aside, but clearly watching to make sure all were behaving appropriately. As we greeted her, she nodded regally. "You may call me Sim."

We were fortunate. From what I heard, female yeti names were even longer and more complicated than male names.

There were few obvious differences between yetis to the uninitiated. They were all big, had white fur, etc. I could distinguish Tim, because I knew him so well. As I studied his family, I noticed other differences. Some were more obvious than others.

Sim was a little shorter than the others, and used a stick as a cane. She didn't seem to need it though. Clya kept her fur very long and braided it. That was a recognized symbol for a yeti involved in the fishing trade. Tim's dam, who we were encouraged to call Lity, wore a woven leather belt, with a knife on it, proving her a very decorated huntress. Ren had blue eyes, which was very rare among yetis, and there were several legends about what that meant. Tim's sire, Kris, was much bigger than any of the female yetis and noticeably larger than Tim. According to Tim, he was a builder.

Introductions were made all around, but I was willing to bet that only Tim would be keeping everyone's name straight easily. There were some jokes about using name tags, which might not have been a bad idea.

"I brought a surprise." Sim said once all the names had been exchanged.

"Oh? That was very kind of you, Granddam," Tim said cautiously.

The aged yeti nodded imperiously before letting out a sound I couldn't duplicate if the fate of the universe depended on it. Best I can describe it is a cross between a whistle and a growl. Whatever it was, it caused two very large white bumps to stand up and run towards us.

My first instinct was to run. Then I realized they were polar bears. My second instinct was to run screaming. I managed to resist both of those and look towards Tim. He was smiling, so I probably didn't need to panic. It didn't escape my notice that he moved forward, blocking the rest of us from the onslaught. Since he was the only one capable of dealing with an over enthusiastic polar bear, that seemed like a good idea to me.

After some petting and pet talk to the bears, Tim turned to us. "This is Blizzard, and this is Whiteout. Why don't you come one at a time, and I'll introduce you to them?"

That was a good idea. Tell the large, potentially aggressive animals that we were friends. However, I really didn't want to get close to the bears. Neither did anyone else, if the lack of movement was any indication.

"Violet?" Tim looked at me. Not surprising, I was the closest to him. Pasting on a smile I didn't feel, I took a deep breath and walked forward. Tim should be able to move me out of the way if they attacked. I hoped.

"Blizzard, Whiteout, this is my friend, Violet." The bears sniffed at me, but let me pet their noises and heads like Tim suggested. "Good, they like you." Lucky me.

I moved out of the way and Arie went next. One by one, we all went through the introduction. Everything was going smoothly, until it was Adrian's turn.

As soon as Adrian stepped up, the bears started growling. Tim said something to them that the translation spell didn't translate. The bears settled a little, but as soon as Adrian moved, they were growling again. One of them, Blizzard, I think, tried to snap at him. Tim gave the bear a smack on the nose and said the same word again, stronger. Adrian had backed up a few feet and decided he didn't need an introduction.

"My apologies, I hadn't realized they would be here so I didn't think this would be an issue. Unfortunately, for whatever reason, polar bears do not seem to like cats."

Adrian eyed the bears warily. "Tell you what, I'll stay away from them, and you keep them from attacking me. We'll call it even."

Tim looked like he was trying not to smile, and failing. "I would be a poor host indeed if I were to let my pets attack my guests."

Everyone else was introduced to the bears with no problems. Adrian just stayed behind the crowd almost glaring at the polar bears. To add insult to injury, they loved Allison. They kept licking her hands and trying to lick her face. Everyone found that hysterical, probably at least partially because we were tired.

Next, we checked into our hotel. Allison, Arie, Ilse, and I shared a room, while Kara, Denise, and the Ice Twins shared another. Adrian roomed with Slate, though there was room for Tim there, too. Not everyone was thrilled with the room arrangements, but no one said anything. It was very kind of Tim's family to invite us over in the first place.

After checking in, and changing into warmer, dry clothes, we went down to meet the yetis for dinner. It suddenly occurred to me that I still didn't know Tim's last name or even if he had one. Maybe I should ask.

I was neither the first nor the last one down. Adrian was outside, in panther form, running around while Blizzard, Whiteout, and a few other polar bears were chasing him. I don't know about Adrian, but the bears sure seemed to be having fun. "Adrian, stop teasing the bears," Allison called.

The panther took half a second to shoot us an unhappy look before jumping onto the back of the closest bear and leaping from bear to bear before pouncing to the ground and dashing towards us. His move surprised the bears enough that a few ran into each other, and the rest were disoriented enough that Adrian was able to get away, transform, and basically hide behind the rest of us.

"They're crazy," Adrian panted. "Absolutely crazy."

"They were playing with you," Ren said. "They wouldn't hurt you."

Adrian snorted and made sure that he always had at least one yeti between him and the bears. I bit my lip to keep from laughing and wondered if it would be mean to buy him a stuffed polar bear from the hotel gift shop. Probably. Besides, I didn't have any money in this currency. Oh, well.

Dinner was, well, weird. The food was mostly fish, but I didn't recognize a lot of them. I'm not a huge fan of fish, but I wasn't willing to complain or cause trouble. Ilse had brought her own 'food' and I could have done the same.

There was a hot drink that I couldn't identify at all, but I suspected might have had alcohol in it. Whatever it was, it certainly helped warm me up. Though I was *finally* building up some cold resistance. Still, North Pole. Cold, ice, snow, polar bears. My meager cold tolerance and my clothes meant for temperatures about twenty degrees warmer were no match.

The conversations were interesting. As I got sleepier and sleepier, I didn't talk, but I listened. Tim's sisters were having fun picking on him. He was the reader of the family, which more or less equated to dreamer. They weren't mean about it, even if his parents seemed to be hoping he'd settle down and pick a 'practical' trade.

Arie was helpful there, since she was also a literature major, had taken some of the same classes, and kept mentioning how well Tim was doing in class. It helped get past some potentially awkward moments.

Only to end up in a worse spot when Kara mentioned that Tim and I had dated once. Other than Tim and me, Kara, Ilse, and perhaps Denise were the only ones to know about that. Everyone else was obviously unaware.

"You two dated?" Arie choked on it. Adrian looked almost betrayed; Allison and the Ice Twins just seemed surprised. Slate didn't react at all, so perhaps he knew too. Tim's family was suddenly eyeing me like a patch of ice they were testing the strength of.

"Um, yes. Well, Kara arranged a blind date between us, in late August. It was how we met. We watched a durchy game, got coffee, talked, and decided to remain friends," I said, trying not to slink under the table.

"Nothing more?" Clya asked.

"Nothing." There was no way I was going to mention that he asked me to the Halloween dance, even if we didn't end up going with each other. "We enjoyed the night, but…" I trailed off, letting everyone come to their own conclusions.

"Whose idea was it?" Arie asked, feathers still ruffled.

"As I recall, the decision was mutual," Tim said. About time he spoke up. I nodded quickly in agreement. Tim had said it first, but if he hadn't, I would have.

Slate, bless his stony heart, changed the subject by asking about the Festival of Ice. The conversation never got back to Tim and me supposedly dating. Not that I was complaining.

***

Dinner finished and people dispersed. I was tired and more than ready to go to sleep. I wasn't sure what time it was here, but it was almost two in the morning at Wollaston Lake. Ilse wasn't tired yet, and wanted to stay up talking to Ren about yeti folklore. Allison and Kara were playing with the polar bears, teasing Adrian to join in. Arie was talking to Tim, so I figured I would have privacy for a while.

I had barely changed into pajamas when Arie came in and locked the door. "I think it's time we had a talk."

Chapter Nineteen
Another Point of View

My eyes darted from the harpy to the locked door and back again. Fatigue receded as fight or flight instincts started to kick in, but I still had hopes to minimize this. "Arie, I'm really tired. Can this wait?"

"No, I don't think it can." Arie approached me slowly. "In fact I think we've put this off for too long as it is." Was she expecting a fight?

I sighed. "Fine, just give me a minute." I walked to the small attached bathroom and splashed some frigid water on my face. After drying it off, I went back to the bedroom, but tried not to get too close to the harpy. "Okay, what do you need?"

"What are your intentions towards Tim?"

A slightly strangled laugh emerged from my throat. "What? Shouldn't I be asking you that?"

"Should you?" She eyed me like a worm on a hook. "I expect an answer."

Steel stiffened in my spine. "Fine, I'll answer you if you answer me."

"You first."

I nodded. "Fair enough. Tim is my friend. A good friend. Not one I'm interested in dating, but one I don't want to see hurt. Your turn."

"Who decided to be friends? You or him?"

"Does it matter?"

"Yes."

"He did." It was the truth if not the whole truth. But it was what she needed to hear. "Now, your turn, what do you want?"

"Why is that your concern?" Arie asked.

Alright, enough playing. "You came to me. You started interrogating me. Now, I know you don't like me, and quite frankly, I haven't seen much to like about you either. But you know what? Tim is my friend. He seems to like you, and as far as I can tell, you like him. That is the *only* reason I haven't told him what a self-centered, snobbish, *prey-thief* you've been to the rest of us." 'Prey-thief' wasn't exactly what I meant, but it was a serious insult to harpies, and would get my point across.

"Why, you–" Her eyes were huge, as her wings fluffed up, possibly an instinctive intimidation technique.

"You have. Don't bother denying it," I cut her off. "But that doesn't matter right now. I will not interfere with your relationship with Tim, including telling him about what you've been like to us. But if you hurt him, I will make your life miserable." I'd find a way. Besides, I was sure to get help.

For a moment, I wondered if I had gone too far. Then Arie actually laughed. "Very well. But I won't stand by for you hurting him either."

"Agreed. Can I sleep now?"

She gave a grunt that sounded affirmative, so I crawled into bed while she took some clothes into the bathroom to change. I was still getting comfortable when she came back out. Unsurprisingly, she took the bed on the opposite side of the room, as far from mine as she could get. "Did you unlock the door?"

Arie didn't say anything, but I heard her unlock the door. Then I heard some strange sounds so I opened my eyes. Arie, instead of climbing under covers, had removed the blankets and top sheet from the bed and swirled them around. Once arranged to her satisfaction, she climbed into her 'nest', and sat down, pulling a few blankets around her. Interesting.

She must have felt me watching her because she turned to me. "Is there a problem?" Her voice had a bite to it.

"No, I just… I didn't know that was how you slept. It surprised me a little."

"Humans," She muttered just loud enough I could hear her, before wrapping her wings around her.

I rolled to my side, and sat up, leaning on my elbow. "What is your problem with humans anyway?"

She looked up at me in surprise. "I don't have a problem with humans." Her sincerity shocked me into silence for a moment.

Only for a moment. "You've hated me from the instant you found out I was a human."

"I never hated you. I don't *like* you, but I don't *hate* you." She looked almost *hurt* at the accusation.

It was on the tip of my tongue to say something along the lines of her fooling me, but this was the closest to civil conversation we had shared since I met her. I wasn't going to sabotage that with sarcasm. "Why do you dislike me? You never even gave me a chance."

"Why are you at Hyde?"

What an odd question. "I want to study genetics. Hyde has an amazing program for that. A teacher recommended it."

Arie shook her head. "No, that's why you *want* to be at Hyde. Why *are* you here?"

"I was accepted, and came?" Did she know?

"Hyde needs humans to stay open," She said, bitterness spreading from her voice. "They need humans desperately. I chose Hyde for its' reputation for academic excellence. I excelled in my studies for years and got a perfect score on my graduation tests. Even so, it was stiff competition. I almost didn't get in. You on the other hand… They accepted you, not because of your grades, your admission essay, or anything like that; but because they thought you would adapt well. You could practically sleep through your classes and they would still make sure you passed! How is *my* education worth anything if *your* grades are being kited?"

The anger and accusation took me by surprise, but not as much as the reason. I'd be mad too. "Whoa, easy! First things first, why do you think my grades are being kited?"

Arie snorted. "I've seen you in class."

"Mostly you've seen me in Foundations of Literature. A few weeks in Prominent Forms of Government, right?" She nodded. "Lit was a struggle for me, I admit. It always has been and this was worse. Ninety percent of the material was new to me. I struggled and worked, and pulled through with B+. That was my lowest grade of the semester." Arie started to say something, but I talked over her. "I got an A- in History, and A's and A+'s in the rest. Dr. Gronk even agreed to let me enroll in an upper level class based on my Bio I grade; something I doubt he would do if he was artificially inflating my grade. These grades, by the way, are pretty typical of the grades I got before Hyde. Government, again, most of this is new to me, but I'd say I'm doing fairly well."

Arie paused, considering it. "Certainly better than Lit."

"You are making an assumption based around my worst class. Hardly a decent representative sample. Surely you have some classes you struggle in more than others." Arie didn't say anything, but she at least looked like she was thinking it over. "I understand why you're mad, I would be too. Actually, I *am* mad. I want to be accepted for my own merits, my grades, etc. Not just because I'm human. Is the school kiting my grades? I don't think so. It never occurred to me, and I've seen no evidence of it. I really hope they aren't. The grades aren't worth anything if you don't earn them."

"Exactly!" Arie burst out. The fact that we agreed seemed to startle her, though.

"Look, you don't have to like me. I'm not expecting miracles. But I'm not an idiot, or 'wormbrain'. I am working hard to succeed in classes. Don't just write me off as a moron because you saw me struggling in one class."

I think Arie would have said something to that, but Allison came in then. "Wow, you two are still up? I'm going to bed. I'm exhausted."

***

We met in the snow caves for breakfast, at about seven Wollaston Lake time. Much too early, considering how late we were up the night before, but we were trying to accommodate Ilse. Normally she would have gone to bed by now, but she was staying up 'late' to eat with us. It wasn't like she had to worry about sunlight, since we were in the North Pole in winter. Some of the rest of us had problems with the lack of light, though. Or at least I hoped I wasn't the only one. Not that Wollaston Lake was much better, but there was at least some light and dark in each day.

There was fish for breakfast, caught by Clya. Happily, there was also toast and porridge. It was a much quieter meal than dinner was, because most of us were half-asleep. The yetis weren't though. Maybe they didn't need a lot of sleep.

"We are approximately two miles from the center of the North Pole," Tim said, apparently under the mistaken belief that we were awake enough to care. "Sleighs are available for rental for that purpose if there is interest. Perhaps tonight, when Ilse can accompany us?"

I rubbed my eyes. Great, more cold. On the other hand, when were we ever going to have this opportunity again? "That could be interesting. Um, what pulls the sleighs?" I hadn't seen any sign of horses, who probably couldn't survive in this weather anyway, or dogs.

"Polar bears, Silly," Ren said. "What else?" Actually, she said 'Fluffhead' but the meaning was the same.

"Ah, of course." I nodded and forced myself to eat a little more. I was definitely going to bed earlier tonight.

"I'm not sure that's a great idea." Adrian said, sparking several smiles around the table.

"Trained sleigh pullers would be muzzled during the journey," Tim said. "It may also be possible to mask your scent for a short time."

Adrian grunted something that could have meant anything, before stretching in a way that had me, and a few others, wincing. "Yeah, I think I have something that might work."

It was Clya who finally brought up the elephant in the room. "Oh, you lot just go back to bed. You obviously want to. You won't miss much."

There were some token protests, but Tim reassured us that he'd spend some time with his family and wouldn't do anything exciting without us. "Besides, if we do journey to the center of the pole this evening, then it would be prudent to be well-rested."

Ilse was the first to respond. "Well it is my normal hour for sleep anyway." She bid us all a good night and went back to the hotel.

Slowly a little at a time, the rest of us followed. Apparently my talk with Arie had gotten her thinking or something because she was watching me now. Either that or she was in the 'stare at nothing' stage of tiredness.

When I got to the hotel, I saw Adrian curled up in panther form on a couch in a quiet corner of the hotel lobby. Allison was sitting next to him, absently playing with his fur. The big cat looked up briefly when I came in, but settled back down to sleep when he saw it was me.

Allison saw me and waved me over. I semi-stumbled to the couch, shedding my coat as I walked. Taking a seat on the other side of the sleeping panther, I looked over at Allison, hoping she wasn't going to try to make me think. I was getting warm, the couch was surprisingly comfortable, and Adrian was soft and warm. "Hmm?" I asked in a low voice.

"What happened last night?" Allison asked in a normal voice.

"Adrian's trying to sleep," I whispered.

"And he'll wake up faster to a whisper than he will to normal volume, trust me."

I shrugged. "Oh."

"So?"

"Hmm?" Sleep was beckoning, couldn't she see that?

Allison smirked. "What happened last night?"

"When?" Only after I said that did I realize what she meant. "Oh, you mean with Arie?"

"Yes, exactly."

Nice, comfortable sofa. Nice, deep, comfortable sofa. "We talked." My eyes wouldn't stay open.

I barely heard Allison say, "Goodnight."

***

Something was wrong. My brain was fuzzy; my thoughts weren't clear. I was in a room that seemed only vaguely familiar. I had been there before. It was important. But I couldn't figure out where I was.

"Hey, are you ready?" A male voice said. I had heard it before, but didn't know it well. Who was it? But part of me did know the voice, recognized the owner.

"Why are we here? This is a bad idea," I said. Only *I* didn't say it. It wasn't my voice. It was… Adrian's? Could it be? I must be dreaming. But why would I dream I was Adrian?

"Trust me," The voice said. I, maybe Adrian, turned. It was a guy, about our age. Morris! It was Charles Morris! It had to be. But that look, that smile. Instincts said run.

Dream-Adrian must have agreed. We turned, trying to dash for the door, when all our muscles seized up painfully, leaving us a heap on the floor.

"Oh, no. None of that," A female voice said. It sounded vaguely familiar, but I couldn't place it. "I've been waiting too long for this." Our eyes darted around, searching for the woman, but she wasn't in sight. "You should be proud, Adrian Char. You are going to be the foundation of a new age. I am sorry you won't survive to see it, but such changes are always wrought in blood."

We were lifted without hands and floated to the middle of the room. Candles were visible at various spots. It was the ritual! Then pain racked through us as we were forced into panther form. Scents became stronger, sounds more prevalent. Two heartbeats besides ours. The female was wearing perfume, it smelled like sandalwood.

"You need to be a cat for this to succeed. Perhaps for the best. If I understand correctly, that means you won't feel as much pain while being skinned." Fear ran through us like water. "It is necessary, I'm afraid." The woman started moving, we could see her from the corner of our eyes, but not clearly. "Hmm, perhaps I'll get a coat out of the deal, keep it from being a total waste."

She stooped, coming up with something in her hand. Something shiny. A knife. "Keep watch on the door," She ordered.

"Alright," Morris answered.

Bile rose up in our throat, fear and betrayal twining in a sickening mixture. We tried to talk, to shout, but couldn't. The woman came closer, muttering something under her breath, as she prepared to make the first cut.

No! We weren't going to go through this. This was a dream. Wake up!

She started to drag the knife slowly, painfully, over a spot near the collarbone. Hair was in our face but we couldn't tell the color in this form. Wake up!

Who was she? Then, as if answering my question, she looked us in the eye. "You!"

My own shout woke me up.

Chapter Twenty
Bonds of Friendship and Family

I might have written the whole thing off as a dream if Adrian hadn't roared out at the same time I shouted. Allison turned to us, eyes glowing. "Adrian, transform. Tell me what you dreamed, now. It's important."

Adrian did what she said. Between the two of us, we filled her in. For some reason, I seemed to remember more of the details than he did. Finally we go to the end. "And? Who was it?" Allison asked, when we mentioned her looking us in the eye.

I opened my mouth to tell her. "It…" I choked. "No, no, no!" I hit the couch arm in frustration. "I can't remember!"

Allison deflated, and Adrian growled. "Must be some spell. I can barely remember the dream, and you can't remember the most important part."

"To be expected, I guess," Allison said. "After all, why should this be easy? Still, we learned something. Violet, you recognized her, right? It wasn't just Adrian's memories?"

I thought about it for a moment, before answering slowly, "Yes. Morris, I recognized mostly because Adrian did, but I recognized Morgana on my own. Possibly better than Adrian did."

"So, perhaps someone you know better than I do," Adrian said.

"Well, that really narrows it down. I only know about five magici. One's a guy, one isn't here, one specializes in elemental magic. Two specialize in illusionary magic, but I don't know any of them well."

Allison sighed while Adrian leaned his head back. "Name them."

"Okay, there's Mark, who I met at the club. Well, I met Cory, too, so I guess that makes six. My high school biology teacher is a magicus, her name is Linda Green." The Chars shook their heads.

"Never met her." Adrian said.

"Didn't think you had." Though I was glad to have her off the list. "Rachael is an elemental magicus."

"Her, I've met," Adrian said. "I think she's in one of my classes."

"Then there's Morgan and Professor Collins."

"Met them, I think. But I don't know them well."

"Still, that limits the field, a lot, right?" I asked, hoping to be of some help.

"Some," Alison conceded. "But there is also the possibility that you know someone without knowing they are a magicus."

That was very possible. Asking 'What are you?' was considered rude. I huffed in frustration. "Okay, we still have too many candidates. How about another question? How did this happen? People do not normally share dreams."

"That's true. Even," Adrian lowered his voice, "defender psychics don't have a history of this."

"You're right," Allison said, eyes in the distance as she tried to reason it out. "However, I don't think there's a precedent for a defender psychic and his primary protectorate also bonding as part of an oath."

My eyes widened as I sunk back into the couch. "I hadn't even thought of that. You know, I think this explains a few things. Adrian, have you been having nightmares about this for a while?"

He hunched over, not wanting to answer. "Off and on, pretty much since it happened. I don't remember much of them on my own. Sometimes a scrap of words, or a feeling of pain, or fear. I remember someone wanting a fur coat."

I shivered, and Allison swallowed hard. "Do you sometimes sleep during the day?" I asked.

That got me a weird look and a shrug. "Sometimes. I do take night classes."

"The average length of a dream is usually under a minute," I said, mostly to myself.

"Usually only a few seconds," Allison said. "Though your nightmare seemed to be about a minute long."

"That's it, then." They were looking at me like I was crazy. Couldn't blame them. "I've been getting mini-panic attacks. They last under a minute, and leave me very disoriented. I haven't mentioned them to anyone, but I wondered why you didn't seem to know about them." I looked at Adrian. "You never said anything because it isn't my panic. It's yours! I'm picking up on your dreams."

Adrian winced, and opened his mouth to say something, but Allison spoke first. "That is entirely possible. A bond like that changes people. It's a little surprising we haven't noticed more changes. You may well be picking up on a few others as well, though because you and Adrian already have a bond, of course it would deepen."

I thought of a few other times my emotions seemed to come from nowhere. "Okay, now is this happening to anyone else? If so, how do we figure out who we are feeling?"

"Tonight we'll have an emergency meeting," Allison said. "We just need to figure out a way to keep the others occupied."

***

It was a little tricky, but we managed to get everyone together before our planned trip. Arie and Tim's sisters spent some time comparing Tim stories and beauty tips. I didn't see the connection between the two topics, but they were having fun. In case Arie got bored with that, Slate was flying around, trying to challenge her to a flying race. It kept them distracted enough that we could borrow Tim and commandeer the other girls' room. It was less likely either of them would check this room.

I told everyone about the dream, because Adrian seemed to remember less about it now than he did when he first woke up. I could almost taste his frustration with the situation. Actually, I might have *really* felt his frustration. After that, everyone thought about it, trying to find anything similar in their experiences.

"I think you might be right about sharing emotions," Krystal said slowly. "Bria and I have always had some sense of each other, but it's now a lot stronger. We seem to know where the other is; sometimes we practically know what the other is thinking."

"Again, it's working on a previous level." Allison nodded. "Okay, anything else happening?"

Adrian spoke up, "I think my bond, as a defender psychic, has widened. Violet is still my primary, but I may be sensing the rest of you, a little bit. When the door exploded, I knew Violet wasn't the only one in danger, but I wasn't sure who else was there. Now that I know it was the yeti, I think I'll recognize him again. It isn't as strong as my bond to Allison, but it may get there."

There was silence as we digested that. "This could be advantageous," Ilse said. "Especially if we can all develop a sense for each other. If we all knew when another was in danger…"

"But it might not go that far," Kara pointed out. "Has anyone sensed when someone else was in danger?"

No one spoke up. Finally Denise suggested, "Maybe we have but don't know what we were feeling?"

Time to be scientific about it. "Okay, Adrian, what does it feel like when you know I'm in danger, and how is it different than what you feel when Allison is in danger?"

Adrian let out a breath and leaned back, closing his eyes. "Danger has a taste. It's sharp, and sparks like biting aluminum with a filling. It pools in my stomach and blood rushes to my limbs. I have to move, have to do *something*. When it's Allison, I, well, I hear bells. Just a little bit. For Violet, I smell sugar cookies. For some reason, I've always associated you with sugar cookies," He said, more to the floor than any of us. "For the yeti, I smelled snow."

"Again, probably something you associate with Tim. I wonder why you hear something for Allison, but smell something for the two of us." Why sugar cookies, anyway? Not that it was bad, just a little surprising. I would have expected him to associate me with the flower or the color.

"I had strings of bells in my room when I was a little girl. I would play them to make music. Or just noise. Adrian probably remembers that, and has always thought of me with bells."

"So, even if we were to start sensing each other, we might well use our own associations instead of using Adrian's," Tim mused. "For example, if I were to connect Violet to the taste of coffee, I might experience that."

"Or maybe you'd taste purple. That's a pretty good taste."

Denise got a few odd looks for the statement, but no one said anything. I made a mental note to look up synesthesia when we got back, but this wasn't the time. "Still, the sense of danger is the same each time? Just a little different to tell you who is in trouble?"

"Basically."

"Does anyone remember feeling like that?" Allison asked. No one did. "Okay, pay attention if you do. Anything else that might be odd?"

"I wasn't very tired the last two transformations," Kara volunteered. "Usually I'm exhausted, or at least drained."

I thought about it for a minute. "Wasn't your last transformation Christmas Eve?" She nodded. "I was tired. I was all hyper the day before, and I couldn't figure out why, but I had no energy on Christmas."

"That would be December 25, would it not?" asked Ilse. "I was also unusually fatigued."

A few others agreed. Final consensus was that no one was as tired as Kara would normally be, and not everyone seemed to be affected. We decided that we were sharing energy. Kara's next transformation was coming up soon, and we'd see if it happened again and if it involved the same people.

"I think I'm getting more cold resistance than I had before, but that might be natural," I said. It was a relative term though, I still normally needed at least two or three layers of clothing.

"Same here," Denise said.

"You two do have less cold tolerance than the rest of us, it's possible that the bond is trying to build that up," Allison hypothesized.

We might have continued, but Arie came by then, wondering if we were going to the center of the pole or not.

***

The trip was cold, but we bundled up and buried ourselves under blankets. Polar bears are fast enough that it wasn't a long trip. There was an actual pole in the center. A brass one; that said, "It's all South from here." We took lots of pictures: of the pole, of people standing around the pole, and finally a group shot. Good thing my camera was digital. I still remembered film cameras and didn't want to even imagine trying to explain these pictures to a developer. There was no way I could explain these back home.

Most of the rest of the weekend we spent trying to pick up on each other's emotions and other changes the bond may have made. The meditation lessons Ilse gave us helped a lot. Close proximity helped too. Allison and I talked it over and decided that I was probably able to share Adrian's dream because we were both asleep at the same time, touching each other. We debated on trying it again, hoping to find out a little more about what happened, but the odds weren't good. We couldn't predict when Adrian would dream about it, or that we'd pick up on his dreams instead of mine; even ignoring how hard it would be to arrange us both falling asleep at the same time. Besides, even if we did luck out with all that, there was no guarantee that we'd learn anything new, or that I'd remember once we woke up. Whatever spell was on Adrian was clearly affecting me at least a little.

I was getting better at telling when the emotions I was feeling weren't mine, but figuring out whose they were was harder. I could identify Adrian's with about ninety percent accuracy; he made me think of dark chocolate. Ilse's emotions had a different feel to them. So did Tim's, but I didn't pick up on him often. The rest I struggled with. Still, it was better than I was doing a few days ago, and I could only get better with practice.

On the night before we left, I woke up near tears. I tried to calm myself down with deep breaths, and figure out what went wrong. How did I feel? Homesick. I stifled a sob. I missed my home, my family. Was it my feeling? It could be. I had been homesick more than a few times since coming to Hyde, but I generally didn't wake up crying because of it.

So, someone else's? I closed my eyes and tried to analyze it. Did anything seem odd? I licked at the roof of my mouth, something that sometimes helped me discern another's emotions. Did I taste pine? It wasn't real, but phantom pine. Okay, that ruled out a few people right there. Adrian wasn't in the running. Neither were Ilse or Tim. Denise, the few times I had picked up on her, made me think of sunshine. So, Allison, the Ice Twins, or Kara.

Allison was in the room, but she was asleep. As far as I could tell, she was peacefully dreaming. I got up and slid my robe on, all while asking myself what I thought I was doing. I couldn't go pounding on doors and waking everyone up. But I couldn't leave this alone either. Making sure I had my key, I left the room as quietly as possible. Neither Arie nor Allison stirred. I had no idea where Ilse was.

I hesitated at the other door, but ended up not knocking. Instead, I followed my instincts. My instincts and my feet led me to the end of the hallway, where someone was sitting on a chair, staring out the window, and quietly crying.

It was too dark to see who it was, so I got closer. Ah, I should have known. "Hey." It was almost a whisper. She stiffened and turned to me. "Are you okay?"

"I'm fine." The tears in Kara's voice betrayed her.

I came closer, looking more out the window than at her. "You miss them, don't you? Your family?"

Out of the corner of my eye, I could see her bite a lip before nodding. "It's my brothers' birthday. I've never been away for a pack birthday before. I just…" Tears took over.

It was painful seeing her cry. The ever-optimist, the always cheerful one. I gave her a hug because I didn't know what to say. She grabbed me back, shaking with sobs. "I miss them. I really miss them. Ever since I started school. I don't know if I can do this!"

Violet, you selfish girl. Did you think you were the only one with problems? Didn't you see your friends were unhappy? Blind, selfish, stupid girl.

There was nothing to say, nothing to do but hold her. Finally she calmed, and gave me a sheepish smile that didn't come close to looking real. "Sorry about that. We're close to full moon. I'm always more emotional then."

"Nothing to apologize for. I've had some rough patches myself." How was the best way to word this? "I didn't realize you suffered so much from homesickness."

Kara shrugged. "When you're part of a pack, it defines you. Life isn't right when you are too far away for too long. Normally I have it under better control, but today, it was just… It hit harder than I expected."

"Look, I don't know anything about being part of a pack, but if there's anything I can do; even just be there when you're lonely, let me know."

"Alright, but I'm there for you too, when you hit your rough patches," Kara promised. At least she seemed to be feeling better.

I smiled and nodded, wondering if I would ever dare go to her. Before I could think of a decent response, a look of absolute awe came over her face.

"Hey, look! It's the Northern Lights."

I turned, gasping in wonder as green ribbons of light danced through the sky. There were hints of red and blue too. "We're lucky. I don't know about this dimension, but in mine, the Aurora Borealis is most common in Mid-March. Red and blue are also rare."

"It's beautiful," Kara whispered.

"Should we wake the others?" I asked.

We hesitated but eventually decided to. It was only a little over an hour before we were supposed to be getting up anyway. I don't know how Kara made out, but I learned something very interesting. Allison is *not* a morning person, by any stretch of the imagination.

Arie snarled at me when I woke her, but as soon as I mentioned the Northern Lights, she got up on her own, apparently all was forgiven. Allison, on the other hand, threw things at me before burrowing under the blankets. I was willing to drop it then, figuring she could decide her priorities on her own. Arie, however, ripped the blankets off her and laughed.

"Go wake the guys. I'll make sure she gets up," the harpy promised. Shaking my head, I finished getting dressed and took her advice. Judging by the screech that was cut off when I shut the door, I was none too soon.

Waking the guys was easy. We had been loud enough to wake Adrian, so as soon as we told him why we were making so much noise, he agreed to get Slate up and meet us outside.

It was a quiet group who watched the lights dance before one by one surrendering to necessity and getting out of the cold. Breakfast was a pensive meal. We were heading back to the school afterwards, but no one wanted to talk. Maybe it was to savor what we saw. Or maybe we were just asleep. Probably a bit of both.

Kara was smiling again, but for the first time, I could look past it. She wasn't completely happy, even if she wasn't as depressed as she had been earlier. Even if I knew what to say, there wasn't a private moment to say it.

We said goodbye to our hosts, thanking them for having us over. I kept feeling like we should have a gift, but both Tim and Ilse assured me that wasn't part of yeti culture. They generally didn't care much for most material possessions, and other than feeding guests, giving food said you thought the recipient was a poor hunter. Considering that was a major insult to yetis, that didn't seem a wise move.

"So, Pink Panther, want to say goodbye to your new playmates?" Allison asked, waving at Blizzard and Whiteout, both of whom stood up and tried to pull at their leashes.

"I'll say goodbye from here," Adrian said, backing away several more feet.

I laughed, but I also went over and slipped my mitten and glove off for a moment. I hadn't actually felt their fur yet. It was stiff and coarse, and cold, of course. But now I could say I pet a polar bear.

We waited in the warm train station, giving Tim a few minutes to say goodbye. Fortunately, the ticket master here was less rude than the previous one; not believing the stories of yetis being dumb enough to try eating rocks. Though, having met other yetis, I could see that the average yeti wasn't an academic. Their culture was one that prided itself on finding the simplest, most straight-forward solution to any problem. If it meant using brute force, all the better. But that didn't mean they were dumb. That philosophy worked well for them most of the time.

There wasn't an express train from the North Pole to Nanooktiw, probably because Nanooktiw wasn't that big. Still, even with several stops, it only took us about an hour and a half to make the trip. From there, we met up with the teleporter that the school had arranged to pick us up. Very nice of them, though Ilse said it was probable the school wanted to get the dimension stabilizing spell back on us as quickly as possible.

Once we were back at the school, and properly 'enspelled', if that's even a word, we dispersed. Ilse was up late for her, and the sun was actually trying to rise. Part of me wanted to watch it, since I hadn't seen the sun in about three days, but I was also tired and wanted to crash for a few hours. I said goodbye to the group, thanked Tim again, and went to my dorm.

Ilse went straight to bed, but I decided to write a couple quick emails to let my parents and Jesse know I was back. I could have called Jesse, but I didn't want to talk to him yet.

Mom had sent a quick email, semi-apologizing for the misunderstanding, reminding me to remember my manners, and wishing me a good time. My email back was short, basically telling her I was back, I had fun, and I'd write more after some sleep.

More surprising was the email from Jesse, apparently sent last night. With some trepidation, I opened it.

You were right. I shouldn't have gone behind your back like that. I'm sorry. Hope you had fun. You should know, I've officially transferred. I leave Wednesday. Hopefully you'll be willing to talk to me before then.
Jesse

Chapter Twenty-One
Those who Leave

I sat in the coffee house at the library, drumming my fingers on the table. I kept trying to stop myself, but it didn't work for long. Jesse had agreed to meet me here when I emailed and asked him to. I wasn't sure what I was going to say, but we had to talk. He would show up, wouldn't he? A deep breath. There he was.

He nodded to me, but went to get a coffee first. I took the time to try again to force my fingers to stop moving, and push down nerves. Why was I nervous anyway? It wasn't like I could do anything about his choices.

"Hey," Jesse said quietly, looking like he was trying to gauge his welcome before sitting.

"Hey." An almost exact replica of his tone. Jesse sat down. "How was your weekend?"

"Okay. I got a lot done. Thinking. Packing. You?"

"I pet polar bears, stood at the top of the world, and saw the Aurora Borealis."

Jesse shook his head with a laugh. "I think your weekend beat mine."

"Why are you leaving?"

"I told you I would," Jesse said with surprise, then took a sip of coffee. Must have been too hot; he winced.

"Yes, but why now? Why not finish the semester? Wouldn't that be better?"

Jesse rubbed absently at a scratch on his hand. It was a wide one that I knew for a fact hadn't been there when I left. "No, I'm pretty sure it wouldn't. You were right about the anti-human sentiment. I don't want to talk about it." He cut off my questions before I could ask them. "I made arrangements to go somewhere else, closer to home. They start late enough that I can still get in if I leave this week."

I took a sip of my coffee so I had an excuse not to talk for a moment. "You aren't going to change your mind, are you? No matter what."

"No, it's too late now." He seemed almost sad about that. Then he put a hand on mine. "Violet, seriously, what do you hope to accomplish here? Come with me. You're smart; there are other great science programs. Why stay here?"

"Oh, Jesse." I shook my head. "Where else can I take a weekend trip to the North Pole? Or have class with a dragon? Or learn about magic, real magic? If it's too late for you to stay; then it's too late for me to decide to leave. That world is too small for me now."

Jesse slumped back, folding his arms over his chest. "You're leaving everyone you know behind. That isn't fair to anyone."

"That is the worst part," I agreed. "I'm doing everything I can not to burn bridges, but…"

"I could make you come," Jesse said, studying me.

I had to stifle a laugh. "How? Drag me on the plane, kicking and screaming? Somehow, I think you'd get stopped at security."

"I'll tell your parents you're in trouble."

I sobered in a heartbeat. "No, you can't tell them anything of the sort. I've told you, again and again; you cannot reveal anything about the dimensions or Hyde that isn't generally known. The consequences can be unbelievably severe."

He leaned back, staring at the ceiling. "I'll have to tell them something. I mean, I didn't even stick out a month. You don't think they'll want to know why?"

"You got a better offer? It's too cold? You can't join the sports teams? You don't want to learn French?"

He chuckled. "Maybe." A long pause. "Are we okay now?"

"Are you going to try to tell someone something you shouldn't?"

"I'll be good," He promised with a crooked smile.

I nodded. "If this is what you want, really want; I'll go with you to the airport. That way you won't have to try to figure out a way to return the snowmobile."

"Wednesday at noon."

"I can do that."

We made small talk for a while, but it was awkward. It was a relief when he excused himself to finish packing. Since I was already in the library, I decided it was a perfect time to do some research for my paper on the rules and limitations of magic.

I went to the section most likely to have what I'd need, only to find a tall guy with messy dark hair had commandeered one of the tables, covering it with books, including most of the ones I need.

"Um, excuse me? Would it be possible for me to borrow a few of these?"

He looked up at me owlishly. "Oh, sorry. I guess I wasn't thinking about someone else needing them. What do you need?"

"Well, I'm doing a paper on the rules and limitations of magic."

"Oooh! That's what I'm working on. Trying to find a way around the limitations. Can I help?"

"Sure, thanks." I sat down. "I'm Violet."

"Call me Nocht. I don't use my real name."

I stifled a smile at that. "Okay, Nocht. Are you a magic user?"

"Of course. I'm a magicus. Did you know that all magici specialize in a particular area?"

"I had heard that."

"Right, but I'm looking for a way to be good in all areas."

"Is that possible?"

He smiled, clearly enjoying his topic. "I'm certain of it. Okay, some of it is natural skill. Like, I'm an elemental magicus, and I'm best at fire. Which really stinks sometimes, because when you have a good flame going, all someone has to do is douse you with water to bring you out of it. Water is more subtle and requires more effort to control or use. You lose it if you can't see the water. Stuff like that. This book is the best I've found about elemental magic." He held up a book titled, 'Lightening from your fingertips, fire from your eyes, and water from your tongue.' "It's a little informal, though."

"I can see that." Maybe I could make this work. "How about some of the other kinds? Say, illusions?"

"Good question. Now, a good illusionist is going to be hard to see through. But even the best can't make you feel something too far from reality. Now, if you really believe you'll feel something, you might. But if you close your eyes and reach out- poof! Just air. Also, there's usually a slight ripple when they make an illusion change or move. Oh, and you will never smell an illusion. Most magici aren't good enough to have an illusion going when they aren't looking at it."

"I've seen tactile illusions before."

Nocht frowned. "Probably not a magicus then. Or it was a magicus working with someone. Or you were expecting to feel it."

All were possible. "Alright. And rituals, they are really precise, and can't be interfered with in the slightest, right?"

"Right, and you have to be incredibly detail oriented." His smile faded. "I'm pretty bad at rituals. Which stinks because that's one of the only ways to really get skill in another area. Well, practice helps, but that only goes so far."

I frowned. "What rituals can you do to get skill in another area?"

He flushed and looked around, before lowering his voice. "Keep in mind that some of these are really, incredibly illegal and I would never ever do them or encourage someone else to do them."

I nodded at the disclaimer. "Like what?"

"Okay, from the most benign to the worst, there is buying an enchanted artifact, usually an amulet or a ring. Someone puts a little bit of their magic in a gemstone and someone who isn't as good buys it. It's perfectly safe, because so little magic is transferred and the magicus in question builds it back. Usually slowly, so most only do it as a last resort. That means these are rare and expensive, and/or family heirlooms. For example," He waved a hand, allowing me to see the onyx ring on his hand, "my Grandmother had this made for me before she died. This helps me in charms."

"It's pretty. Why a gemstone?"

"They hold magic best. Well, some of them do. Like, you're wearing an amethyst necklace. Amethyst is great at holding magic. It can hold an enchantment for centuries, but not a very powerful one. Onyx holds a little more power, but I can't expect it to last as long. I can pass this on to my kids, but they probably won't be able to pass it on to theirs. Emeralds, rubies, and turquoise are on the other end. They hold loads and loads of magic, but only for a few years. If you do it right, you can sometimes arrange it so the magic flows into the wearer, becoming permanently theirs. But that's dangerous, especially if there is an incompatibility between magics. It also won't work on a non-magic user. I think."

Interesting information, but we had gotten off track. "What else can you do to boost your abilities?"

"There's the blood ritual. That, surprise, surprise, requires a little of your blood. Technically legal, but strictly monitored, since people have gotten themselves killed getting that one wrong. You can also only do it twice. Ever. In your entire life. And there's no way of knowing ahead of time how successful the ritual will be."

I nodded carefully. "Okay, what else?"

"You can share magic with a willing participant, but that only works for really short term. Both participants pay a double price for it, but that magic is more powerful than anything a single person can cast. Then we get darker. Sure you want to hear this?" He gave me a skeptical look.

"I don't have the least erg of magic and couldn't do any of these even if I wanted."

That seemed to reassure him. "Okay, frowned upon, but not technically illegal, is the sacrifice ritual. You have to kill an animal. This gives you a temporary boost in a particular area."

I swallowed bile back. "Why isn't that illegal?"

"Because the High Magi don't want to make it illegal in case they ever need it. I don't know if there's any truth to them, but there are legends of heroes defeating supposedly unbeatable foes after a sacrifice ritual. There are also stories, probably true, of people getting addicted to the rush and having to sacrifice more and more until they reach the worst. Stripping another magicus of his magic; or human sacrifice. Well, sentient, really. Not just human. Both are illegal and lead to death."

"So a magicus can be stripped of magic?" We had discussed whether it was possible.

Nocht nodded, looking serious. "It's a death sentence. They die a slow death without even a spark of magic to keep them alive. You aren't a magicus, you can't do magic, but you still have a spark. It keeps you alive, and makes it so spells can be cast on you. Without even that... well, they wither away and die. It's been used as capital punishment before. Sometimes the magic goes to restore the victims of a power-mad magicus, sometimes it gets released to Free Magic."

I shivered. Had it gotten colder in here? "Wow, that's creepy."

"Yeah, there are a few rituals in between. Stealing magic, but not all of it. Still illegal though. I'm trying to figure out a few of these. Not so I can do them! I'm trying to find legal, safe, non-deadly ways. Much preferable."

"I would definitely have to agree with you there." I looked down at my notes. "Okay, this is fascinating, but a little advanced for what I need."

"Right, okay. Rules. Magic always has a cost. Usually that cost is mostly made up of your energy. Some magic is always 'lost' which means it doesn't stay with the caster or go to the spell. It goes back to Free Magic. Rule Two, magic is neither created nor destroyed. Magic is in casters, in spells or Free. Casters regain magic over time, but it's from Free Magic. Rule Three, Free Magic means that no one controls it, not that you can get it for nothing."

"Makes sense. Nothing is truly free." First rule of economics.

"Right. Rule Four, magic always leaves a signature. Now, here's where it gets tricky. If I cast a fire spell," he opened a hand to reveal a black-blue flame, "it would have my signature. If I used my ring to cast a charm, it would have elements of my grandmother's signature. Depending on how much I'm relying on it, it may be almost completely my grandmother's signature or a mix between hers and mine. Rule Five, magic will not change the basic essence of an object. I can put any charm I want on this book, but it will still be a book. I can burn it to ash, and it's still paper ash. I could, if I had the ability, and I don't think anyone does, turn this book into a skyscraper, but if you examine it microscopically, you'll still see paper cells. Rule Six, you can't turn something non-living into something living, or vice versa. Well, technically you can turn something living into non-living, but it will die very quickly."

"It... will... die." I checked my notes. "Is that legal?"

"Short answer, no. Long answer, not really, except... High Magi are good at making sure they have loopholes."

"I can see that." I frowned. "Hey, I saw that once. On my first day. Someone turned a Solurt into a cake."

"Solurts have better tolerance than most races, since they aren't matter in the same way. But I'm also betting it wasn't for long."

"Less than a minute. Probably less than twenty seconds."

Nocht nodded. "Yeah, even you could survive it for that long. But it would be very unpleasant, much more than it would be for the Solurt. It was probably an accident. They can be more susceptible to transformation just because, like I said, they aren't matter the same way you or I are."

"I think I can see that."

He smiled. "Okay, limitations are easier. You have to understand a spell, really know what it's going to do. You have to believe it will work, and have the power necessary to make it work. That's what I believe anyway. There are words, and gestures, and props, but I believe that's just to help you focus on what you're doing."

That might be why he struggled with rituals. "You've put a lot of study into this, haven't you?"

He perked up, a huge grin on his face. "I want to be the first magicus to be good at everything! I'm sure there's a way."

"Well, good luck. Hey, Nocht? I have to go meet someone now, but I'd like to talk to you about this later, would that be possible?"

"Sure." He tore off some paper from his notebook and scrawled his name and number on it. I gave him mine too, to be polite. I wondered if Ilse might find some of this interesting. She'd be wondering where I was.

***

I raised an eyebrow as Jesse took his normal seat next to me in Tuesday's Government class. "Hi. I'm a little surprised you're here." He was leaving the next day, so it wasn't like it would matter what he did.

He shrugged. "I skipped one of the law classes, this morning, but I decided to come to this one. Wanted to talk to you."

"You can, you know. I mean, I have Genetics after this, but I can make some time afterwards."

Jesse nodded, looking ambivalent. "Hey, been meaning to ask. Do you want my textbooks? I mean, I can't take them back home. You can sell them at the end of semester book buy back, and earn a little extra spending money. They do that here, right?"

"Yeah, pretty sure. I kept mine. Do you want the money I get for them?"

"No, you can have it. There won't be much if it's anything like the colleges I've seen."

Nice of him. "Thanks. Sure you don't want them, though? A memento, or something? Yeah, you'd have to be careful no one saw them, but…" Jesse was vehemently shaking his head.

"No. You take them. Sell them back, read them, turn them into paper airplanes, burn them, I don't care. I don't want them." He rubbed at his hair. "I just… want to forget."

"Jesse–" The teacher started talking, so I couldn't talk to him. I wouldn't have a chance after class either. Maybe I could talk Jesse into having dinner with me. Might mean not eating with Ilse, but she would understand.

As the teacher started talking about the main governments of dimension 3a and 3b (oligarchy, feudalism, matriarchy in a few places, and a plantarchy, or rule of people who proved able to control a particular type of plant in the area); I noticed Jesse flipping around the pages of the textbook, nowhere near our current unit. Oh well, it wasn't like he was sticking around for the quiz. I would be, so I was trying to ignore him and pay attention to Dr. Kraes.

It was a lot harder when he elbowed me for attention. Stifling a huff of annoyance, I turned to him. He pointed down to something in his book. The first word to catch my eye was 'Char', so I quickly skimmed the section.

In dimension 13a, the dimensional government is called a Hall *with the members known as* Hallmen. *The Hall, in its' current form owes much to the Char family, particularly Arthur Char and his son Percival Char. Both served as Hallmen for many years, acting as a form of stability for the Hall. For more information about the formation of the Hall, see chapter ten, section two. For more information about the Chars, see 'The Hall Monitors' by this author.*

I had to read the information twice before I could be sure I understood it. While I was reading, Jesse had written on his notebook, *Any relation to your friends?*

Maybe. I shrugged. If so, no one had told me. Which would be a little odd, considering I knew Ilse had done a background check on Adrian. I would have to ask one or the other. On the other hand, whether he was or not, I still had class to get through.

Jesse dropped the subject, seeing I didn't have an answer, and went back to reading. Only to try to get my attention again a few minutes later. This was getting very aggravating.

This time when I turned to look, it was a painting of the first Hall. Even without the caption, I could tell which one was Arthur Char. He looked almost exactly like Adrian. Getting through class was going to be harder than I thought.

***

Adrian was hanging around my Genetics classroom when I got out. He didn't usually show up after this class, but I was glad to see him. I think. "Hey, how did you do on your math test?"

"Not too bad. I hope to do better on the next. You have a few minutes?"

"I have two hours. And a few questions."

Adrian nodded, and led the way to the library. It was the closest building where we could find somewhere private to talk. "Coffee?"

"No, but a hot chocolate would be nice." I unzipped my jacket as he grabbed a place in line at the coffee shop in the library. It wasn't too crowded, so we were able to get our drinks quickly. The library didn't have a rule about no beverages allowed, but students were punished severely for damaging books.

We found an empty study nook, and I turned to Adrian, "Okay, I have some questions, but you go first."

"Fine, do you know why your cousin is accusing me of lying to you?" Adrian looked genuinely puzzled and even more so when I started laughing.

"Actually, that's related to my question. Jesse was looking in our government book, when we found mention of 13a's dimensional government, the Hall." Adrian groaned. "I see you know what I'm talking about. You're related?"

"My grandfather and my father. Didn't you know that? I thought for sure your roommate would have told you."

I shook my head. "No. That she didn't mention. Come to think of it, I think I cut her off from telling me most of it. Said it wasn't my business."

"Is it now?" Adrian asked.

Was it my business? "No, I guess not. I mean, it doesn't really change anything, does it?"

Adrian slumped back with a sigh. Was that relief? "No, it doesn't."

"Since you are a chem. major, I take it you don't plan to follow in the family footsteps?"

Adrian scoffed. "Me? As a politician? No. Even if I wanted to, and I really, really don't, I couldn't. Maybe someday they'll forgive me for that." Judging from his reaction, Adrian didn't mean to say that.

"If you want to talk–"

"I don't. Is your cousin ready to leave yet?" Adrian interrupted.

"Pretty close. He's giving me his textbooks."

"Makes sense, I guess. When are you leaving?"

"He's supposed to be at the airport about noon."

Adrian frowned. "I have a lab tomorrow, until 12:15, so I can't help. Allison might, no, wait; she has a committee meeting tomorrow."

I chewed my lip. "So I'd have to rent one of the larger snowmobiles. Right. Okay." Hopefully I could actually use one of those. Shouldn't be too hard. Adrian didn't seem happier with the results than I did. "So, any new information? Dreams?" I doubted it, I hadn't had one of those panic attacks.

He shook his head. "No, nothing." He gave a wry grin. "I suppose I could go around trying to figure out who wears sandalwood perfume."

"Better you than me. I'm not sure how well I'd recognize sandalwood on my own." It was clearly Adrian who had recognized the scent.

"Allison used to like it. Had a bunch of candles with that smell. I guess she used it so often she got tired of it; she hasn't bought any in a couple years. Doubt she'll get any again."

I nodded. I certainly wouldn't, if I were her. Adrian hadn't said anything about it, but it was very clear that he would never be able to smell sandalwood without thinking about how he was nearly sacrificed in the training room.

***

Jesse and I did have dinner together that night, and he gave me his books, some of the food he had accumulated during his stay, and one of his sweatshirts. He said he wouldn't need them and it was easier than packing. I didn't argue. At least the sweatshirt wasn't overwhelmingly masculine.

It was a pretty quiet dinner, but at least we didn't fight again. I had been worried we would.

To take Jesse to the mainland by noon, I had to slip out of Bio II early. When I explained the situation to Dr. Gronk on Monday, he agreed to let me leave a little early, as long as I sat near the door so I didn't distract the other students too much. I reminded him again, before class, so he gave me a subtle nod at eleven-forty, letting me sneak out the door.

Jesse was waiting at the dock, luggage ready. I rented one of the larger snowmobiles, with a trailer. They were more expensive, slower, and less maneuverable, but it would fit us and his luggage, so it was worth it.

"You can still–"

I cut him off before he could say it again. "Put your helmet on. We don't want to be late."

We were cutting it close to noon by the time we got to the mainland, but I wasn't too worried. Jesse's plane didn't leave until one. Yes, the airport said to be an hour early, but the airport was tiny, and didn't seem to worry a lot about security.

By calling ahead, we were able to arrange a taxi to meet us. Jesse paid the man while I finished unloading the luggage. The taxi driver asked me if I wanted a ride back, but I turned him down. I could walk.

Jesse took his suitcase, ready to go in, before he turned back to me. "Come with me. Please."

I laughed. "Maybe you aren't aware of this, but I don't have a ticket, my passport is back at the college, I have nothing packed, and most important, I don't want to leave."

Jesse started to say something, but I didn't hear him. I was too distracted by the sandy-haired young man nearby, watching us with a pained expression on his face. He looked familiar but I was sure I had never met him before. Then recognition slapped me in the face. "Simon? Simon Nicols?"

Chapter Twenty-Two
Deadly Information

Both men looked at me in confusion. "Do you know this guy?" Jesse asked.

"Yes, have we met?"

"No. No, I've never met you. I saw your picture. You won, um, a competition last year."

Simon laughed bitterly. "Yeah, I did. Just before everything fell apart. Are you part of that club?"

"No, I was just a visitor. I'm totally without that kind of skill." Wow, it was hard to talk about Hyde outside it.

"You're lucky." Simon turned to Jesse. "You're leaving?"

"It's dangerous there."

"You have no idea." He turned to me. "If you're smart, you'll leave too. While you still can."

"I'm not leaving. Jesse, you have a plane to catch." I ignored his sound of protest. "Simon, you don't have to answer this, but why did you disappear? I talked to someone who said you didn't bother to tell anyone anything."

He stared at me for a minute, and I had almost given up hopes of an answer when he finally spoke. "What the heck, can't hurt now. I'm dying."

"Dying?" Jesse squawked. "The school killed you?"

A wry smile. "Close enough. They haven't found my killer yet. I keep waiting around, hoping they'll find the one." He looked around to make sure no one was listening. "The one who stripped away my magic."

I gasped. "What? Someone… And you don't know who did it?"

"No. A few days later, some big brouhaha happened, and everyone focused on that. As soon as I could get out of the infirmary, I left the island entirely. Even their spells can't affect me anymore."

"Because you have no…" Jesse trailed off. "So they shouldn't be able to affect me! I mean, they took almost everything off anyway. But–"

"You still have your spark. I can tell. Be glad. Otherwise…" Simon held up his hands. They were practically translucent, skin paper-thin, with veins sticking out like blue wires.

"Why did you leave?" I asked.

"What, let them watch me die? My classmates, my friends, my girlfriend? I don't need their pity." He looked away. "I never told them what happened. Besides, the island would drain me faster."

That was interesting, but something else struck me. "Girlfriend?"

He smiled, a true, albeit small, smile. "Rachael. Her name is Rachael." The smile transfigured to a scowl. "The powers alone know what she thinks happened to me."

"Jesse, plane. Rachael, an…" no one was nearby, so I whispered, "elemental magicus? I think she's an RA in my dorm."

"Probably. She was an RA last year, too. I've caught a glimpse of her occasionally, when she comes to town. She doesn't know I'm here."

"But, shouldn't she know? Doesn't she have a right to know? To, well, say goodbye? Don't you?" That sounded callous, didn't it? I didn't mean to.

His eyes sharpened, making his features, already gaunt, look like they would tear through the skin. "It's better this way. She doesn't need to know. At all."

I backed up a step, hands raised. "I understand. I won't tell her." Rachael's right to know might or might not trump Simon's right to privacy. Either way, I didn't have the right to interfere.

Jesse, who *still* hadn't left, turned to me. "See, if this could kill him, what chance to you have? I'll lend you the money for a ticket, just come home."

"You would be wise to listen," Simon said.

I opened my mouth to say something to both of them, before suddenly doubling over in pain, falling to my knees. Something sharp and electric filled my mouth and taste buds. I could feel my blood flowing. Dark, bitter, chocolate lingered on my tongue. "Adrian!"

Two people were helping me stand, but it took a moment for me to recognize them as the people I had been talking to. Adrenaline kicked in, making my thoughts fly. "Jesse, get on your blasted plane before it takes off without you. Simon, I'd like to talk to you later, but I have to go *now*!"

Neither of them had any clue what was going on, but Simon at least knew enough to go with the flow. "Go. Be careful though, and remember my advice."

I think I said goodbye to them, but I couldn't swear for certain. Adrian was in danger and I was miles away. I ran and didn't look back.

***

As soon as I got to the island dock I could see a crowd forming. That seemed a good place to start. Then I saw Allison on the sidelines, white, squeezing her hands over her mouth. She was clearly trying not to cry, trying not to get in the way. She was successful in the latter if not the former.

I turned to look at what she was staring at. There were several people there, clearly doing something, but it wasn't until I got closer that I could see what. I realized they were all healers before I realized what I was looking at.

An unconscious body, badly burned and bleeding faster than they could heal. Swallowing the bile rising in my throat, I looked closer, already knowing what I would find. It was his coat I recognized first. That black duster of his that he wore everywhere. Oh, Adrian.

I couldn't do anything for Adrian. He was injured far beyond what my meager first aid training could handle. Healers, people much better trained and equipped than I was, were already working on him, doing everything they could. So, if I couldn't help Adrian, maybe I could help Allison.

Giving the working healers a wide berth, I went straight for Allison, trying to ignore the sight of Adrian hurt, the smell of blood, of burnt flesh. "Allison, wh–"

She looked in my direction, but she couldn't see me at first. I could tell the exact instant she recognized me, as she latched on to me, tears soaking my coat. Maybe I was holding her up, maybe she was holding me up, or maybe it was mutual. I tried to think of the facts I knew. Adrian's lab was in Victor. He was maybe two hundred yards from the building now. Somehow, something or someone attacked him in plain sight in the middle of the day, without anyone seeing anything.

I watched the healers working on him, eavesdropping shamelessly while hoping Allison didn't understand. I didn't understand everything, wouldn't have even if I was a licensed doctor thanks to Hyde's unusual medical methods. But I could understand that he was in bad shape. Very bad shape. They couldn't even teleport him before stabilizing him, and something was preventing them from doing so.

I don't know how long they were there, trying to patch him up. It could have been ten minutes, it could have been five hours. I truly couldn't say. The others joined us. Perhaps they heard the rumors, or maybe they felt it too. I neither knew nor cared. Even Ilse came out, draped in veils to protect herself from the sun; a supportive, if cold, hand on my shoulder.

Finally, after forever, they decided they had him stable enough to teleport him. Without a word, we headed to the infirmary. They let us wait in the waiting room, warning us it could be a very long time before we heard anything.

It was over an hour before the silence was broken. Ilse, still wrapped protectively, looked to Allison and me, the first two on the scene. "Do you know what transpired?"

Allison didn't answer, probably still in shock. She hadn't let go of me since I got there. "I don't. I was taking Jesse to the airport, and I…" I rubbed at my still upset stomach. "I had to come back." Good enough. They'd understand.

Allison shuddered. "I knew something was wrong, but I didn't know what. Then I knew it involved Adrian. I think he was agitated. Then… I was on my way when security found me." Her voice was spacey and her eyes distant. Another shudder and she was back with us. "He'll be alright, won't he? I can't lose him, I can't!"

I tightened my hold on her, and somehow spoke through a throat shrunk to the size of a straw. "Hey, this is Adrian. He's stubborn. The original hardhead, right? He'll be fine. Let something like this stop him? No way!"

My voice was shaky and hinted of tears, but no one called me on it.

I wondered if anyone else knew he crashed at least once before they transported him. No one else had reacted, so I might be the only one who knew he technically 'died' once.

Allison patted my arm, nodding a little. "Yeah. You're right."

Silence held court. Shock slowly gave way to boredom. It felt wrong, to be bored while waiting to hear news about a friend, basically if he would live or die. I was worried, terrified even. We all were. But I was also sitting in a color monstrosity, doing nothing. We weren't even talking. Along with boredom, worry, and some guilt, there was frustration and impatience. I felt like I would explode if I didn't hear something soon; while at the same time I was terrified of what we might hear.

To complicate things, it wasn't just my emotions I was feeling. I knew I was picking up on everyone else, even if our feelings were so similar I couldn't distinguish whose emotions were whose.

Kara sat on Allison's other side, arms around her, hands on me, trying to be there for both of us. Ilse was on my other side, every so often rubbing tension out of my shoulders, letting me hold on to Allison without my arms cramping up. The Ice Twins were leaning on each other on another sofa. Tim sat next to Denise on the other side of the room, both to offer her comfort, and possibly to try to listen in on what the doctors were saying. If he could hear, he wasn't sharing.

Hours passed. At times I could have sworn it was days. About eight, someone, I think it was Tim, suggested we eat.

Allison looked scandalized. "I can't leave! They might come out any minute!

"What if we went in shifts?" I suggested. "Half go now, and when they come back, the other half go."

"Good idea," Kara said. "It could be some time before they come out, and we want to be sharp and alert to understand when they do. Plus, what if they let us see him and you faint of hunger?"

That got a small smile out of Allison. "Alright, you win. But I'm second shift."

"What if that side of the room goes first?" I waved to indicate Tim, Denise, and the Ice Twins. "We'll go when you come back."

They left and came back. Still no news. Allison was clearly reluctant to leave, but we managed to get her to the cafeteria, and even if she just picked at her food, a few bites made it in her mouth. Her mind was still in the infirmary and her body wished to join it.

I took a couple minutes to use the restroom, something I had needed and tried to ignore for an hour. That was when I learned I had scraped my knees earlier. It took a moment for me to remember how I had done that. I had fallen when I felt Adrian in danger, then had been so focused on that, I hadn't even noticed. Oh well, they weren't that bad, though of course now that I knew about them, they hurt.

We ate quickly and hurried back to the infirmary. Apparently we had good timing, because almost as soon as we got back and sat down, Dr. Zyloas came out. "Family of Adrian Char?"

Allison leapt to her feet, dragging Kara and me along for the ride. "I'm his sister. We're his friends. Please, he's…"

Dr. Zyloas held up a greenish hand. "We've stabilized him. It's still touch and go, but we remain cautiously optimistic. We'll know more in the morning."

I truly hoped I was the only one who knew that meant, 'We'll know more if he lives to see morning.'

***

They only let Allison in that first night, and only for five minutes at that, before chasing us out and telling us to get some rest. Even Ilse was dragging and this was the time she normally got up. Unfortunately, she had three classes tonight. I might have been willing to skip them, under the circumstances, but Ilse wasn't. Then again, considering the oath, perhaps it was best she didn't. We both knew that she would come back and collapse as soon as her last class was over. She did make me promise to wake her if anything happened.

Allison didn't want to go back to her room, where she would be alone. It was on the tip of my tongue to invite her to spend the night in our room, but Kara beat me to it. Allison agreed quickly.

We walked back to the dorms as a group. No one wanted to be isolated. Not while we had no idea what attacked Adrian. Tim was not pleased to be escorted instead of doing the escorting, but we pointed out there were seven of us, and one of him.

I made Ilse promise to have security walk her to and from classes. I knew she could take care of herself, but so could Adrian. Perhaps she was worried too, because she didn't give me any grief about it.

We stayed in the lobby long enough for Allison to sign in as an overnight visitor. Rachael was the RA on duty. She had heard what happened, probably the whole school had, and offered her condolences. Denise thanked her for the group. None of the rest of us spoke much, or at all.

The suite was quiet and unnerving. Part of me wished I had spoken up about inviting Allison faster. On the other hand, if things got too much, I had absolutely no doubt I could go to Kara and Denise's room at any time. To distract myself, I checked my email. Jesse wrote. He was back home safely, and wanted to know what happened to Adrian this afternoon.

Was it only this afternoon? It felt like years. I told him the truth, well, parts of it. Adrian had been attacked and was hurt. We didn't know how badly and were still waiting for news. Don't tell my family. Once that was done, I shut down the computer. The hour was technically early, but I was beyond exhausted. I changed for bed and spent the night alternating in praying Adrian recovered soon and trying not to think about it at all.

That, scarily enough, set the pattern for the next few days. Each day they told us he was better than he had been the day before, but they wouldn't say more than that and that they were cautiously optimistic. I'm not sure it is possible to hate a phrase more than we started hating that one. I think it was the third day that Allison lost it and demanded to know, in plain language, what happened to her brother, was he going to recover, and when? Basic answer, near as I could tell, was unknown magic, probably, and our guess was as good as theirs. If Allison had had any energy left after her fit she might have hit someone.

On the fourth day, or maybe the fifth, they started allowing other visitors, with Allison's permission. On the second day, there had been some question of whether or not the senior Chars would come. Allison had informed anyone who asked that *she* was Adrian's medical proxy, and glared down anyone who didn't drop it after that. Since Kara swore that Allison had called her parents the first night, telling them everything, no one really wanted to question more than that.

While Adrian's being allowed visitors was a good sign, and I desperately wanted to see him, I was also afraid. Terrified would probably be a better word for it. The few times I did fall asleep, I often had nightmares of seeing Adrian so badly hurt. Every time Allison left his room, she was crying. So I let everyone else go first.

It was late on the sixth day that I took my turn. The healers had finally said, earlier that day, that Adrian would almost definitely survive, and probably make a full recovery. As soon as they could figure out why he wouldn't wake up.

Allison was there, like always. She had noticeably lost weight, and her eyes were permanently red. Her hair was limp and she moved like one in a daze. When she looked at me and smiled I wanted to scream. This wasn't real, how could it be real? Instead, I tried to smile back. I doubt my smile was any better than hers. "Hey, how are you doing?" I sat next to her.

"The same. How did you do on your math test?"

"Not too bad. I hope to do better on the next."

"Good." She picked up Adrian's hand. It was pale and lifeless, but it looked better than his gray face. "Adrian, Violet is here to see you. She's worried. Like I am. Wake up and tease us for being such worrywarts."

"Can he hear us?" I asked.

Allison shrugged. "I don't know. The healers can't give me a definitive answer. I think he can, though, at least a little."

I nodded. "Have you been here all day?" I asked, even though I knew the answer.

"Of course."

She wasn't going to be happy with this, but I had to try. "Maybe you need a break. Even just to get out of here and have a coffee."

"But Adrian–"

"Would tell you to take care of yourself. Have you even had a shower since he ended up here?"

She deflated. "You win. I'll get a coffee. But I'm not staying away for long."

I smiled. "I wouldn't expect anything else. It will do you good. Just don't go alone."

"I won't." She stood up and stretched, her back popping a few times. "I guess I did need to get out of that chair before I took root. I see Tim's in the waiting room, he'll probably walk with me. Do you need anything?"

"No, I'm good." I waved as they left. Tim had agreed to Allison's request almost before she finished asking. Maybe he was going stir crazy as well.

With Allison gone, I was alone with Adrian. Which wouldn't be so bad if he wasn't doing a wonderful job impersonating a corpse. Trying to push that thought from my mind, I examined the room. It looked like a standard Hyde infirmary room. Adrian was on a hospital bed. There was a bag on an IV post, but instead of traveling by tube and needle, there was what appeared to be a bright blue sticker on the bottom of the bag, matching a bright blue sticker on his arm. The contents of the bag seemed to match a bottle on a table next to the bed. By squinting, I was pretty sure it said 'Nutrient Solution'. There was another bottle, a medicine I didn't recognize.

There wasn't a standard medical chart, but there were a few notes. I recognized his blood type, and that he had been given at least one transfusion, but that was all.

A phone was on the opposite side of the room, near a fire extinguisher, because fire preventing wards don't work well with healing wards. A trash can, and a medical cart, probably where his medicines were stashed, finished off the rest. Not particularly interesting.

With a shrug, I tried talking to Adrian. "I hope you don't mind, but Allison was ready to pass out. She can't be there for you when you wake up if she's hospitalized for exhaustion herself." Silence.

"You'd probably be embarrassed if you knew how worried everyone has been. I know you don't like being the center of attention but you are practically all anyone's thought about. Well, there's classes too, but hey." More silence.

I closed my eyes. "I wish you'd wake up. I'm scared. We all are. We need you okay. Being able to tell us what happened would be a bonus." I squeezed his hand. It wasn't cold like I was afraid it would be, so I continued holding it.

"Do you remember our date on the mainland? You said you'd always come when I was in trouble. Why couldn't I help you this time? Why aren't you coming?" The tears I had kept locked away since the first night threatened to make an appearance but I forced them back.

"Are you alright?" A voice at the door asked, causing me to nearly fall out of my chair.

"You startled me." I said, turning to face Ilse.

She looked ill at ease herself. Her hands fluttered at an emerald necklace, simpler than her usually style, and unless I was mistaken, that was the dress she wore yesterday. Ilse never re-wore clothes that quickly. "I didn't mean to."

She came to sit next to me. "How did you do on your math test?" I asked.

"Fine."

"Just fine?" I scratched at my eyebrow, than down the side of my face.

"I did well," She responded.

I nodded. "Will you excuse me a moment? I'm supposed to call Kara if someone joins me. She was worried about me being here alone." I didn't look at my companion.

"Of course, good idea."

I walked over to the phone, trying to keep my eyes on Adrian the whole time. I barely looked away long enough to dial the number. Fortunately, Kara answered on the second ring. "Hello?" She sounded drained.

"Hi, Kara. It's Violet. I just wanted to let you know that Ilse joined me. I know I promised to tell you if anyone came. Oh, I asked her about her math test. She said she did well. I thought you'd want to know."

"I'm on my way."

"Hmm. Oh, Allison and Tim went for some coffee. They should be around somewhere."

"Okay, got it." Kara hung up.

I hung up too. Taking my seat, I looked at Adrian, who was finally looking like he was starting to stir. For the first time, I prayed he'd stay asleep a little longer. Don't wake up, not yet.

Leaning back, my nose tingled with the scent of sandalwood. Could Adrian smell it? Was that what was waking him? I hoped not. He'd probably panic if he woke to that scent. Had we mentioned sandalwood to the group?

My prayers either were or weren't answered, depending on how one looked at it. Adrian was clearly waking up. My companion noticed too, jumping to her feet. "He's waking up! I need to…" She started to reach for the mystery medicine bottle.

I grabbed her wrist and pulled back as hard as I could; jolting her off balance. "Oh no, I think you've done enough damage, Rachael."

Chapter Twenty-Three
Back to Normal?

She stared at me, mouth gaping, before recovering. "Violet, I think you're under a little too much stress."

"How many times did you think I'd fall for that? You pretending to be one of my friends? We came up with a code, you didn't know it. Either of them, actually. You aren't using the right speech patterns. Ilse doesn't react to stress by fiddling with jewelry, unlike, say, Rachael. That's a very nice necklace. One exactly like I remember seeing Rachael play with several times while on desk duty. I always had to be careful not to accidentally hypnotize myself watching you."

I hadn't let go of her arm. At worst, Kara, and probably a few others, were on their way here. At best, someone had thought to call security and they were right outside. All I had to do was stall.

"Rachael is an elemental magicus, not an illusionist," She argued.

"I know, that's what threw me for the longest time. Even when someone practically threw the answer at me. Jewelry can be charmed to hold magic, allowing a magicus to use a type of magic they aren't dominant in. Emeralds hold a great deal of magic for a relatively short time. Allowing you to specialize in elemental magic, and illusionary, the two kinds that have been causing us the most problems. That's Simon's magic, isn't it? He's out there, *dying*, because his girlfriend, who he didn't want to hurt, is using his magic to *destroy* the school!"

With a flicker, Ilse disappeared, replaced by a white-faced, wide-eyed Rachael. "Simon? Simon's magic? No! You're lying!" She shoved her free hand in my direction. The hand never touched me, but I went flying, hitting the bed hard enough to see stars.

Adrian grunted. I had almost forgotten he was waking up. "Rachael. It was–" He ground out.

"Shut up!" Rachael screamed, tossing a ball of fire at us.

I grabbed Adrian and pushed him to the floor, rolling over the bed and somehow managed not to fall on top of him. He cried out in pain, and I mentally apologized. Where was help? Surely it was coming. Yes, there! I could see security on the way. Unfortunately, Rachael saw it too.

The door slammed shut, infused with pink light. "No, not this time. I will not be interrupted. I tried again, and again. It's a shame it came to this. I actually like you, Violet. So I tried to get you to leave. But you wouldn't take the hint! Not even when I bought you a ticket and left it in your room. So I had to hurt you." The bed started to rattle as winds picked up in the room. "But you never got hurt. Not badly enough to leave. Just lucky, I guess."

Glass started breaking around us. I covered Adrian as best I could while trying to figure out how in the world to stop her, or even just stall her while security took down her shield. Hopefully that was one of her weaker areas.

"Or maybe you aren't so lucky. Because now I have to kill you. It's the only way to succeed." Flames built up around us. I could smell the linoleum melting.

Rachael laughed, but there was no sanity in it. I peeked at her from under the bed, trying to see what she would do next. Her face was a twisted mockery of joy, and the necklace was glowing.

Could it be controlling her somehow? If someone else had stolen Simon's magic and planted it in the necklace, how much harder would it be to add magic to control the next wearer? In spite of all she had clearly done, her shock and horror of using her boyfriend's magic seemed genuine.

If the necklace was controlling her, then if I could get it off her, would there be a chance to reason with her? It was worth a try, if I could do it safely. At very least she wouldn't be able to throw illusions at me to confuse me.

"Why?" I shouted. "Why do I have to die? Succeed in what?"

"To make a better world." She was starting to come around the side of the bed.

The flames were bearing down on us, possibly close enough to singe my hair. Adrian was awake, but he couldn't move yet. It was up to me. But what could I do? There wasn't a lot of water here.

I shoved Adrian under the bed. It wasn't a lot of protection, but it was better than nothing. Grabbing a plastic bottle in reach, I tossed it at Rachael's face. "Think fast! Rubbing alcohol is very flammable."

Maybe it was my words, or more likely, it was seeing something flying at her face, but Rachael pulled back the flames before catching the bottle and automatically reading the label. "This isn't rubbing alcohol. This is nutrient solution!"

I didn't answer her, because I was too busy grabbing the fire extinguisher. Apparently, covering a magicus in flame-proof foam also puts out their fire. Rachael doubled over, gagging. She must have swallowed some. I stood there, extinguisher gripped in my fingers, willing to hit her with the empty container if she tried anything.

Security finally burst through and converged on the shaking magicus. "How…" She rasped out. "How?"

"Just lucky, I guess." Jostop was forcing a pair of anti-magic handcuffs on her. "The necklace, it isn't her magic. I'm pretty sure it's Simon Nicols'. I think it might be part of why she's so…" I stopped not sure how to finish.

"It is," Taria said. When did she get here? "We've known for some time that whoever was causing trouble was using his magic, but we couldn't find out who."

"No!" Rachael shrieked. "It's not his! They wouldn't do that. They wouldn't."

"Who wouldn't?" Taria asked. "Who gave you that necklace? They are manipulating you."

I helped Adrian out from under the bed. Hopefully a healer could actually come in soon and look him over. Not that we weren't paying attention to this. Even if we were ignoring it, we wouldn't be able to for long.

Rachael suddenly started to howl, a deep guttural sound, like an animal having its' throat ripped out. To my shock and horror, she started to shake as smoke rolled off her.

Security tried to stop her. Taria was telling her that she would die if she didn't stop. But it didn't stop. The howl got louder and louder, the shaking was enough to rattle bones, and the smoke was filling the air with haze and the smell of burnt flesh.

I gagged twice. Adrian pulled me down to the ground with him, holding my head to his shoulder. "Don't look. Don't watch. There's nothing you can do," He murmured in my ear.

I cried, knowing he was right. I cried for him, for me, for Simon, and even for Rachael. I cried as she was pronounced dead. I cried as the healer told Adrian that now that he was awake and the magic attacking him was gone, they could heal his remaining injuries, and he could leave in under an hour. I cried when Allison basically fell apart in her brother's arms, both siblings trying not to cry, and neither succeeding. I cried as the real Ilse took me home. I didn't stop crying until I fell asleep.

***

"Hey, you're looking a lot better." I smiled at Simon when we ran into him at Mama Rose's.

He smiled back, "I'm feeling a lot better." He turned to my companion. "So, would you be Adrian? If so, I imagine you're doing a lot better too."

Adrian's mouth twitched a little. "I am. Thank you."

"Don't mind him; it's just been a long two weeks." Was it only two weeks ago that Jesse left, I met Simon, and Adrian was attacked? It had to be. "May we join you?"

"Please." Simon gestured to the other chairs at his table.

Mama Rose, perhaps sensing it was important, did no more than give Adrian a big hug and promised us two more soups pronto. She meant it, too. We were eating in minutes. She had somehow heard he had been injured, and the soup was supposed to help him get back to full health.

"So, were they able to fix your problem?" I asked. Taria had said that they should be able to give Simon at least some of his magic back.

"To an extent. There is always some loss in a transfer, and this had to be... cleansed first." He said, pulling out a familiar emerald necklace. One of us, might have been Adrian, might have been me, stiffened; so I took his hand. Fortunately, Simon slipped the necklace back under his shirt. "I'm... absorbing. Slowly. It's safer that way."

Since it was his magic to begin with, there shouldn't be any complications. Once the corrupting element had been purified and removed anyway. Taria said they were able to do that, I really hoped it worked. It certainly wouldn't be fair for him to get his magic back, only to end up a slave to the one who stole it in the first place.

"I am sorry. About Rachael. About everything." I hoped I wasn't making things worse.

Simon studied the patterns his spoon made in his soup. "Rachael was always an idealist. She had big dreams of a more open world. Someone used that. Used her. I believe she never meant for things to go so far. To hurt anyone. It was..." He tugged at the chain, his meaning clear. "I believe that with all my heart." He would believe that if an angel from heaven came down and declared otherwise.

I didn't say anything about it, though. Maybe he was even right. "I'm sure she was special. I'm sorry I didn't meet her before."

Simon's smile shouted that I had said the right thing. "You would have liked her."

Adrian shifted, and I was pretty sure I was picking up on discomfort from him. Well, she had tried to kill him on at least three occasions. Not to mention the things she had done or tried to do to me. Perhaps it was best to change the subject. "So, will you be coming back to Hyde?"

"I haven't decided yet. Perhaps next year. I would like to finish my education, but I need time to recover fully. Or at least as much as I will. I'll probably never have as much skill as I used to."

We commiserated and ate in silence for a few times. Simon brought up Rachael a few more times. Adrian kept a diplomatic silence, but I tried to be sympathetic and change the subject as soon as I could without being rude. Finally, we paid our bill, excused ourselves and left.

It was a nice day, for February, so we took a short walk on campus. A very short walk. Adrian still got fatigued faster than he liked to admit.

"I wish he didn't keep bringing her up." Adrian said, mostly out of the blue.

"Rachael? It's not surprising. He cared about her. A lot. Even after he found out everything."

"Doubt they told him everything. And I'm sure they haven't told us everything," he grumbled.

I gave him a wry smile. "What else is new?"

"We still don't know who gave her that necklace."

I frowned. "Probably the 'mysterious benefactor'. It would have to be someone very powerful magically. Capable of doing things a magicus can't do." Rachael had been an RA which gave her access to any room in that dorm, but not much else on campus. Chances were that whoever controlled her had more authority than she did. That was a creepy thought.

"Creepy, wearing that necklace."

I almost laughed at the way our thoughts went perpendicular to each other. "I agree, but they purified it. And it's saving his life. Besides, it may be the only thing he has left from her." That was probably one of the saddest thoughts I had had all day.

"I'm not so sure about that."

"Huh?" What did that mean?

"Rachael died wearing that necklace. Do you know how she died?"

"No, I didn't ask." It wasn't something I wanted to think about. Every day I blessed Adrian and Ilse for preventing me from actually seeing Rachael's body. I had seen, and heard, too much as it was.

"She forced her magic out. All of it. While wearing a necklace to absorb magic."

I froze for a moment, thinking about the implications. Adrian rubbed his side, trying to hide it, so I lead him to the nearest building, the library. "She was wearing anti-magic handcuffs. How could she do that?"

"By using her life energy to push it out. That was enough power to override the handcuffs."

"Do you think he got some of her magic?" I held his arm as we went up the outside stairs. There weren't many of them, but they were icy.

Adrian shrugged. "It's possible. Unless he tells us, I doubt we'll know for sure."

I shook my head, as I grabbed the door. "I don't know. I just don't know."

"How's your cousin?" Adrian followed me to one of the benches the lined the perimeter of the shelves.

"Okay. He says he enjoys his new school. He says it's normal. I don't know what normal is anymore."

Adrian smiled. "Don't worry, things will be back to normal around here soon." He was almost cut off by the announcement.

"Attention all students! The blood-seeking creeper vines are loose. All students are to head to the nearest shelter with all due speed. Students inside shelter are not to leave until the all clear has been announced. Trained faculty, please meet at the arranged points to corral the plants. Thank you."

I leaned back, trying not to laugh and failing. "You were right. Back to normal."

Now Out

Moonlit Memories: Book Two

Nightmare's Revenge

By H. J. Harding

Liska is a girl of many faces and more names. Currently she goes by Anna Andrews, a British born college student in West Palm Beach, FL. She prefers to think of herself as Luna Liska, active ninja from the Kikisutai Werefox clan of Japan. It is more comfortable than even her own name.

Liska hoped her second semester of college would be quieter than her first. She was wrong. Within her first week it's clear that last semester's problems aren't over and she isn't fully recovered. Then she has to uncover who betrayed a sworn ally to prove her own innocence. Add in an unexpected encounter from the past that complicates her fledgling relationship with Todd, and classes become the least of her concerns.

And then, there's Nightmare...

Coming Soon!

The Hyde Chronicles: Book Three

The Bishop's Decoy

By H. J. Harding

Freshman year is wrapping up at Hyde. Pity exams are the easy part. Summer means going back home and trying to avoid the problems of Christmas. Between her cousin's interference and an unexpected visitor from Hyde, summer could prove even worse.

But the game at school continues, with the stakes climbing ever higher. Can Violet win a war on two fronts? Can she even survive?

Coming in 2018